JOURNEY'S END

What Reviewers Say About Amanda Radley's Work

Humbug

"*Humbug* is the Christmas cuddle we all want and need this festive season. Once again Amanda Radley has given us characters we can love, a gentle romance and a setting we never knew we needed."
—*Kitty Kat's Book Review Blog*

"This is a classic Christmas rom-com, with holiday cheer and a predictable storyline. I would vote for *Humbug* as my favorite Christmas novel of 2021."—*The Lesbrary*

Under Her Influence

"Light, sweet, and remarkably chaste, this sapphic love story will make as enjoyable a vacation pick as it is an armchair getaway."
—*Publishers Weekly*

"My heart is just…filled with love and warmth! Finally, I have found an author who does not rely on sex to make a book interesting!! I'm probably going to go on an Amanda Radley read-a-thon."
—*Periwinkle Pens*

"Since I'm a big fan of Amanda Radley's romantic comedies, I had no doubt that I'd enjoy *Under Her Influence*. And I did! Her trademark dry wit and family-centered, low-angst romance always satisfies and this was no different. I always seem to learn something about a new industry, too, so that's a bonus."—*To Be Read Book Reviews*

Detour to Love

"If you're on the lookout for well written sapphic romance with stellar characters, wonderful pairings & outstanding plots I whole heartedly recommend any of Amanda's books!!"—*EloiseReads*

Flight SQA016

"I'm so glad I picked this book up because I think I've found my new favourite series! …The love brewing between these two is beautifully written and I was onboard from the beginning. I had some laugh out loud moments because this is British rom-com at its best. The secondary characters really added to the novel and the rollercoaster ride that is this book. The writing is tight and pace is perfect…"—*Les Rêveur*

Lost at Sea

"A.E. Radley knows how to write great characters. And it's not just the main characters she puts so much effort into. I loved them, but I was astounded at how well drawn the minor characters were, especially Elvin and Graham. The revelations are perfectly paced in this story. We find out more about their backgrounds as they get to know each other. The reader can so easily believe everything A.E. Radley writes because she is so observant and makes the world so real in her books. …The writing was beautiful—descriptive, real and very funny at times."—*Lesbian Review*

"Absolutely amazing, easy to read, perfect romance with mystery and drama story. There were so many wonderful elements that gave twists and turns to this adventure on the sea. I absolutely loved this story and can't rave about it enough."—*LesbiReviewed*

Going Up

"I can always count on this superb author when it comes to creating unforgettable and endearing characters that I can totally relate to and fall in love with. A. E. Radley has given me beautiful descriptions of Parbrook and the quirky individuals who work at Addington's."
—*Lesbian Review*

"This story is a refreshing light in the lesfics world. Or should I say in the romance lesfic world? Why do you ask me? Well, while there is a lot of crushy feeling between wlw characters and all, but, honestly that's the sub-plot and I've adored that fact. *Going Up* is a lesson in life."—*Kam's Queerfic Pantry*

"The author takes an improbable twosome and writes such a splendid romance that you actually thing it is possible...this is a great romance and a lovely read."—*Best Lesfic Reviews*

Mergers and Acquisitions

"This book is fun, witty and adorable. I had no idea which way this book was going to take me, and I loved it. Each character is interesting and loveable in their own right. You don't want to miss this one, heck if you have read any of A.E. Radley's books you know it's quality stuff."—*Romantic Reader Blog*

"Charming and quick witted, I think A.E. Radley is an author to watch."—*Les Rêveur*

The Startling Inaccuracy of the First Impression

"We absolutely loved the way the relationship between the two ladies developed. There is nothing hurried about relationship that develops perfectly organically. This is a lovely easy to read romance."
—*Best Lesfic Reviews*

Huntress

"The writing style was fun and enjoyable. The story really gathered steam to the point of me shirking responsibilities to finish it. The humor in the story was very well done."—*Lesbian Review*

Bring Holly Home

"*Bring Holly Home* is a fantastic novel and probably one of my favourite books by A.E. Radley. …Such a brilliant story and one I know I will read time and time again. This book has two ingredients that I love in novels, Ice Queens melting and age-gap romance. It's definitely a slow burn but one I'd gladly enjoy rereading again."
—*Les Rêveur*

Keep Holly Close

"It was great to go back into the world of the Remember Me series. The first book in the series, *Bring Holly Home.* is one of my favourite A.E. Radley books. I love Holly and Victoria; they tick all the boxes for me when it comes to my favourite tropes. Plus, Victoria's kids are adorable, especially little Alexia. She melts my heart."
—*Les Rêveur*

Climbing the Ladder

"Radley has a talent for giving us memorable characters to love, women you wish you knew and locations you wish you could experience firsthand."—*Late Night Lesbian Reads*

Second Chances

"This is an absolute delight to read. Likeable characters, well-written, easy flow and sweet romance. Definitely recommended."
—*Best Lesfic Reviews*

The Road Ahead

"I really enjoyed this age-gap, opposites attract road trip romance. This is a romance where the characters actually acknowledge their differences and joy of joy, listen to each other. I love it when a book makes me feel all the feels and root for both women to find their HEA. Hilarious one minute, heart-tugging the next. A pleasure to read."—*Late Night Lesbian Reads*

Fitting In

"Writing convincing love stories with non-typical characters is tricky. Radley more than measures up to the challenge with this truly heartwarming romance."—*Best Lesfic Reviews*

Visit us at www.boldstrokesbooks.com

By the Author

JOURNEY'S END

by
Amanda Radley

2022

JOURNEY'S END
© 2020 By Amanda Radley. All Rights Reserved.

ISBN 13: 978-1-63679-233-0

This Trade Paperback Original Is Published By
Bold Strokes Books, Inc.
P.O. Box 249
Valley Falls, NY 12185

First Bold Strokes Books Edition: April 2022

_____

CREDITS
EDITOR: CINDY CRESAP
PRODUCTION DESIGN: SUSAN RAMUNDO
COVER DESIGN BY TAMMY SEIDICK

Dedication

For the readers.

CHAPTER ONE

Emily cupped the mug of tea firmly in her hands. She looked at the various papers on the kitchen table. She wasn't one for business and finances; the whole thing gave her a headache. But here she was, having a business meeting with her recently appointed agent.

After so many weeks of telephone calls and emails, it was a relief to have the meeting in person. The only problem was that now Nicole could see her confused expression.

"So, that's the final script that you think we can sell?" Emily asked. She gestured to the piece of paper that Nicole held.

Nicole nodded. "I've spoken to all my contacts, and I think that's it. The remaining scripts that you've written are good, but they don't all work in a theatre environment. They'd need quite a lot of rewriting to get them into a place where they'd be suitable for stage."

Emily picked up the mug and sipped at her tea. She wasn't surprised that only a quarter of her back catalogue had any financial value. In fact, she was still getting over the shock that any of them had made any money at all.

When she had first started putting pen to paper, it was simply as a hobby. She'd read a book when she was in school about scriptwriting, and something had lodged in her brain. The act of taking a story and writing it out in simple script form had been calming.

With her only son in the hospital for weeks at a time over the course of his early years, calm was what she needed. She'd lost count of how many hours she had spent scribbling scripts while Henry had slept.

She felt her heartbeat accelerate. The memories of those times didn't seem to fade. Even now, months since the operation that had fixed Henry's heart, she felt the familiar sense of panic writhe inside her.

She turned to look out of the window and smiled, reassured. Henry ran around the yard, just like any other five-year-old boy would. Olivia playfully chased him.

"Motherhood suits her," Nicole said, following Emily's distracted gaze.

"It does. Henry adores her."

"She adores him. She's already planning an over-the-top sixth birthday party," Nicole confessed.

Emily put down the mug and turned to look at Nicole. "She hasn't mentioned anything to me."

"I think she wants to get the wedding out of the way before she talks to you about the next event she intends to plan into oblivion."

Emily put her head in her hands and let out a long breath. She adored Olivia, loved her more than she thought it was possible to love someone. But if she had to go through another day of Olivia planning an event, she might just kill her.

"Don't worry, you'll be married in a couple of days," Nicole said. "No more discussions about table decorations or photographers."

Emily looked up. "Oh, I expected the discussions about table decorations and photographers. It's the three-hour debate on whether the wedding cake should have a ribbon placed around the bottom of the middle tier or threaded into the icing. When I agreed that threaded into icing looked nice, it started a discussion on the spacing between the exposed thread and then an impromptu math lesson regarding the circumference of the cake."

"Only three hours?" Nicole chuckled. "I think you got off rather lightly there."

Emily smirked. "Next time I'll tell her to talk to you about it."

Nicole shook her head. "No, I've done my time. I've been Olivia's best friend for more years than I dare to say. You're marrying her, you can deal with her micromanagement."

Emily leaned her head on her hand and looked at Nicole with a smile.

"Gee, thanks. And I thought you were here to help me."

"I'm here to be your agent and help you with scriptwriting." She waved her hand towards Olivia. "You're on your own with that."

Emily looked at a piece of paper with some hastily jotted figures on it. It was the total amount of money she was due to receive from current script sales. Not everything had been finalised yet, and most of the money was still to be received. Nevertheless, it was an amazing feeling to think that scripts that had been sitting in a box under her bed were now making money.

But nowhere near enough money.

Her face fell at the realisation that she was still a long way from her goal.

"Problem?" Nicole asked softly.

"No, just thinking," Emily lied.

Nicole was a good friend and a fantastic agent. But she wasn't great at keeping her mouth shut. Emily didn't want Nicole, and by extension Olivia, to know about her desire to pay Olivia back the enormous sum she had used to clear Emily's debts.

It was the only thing in their relationship that they struggled to agree on. Olivia thought money was an object, just like any other. When Emily had been locked in a legal battle with Henry's grandparents, the debts she had accumulated over years of paying for his healthcare had become a huge issue. Once Olivia discovered that the debts were being used as leverage in a pointless attempt at blackmail by Henry's grandparents, she had cleared them without saying a word to Emily.

Of course, Emily had forgiven her for the deception and was grateful beyond words that Olivia had done that for her, regardless of their relationship status. But Emily was determined to pay Olivia back every last cent, even if it took the rest of her life.

It was important to her. She needed to feel that she was on an equal footing with her wealthy wife-to-be. Even though they would never be matched when it came to personal wealth, at least Emily could feel that she didn't owe her anything.

So, while the scripts she had sold would put a small dent in the debt, there was still a mountain to climb.

"Can I make the other scripts sellable?" Emily asked.

"I think so, some of them," Nicole said. "As I said, they'd need a lot of reworking. What you really need is experience working in the trade. A lot of scriptwriters fall down on the same thing, lack of experience. You need to know how a production works in order to know what script will fit into the theatre scene. Little things like too many actors, too many sets, and not enough variety in location. Things like that can provide resistance and prevent someone from wanting to take a chance on an unknown scriptwriter."

"But how do you get experience in something like that?" Emily asked.

"That's the problem, it's an endless cycle," Nicole admitted.

Emily noted the unmistakable twinkle in her eye that suggested an idea.

"However, we might be able to work something out," Nicole said.

Nicole looked from one piece of paper to another. Emily watched her quietly and allowed her to finish whatever thought process she was in the middle of. Being one of the founding partners of Brightview Productions, she was in a perfect position to help Emily realise her dream.

Emily had spent the last few weeks pinching herself to see if she was actually dreaming. She feared she'd wake up one day, and it would all vanish into nothingness.

"This is just a suggestion," Nicole said, "but how about we do a deal? As you know, Brightview is moving into the final production stages for the script we bought from you. We could bring you in as a consultant. You could work beside one of our current in-house scriptwriters and learn the ropes."

Emily opened her mouth to speak, but no words came forth. She closed her mouth again. Her brain started swimming with questions, and she wasn't sure which to ask first.

"Obviously, it would be in London," Nicole continued, seemingly unaware of Emily's bewilderment. "And we begin work on the Monday after your honeymoon. But I think we can work around these details. You'd be getting an amazing opportunity to learn more, to work in a theatre and for a production company."

Emily finally found her tongue. "It sounds great! But there's no way I could afford the flights."

Nicole nodded her understanding. "Well, we could adjust the royalty split that we have set up. You could take less of a percentage, and we can pay for your flights. And, once the production is up and running, we may have something else for you. Or your experience might get you a job here in New York. We'll see how things go and what comes up in the meantime. The important thing is that you'll have firsthand experience at what it takes to put on a production. You'll see the direct correlation between script and production."

Emily felt the familiar palpitations. She tried to think logically about the proposal, but she was overwhelmed.

"I know it's a lot to take in," Nicole said apologetically. "And obviously, there's a time pressure on your decision. But I wouldn't recommend this unless I genuinely felt that it was a good opportunity for you."

Emily licked her lips and placed her hands palm down on the table to ground herself.

"So, hold on, let me get this right. I'd take a royalty cut, but you'd fly me to London and back?"

Nicole nodded.

"How long would I be gone? I can't leave Henry…or Olivia. Not just after the honeymoon. And Henry starts school then…"

Nicole picked up a calculator from the table and quickly input some figures. "Yes, well, it will be a four-week project. So, how about we pay for you to fly to London on a Sunday evening and back to New York on a Friday evening for as long as the project lasts? You'll be away during the week but home at weekends."

Emily tried to calculate all the questions she should be asking, but her mind was coming up blank. She knew it would be an amazing opportunity, but she also didn't want to leave her family for long periods at a time. Especially with Henry starting school. She didn't want to give him extra stress, or make Olivia have to deal with what would be a big event in Henry's life.

"Sorry to throw this at you right before your wedding," Nicole said. "It's just that I can't guarantee Brightview will host another of your plays, and if we do I couldn't possibly say when. But this I can guarantee."

"I understand," Emily quickly said. "And I really do appreciate the offer. It's just a lot to take in. I need to think it over."

"Of course." Nicole started to gather up the paperwork that had been strewn over the table. "Chat with Olivia and let me know what you think."

"I will. And thank you, I know this isn't something you'd do for just anyone."

"I believe in the quality of your work, Emily. You have a style that is quite unique, and I genuinely believe that you have a lot to offer the theatre world in a time where theatre is frankly struggling. You just need the opportunity to see behind the curtain."

Emily picked up her mug and took another sip. She pictured herself standing in the stalls of a London theatre, looking up at the actors on the stage reading out words she had written years before.

It really was a golden opportunity.

Chapter Two

Olivia sat on the edge of the sofa, waiting to stand up and offer help. Even though she knew it would be declined. Emily was very keen on doing most of the household tasks herself, especially the laundry. She claimed that as Henry went through anywhere between two and five clothes changes a day, she felt obliged to take on all the laundry. Which was clearly ridiculous, as Henry's clothes were a quarter of the size of the adults' and Olivia didn't feel that laundry was such an arduous task.

But she knew it was best to remain seated while Emily spoke about whatever it was that was bothering her.

Nicole had left, Henry had been put to bed, and Emily had poured Olivia a glass of wine and ordered her to sit on the sofa. Emily had returned with the laundry basket and started to fold clothes while she explained Nicole's work offer.

Olivia could tell that Emily was slightly agitated, but she couldn't quite figure out why. The fact that she was attempting to fold Henry's tiny socks was an indication of her distraction.

"It sounds like a good idea," Olivia said, hoping that it was the right thing to say.

Emily dropped a half-folded sweater into the laundry basket and looked at Olivia with pleading eyes.

"Really?" Emily asked.

"It's an amazing opportunity," Olivia said.

"But I'll be away from home," Emily said. She picked up the sweater again and started to refold it.

Olivia bit her lip and looked out the window. It was dark outside, and she stared at the tree branches shifting in front of the streetlight. She didn't want Emily to go away. It already felt like there had been so much wasted time between them. She wanted to spend every feasible moment together, even if she knew that wasn't necessarily possible. And maybe not wise.

"You don't want me to go, do you?" Emily asked.

Olivia turned back to face her. "I do. A-and I don't."

Emily waited for her to continue.

Olivia licked her lips and prepared herself. It was one of those conversations. A big one, an important one. One that had the possibility of going oh-so-wrong. They'd talked at length about Olivia's fear of saying the wrong thing. Emily was calm and tried to see the meaning behind some of Olivia's less artful words. But even so, the fear of getting everything wrong worried Olivia immensely.

"I want you to be happy," Olivia said. It seemed like a safe starting point. "I'll miss you terribly during the week. But I can see that this is a great opportunity and one I don't think will appear again."

"I don't want to be away from you," Emily said. "And what about Henry?"

Olivia frowned. "What about Henry?"

Emily gave her that look. The look that indicated that she might have said something stupid.

"I-I mean, of course, I'll look after Henry."

Emily's look softened to one of curiosity.

Olivia snatched the glass of wine from the table and stood up.

"It makes sense. You have an opportunity, and I'm not working at the moment. I will tend to Henry while you focus on your career. I know Henry's routines, he's comfortable with me. I'm sure between us we could make him understand that you need to work. He's always been understanding of that in the past."

Olivia walked in front of the window. She gestured towards the upstairs of the house with her wine glass. "I've been involved in all the discussions regarding his school. I'd made a small list of things we need to prepare. I'm happy to take over in that regard. And then we can make the weekends extra special."

"Really?" Emily breathed.

Olivia looked at her and frowned. It seemed the logical thing to do. Of course she'd watch over Henry. She wasn't sure why Emily was looking at her as if she'd agreed to some horrendous undertaking.

"Absolutely," Olivia said. "This is something you have to do. I know how much you want to be a scriptwriter. Real-life experience is going to be such a break for you. You simply have to take these opportunities when they arise. Henry and I will be fine. Besides, Henry will be at school all day so he'll barely have *time* to miss you."

Emily dropped an unfolded T-shirt into the laundry basket. She looked at Olivia with a smile. "You're incredible. I should marry you."

"You should." Olivia looked at her watch. "In thirty-six hours."

Emily crossed the room slowly, her eyes fixed on Olivia.

"I'm bored of laundry," she said.

Olivia placed her wine glass on the coffee table. "I'll take over," she offered.

Emily took her wrist and spun her around so they were facing each other.

"I'm bored of laundry," Emily repeated, slower this time.

Olivia considered Emily's eyes. Something was up, and she couldn't quite tell what it was.

Suddenly, the penny dropped.

"Oh! Yes, well, the laundry can wait," Olivia said.

Emily smiled and gently tugged on Olivia's wrist. She led her through the living room. Olivia reached out and turned off the downstairs lights as she was steered upstairs.

CHAPTER THREE

Emily critically eyed her reflection in the floor-length mirror. She ran her hands over the front of her white wedding dress, brushing out non-existent creases. Her heart fluttered nervously in her chest.

After weeks of planning, the day was finally here. She was marrying Olivia Lewis. Months ago, when she was working as cabin crew in the first-class compartment of a transatlantic flight, she would never have dreamed that Olivia would become the love of her life. Now, she couldn't imagine life without Olivia.

That thought did little to quell the butterflies racing through her stomach.

Emily had always been pragmatic. She'd always let her head lead her heart, never the other way around. She knew that she hadn't known Olivia that long. Their relationship had gone from dating to moving in together in record time, and the notion of marriage had quickly followed.

But she'd fallen head over heels in love. She knew that Olivia was the one. She'd never experienced the sensation before. Knowing without a shadow of a doubt that you had found your perfect partner. Understanding with heart and soul that looking any further would be utterly pointless.

Sadly, such understanding didn't stop wedding day jitters.

"Mommy, Olivia looks like a princess!" Henry exclaimed as he came bursting into her room.

Emily chuckled and put her hands on her hips as she looked down at him.

"Don't I look like a princess?" she asked.

Henry looked at her thoughtfully for a few moments before shrugging.

Emily turned away from him and looked at herself in the mirror again.

"You're not helping Mommy's nerves," she told him with a sigh.

Henry softly elbowed his way in between her and the mirror to see his own reflection.

"Are you nervous?" he giggled as if the thought were ridiculous. "I am."

Henry made an amused face and then started to reach for his gelled hair. Emily took his hand and shook her head.

"Leave your hair alone, at least until after the photographs have been taken."

Henry nodded and lowered his hand. He looked at his reflection and sighed.

"Why do I have to wear a suit, Mommy? It's tight. And heavy."

She smirked. Henry had recently discovered the art of lying to get his way, and while it worked well with Olivia, she knew when Henry was being liberal with the truth.

"Oh, then I suppose you should go home. We'll go on the honeymoon without you," she suggested lightly.

Henry's eyebrows rose in shock. "I want to go on the honeymoon, Mommy," he argued.

When the idea of a honeymoon had been brought up, Emily had been hesitant. Yes, she wanted to go on a honeymoon and spend time with Olivia, but the timing of the wedding was difficult. It was only a short time before Henry started school, which happened to be the same time that Emily started her new job as a scriptwriter in London. Emily didn't want to spend time away from Henry right before they were both embarking on new adventures in their lives.

Olivia had quickly solved the problem: Henry would join them on their honeymoon. It was just another reason Emily adored her.

Some people would have taken a while to settle into the role of stepparent. But Olivia loved Henry and would do anything for him. Honeymoon plans were quickly changed to include things suitable for a five-year-old boy. And now, Henry was more excited about the honeymoon than anyone else.

"But we're going straight from the reception to the honeymoon, if your suit is too tight and too heavy then you'll need to go home," Emily explained.

Henry's shoulders slumped. "I'll be okay," he promised as if making a great sacrifice on her behalf.

Emily smothered a smile and walked back towards her dressing table. She knew without a shadow of a doubt that Olivia would have raced around, seeking out a new suit for him. And Olivia would probably manage it, too. She smiled at the mental image of Olivia rushing into the local mall in her wedding dress, demanding that a child's suit of impossibly light material be produced immediately.

She looked at her hair, wondering if the complicated up-style was worth the sensation of a hundred hair clips digging into her skull.

"Mommy? Mommy?" Henry stood beside her and tugged on her cap sleeve excitedly.

She turned and took his head in her hands, staring at him intently and responding to his enthusiasm in kind. "Yes, Henry?"

He giggled at her behaviour but quickly put on a serious expression.

"Mommy, I need a kitten."

Emily laughed. She continued to cup his face as she shook her head. "You don't *need* a kitten, Henry. You certainly don't need a kitten. On. My. Wedding. Day." She kissed his forehead and let him go. "We'll talk about it later, I promise."

"Okay," he said reluctantly. He looked at her seriously for a moment. "You're very pretty."

Emily narrowed her eyes. "Are you saying that because you want a kitten or because you actually think I'm pretty?"

"Because you're pretty!" Henry said with a wide grin.

Emily chuckled. "I'm not sure I believe you. I mean, I don't look like a princess like Olivia." She pretended to be hurt and turned away to look at her reflection again.

"But you always look like a princess, Mommy," Henry said sincerely.

Emily looked at his reflection in the mirror and smiled. "Henry?"

"Mommy?" He met her eyes in the glass.

"I love you very much."

Henry frowned, clearly confused as to why the subject was being brought up. He was starting to grow out of the never-ending kisses and declarations of love phase.

"Can you go and get Lucy for me?" Emily asked.

Happy to have a task, Henry turned away and started to run from the room.

"Remember to knock!" Emily called after him, hoping that he'd heard and would in his excitement.

She looked at her reflection again, wondering where the sudden doubt over her appearance had come from. She'd never been one to particularly worry about her looks, figuring that she couldn't do much to change them, so why worry?

But now she couldn't tear her eyes away from the mirrors in the hotel room. And there were a lot of them. Apparently, when you were getting married, the hotel wheeled out every mirror in New York so you could see parts of your appearance never seen before and start to worry about them.

"Knock knock!"

"Come in, Nicole!" Emily called out.

Nicole walked in and stopped dead in the middle of the room. She put her hand over her heart and smiled.

"Darling, you look incredible."

Emily could feel herself blush. "Do I? Are you sure? I'm really nervous."

"Oh, you're supposed to be nervous, I'd be worried if you weren't. Olivia's a basket case."

"Is she?" Emily felt happier knowing that Olivia was also feeling the nerves. Something about her strong and put-together fiancée also being terrified helped to centre her. Strength in numbers, she assumed.

"She is," Nicole said. She took a few steps forward and twirled her finger in the air. "Come on, give me a spin for the full effect."

Emily laughed and took a self-conscious spin.

"Gorgeous," Nicole decided. "Absolutely gorgeous. Olivia's a lucky woman."

"I bet she looks amazing, doesn't she?" Emily asked. She hated being separated from her. Olivia's insistence that they not see each other before the wedding was ridiculous, superstition be damned. She wanted nothing more than to get into the elevator and go down a couple of floors to where Olivia was presumably pacing a hotel room in much the same way she was.

"You both look gorgeous," Nicole replied diplomatically.

Emily frowned. "She's not on her own, is she?"

"No, Sophie's with her," Nicole said. She sat in an armchair in front of the large window and let out a sigh. "Young Sophie who's glowing with pregnancy and also looking gorgeous."

Emily chuckled. "Nicole, you look fantastic."

"Do I?" Nicole perked up. "How nice of you to say."

It was true, Nicole looked great. But Emily always thought that Nicole looked great. Like Olivia, Nicole just seemed to effortlessly look incredible.

Emily was no stranger to looking impeccable, but that was when she worked cabin crew. When she knew that immaculate nail polish and not a hair out of place was fundamental to keeping her job. On an average day, Emily pulled her long, blond hair into a ponytail and was content to wear whatever fell out of the wardrobe first.

Nicole and Olivia were professional adults, sometimes even wearing suits and heels on days off.

"Can I come in?"

"Come in, Luce," Emily called.

"Oh, it's turning into a party! I should have brought some wine," Nicole said.

Lucy hurried into the room. Once she caught sight of Emily, she gasped and covered her mouth with her hand. She let out a little scream before rushing towards Emily and wrapping her in a hug.

No sooner had she hugged Emily, she stood back and started walking around her, looking her up and down.

"You look amazing!" Lucy squeaked. "Oh my God, you look so amazing."

Lucy spun to look at Nicole. "How's Olivia? Does she look amazing?"

"*Everyone* looks amazing," Nicole assured her. "And Olivia is fine. Anxious to get on with the show, but fine."

"Tom is walking Henry through their roles again," Lucy explained. "Just another thirty minutes!"

Emily flopped into the chair at the dressing table. "Thirty minutes? It was thirty-five minutes about an hour ago!"

"It's wedding time, wedding time doesn't follow the rules of normal time," Lucy said. "If you're running late, then every minute you spend is actually ten minutes. If you're ready early, then it's the reverse."

"It's the same as theatre time," Nicole said. "If everyone is ready to go ten minutes before curtain up, then those ten minutes take about an hour."

The comment about work jogged Emily's memory. "Oh yes, I may need to change my flight time arriving in London…"

Nicole raised an eyebrow. "If you talk about work now, I'll pull the fire alarm."

Emily laughed and held up her hands. "Okay, okay, no work talk."

"Is everyone decent?"

"Come in, Simon," Emily called out.

"You're going to need more chairs. Maybe have the wedding here and save on the venue hire," Nicole said.

Olivia's former assistant entered the room. Once he saw Emily he fell to his knees dramatically, his arms outstretched and his face one of awe. "Wow!"

"Oh, shut up," Emily told him. She laughed at his overreaction. He smiled and stood up again. "You look incredible. Seriously."

Emily walked over to him and adjusted his tie slightly. "You look very handsome. Are you wearing foundation?"

Simon nodded excitedly. "I stole some of Sophie's. My skin looks great!"

"It does," Emily said. She held on to Simon's tie. "So, apropos of nothing, what happened at Olivia's bachelorette party last night?"

Simon's eyes flicked down to where Emily was slowly tightening his tie.

"Nothing," he quickly said. He looked to Nicole. "Why don't you ask her? She was there, too!"

"She's kind of my boss now. I can't threaten my boss," Emily told him with a wink. "And if anyone would be stupid enough to organise something silly…like strippers, it would be you, not Nicole."

"No strippers, nothing like that. Promise," Simon said.

Emily readjusted his tie and patted it down. "Good, good." She winked at him again.

"What did you girls get up to anyway? Sophie won't say a word," Simon asked.

Lucy laughed. "What happens at a bachelorette party, stays at a bachelorette party."

"When it suits you," Simon said. "And remember that Sophie isn't drinking, so she remembers everything. She'll be blackmailing you for her silence any day now."

"No, you're confusing your lovely girlfriend with yourself," Lucy told him.

Their playful bickering blended into the background as Emily started to panic. In under half an hour she'd be getting married. Something she desperately wanted, but something that terrified her nonetheless. Why was she so nervous?

Nicole appeared by her side. "Do you want to raid the minibar?" she whispered.

Emily chuckled and shook her head. "No, I'm just really nervous. I want it to be done. I just want to be married. All this waiting around is killing me."

Nicole handed Emily her iPhone. "Angry Birds. It's gotten me through my niece's school nativity, a three-hour flight delay, and a nightmare wait for hospital results."

Emily felt Olivia's lips on hers and almost let out a sigh of relief.

It was done.

They were married.

She was glad that Olivia had thought to hire a videographer because she was already struggling to remember any details of the wedding aside from sheer panic.

From the moment she had seen Olivia standing beneath the flowered archway in the hotel gardens, everything had gone blank. The crowd of people had merged into the background, the violinist's music had become white static in her ears.

She was thankful for Tom agreeing to take on the role of father of the bride and guiding her down the aisle. Without his support, she was sure she would have remained glued to her spot, unable to move. Olivia, being a problem-solver, would have eventually moved the archway to where Emily stood, immobile.

Now, she felt Olivia's warm and soft lips on hers. Everything was returning to normal. She could hear the violins, the sound of the crowd applauding, and Simon wolf-whistling above everyone else. She could feel Henry's hand touching her leg, Olivia's hand on her arm. Soft gestures of comfort that reminded her of the little family they had managed to create.

Olivia ended the kiss and leaned back a little. She looked amazing. Her makeup and hair were perfection, as always, but the passion in her brown eyes took Emily's breath away.

"Are you okay?" Olivia whispered.

"Very okay, especially now that it's over."

"It's not over." Olivia frowned. "There's still the photos, the cake cutting, the meal, speeches, party—"

"Olivia," Emily warned her.

Olivia was still working on identifying when her fastidious attention to detail stressed Emily out. Clearly, this was a time when she needed a little guidance.

"Oh." Olivia's eyes widened. "It…will all be fine. I'm here."

Emily smiled. "Thank you, that's just what I needed to hear."

Olivia beamed with satisfaction. They turned to face the guests, who were still cheering and clapping loudly. They started to walk down the centre aisle, but Emily felt Henry's hand tugging on her dress and paused.

"Mommy?" Henry asked. "About the kitten…"

"Henry, maybe later?" Emily suggested.

❖

"We need sperm."

Emily nearly choked on her food. She turned to regard Olivia with a look that she hoped conveyed now was not the time for such a conversation.

Unfortunately, Olivia took the look as confusion and decided to explain further.

"To make the baby. If I'm going to have a baby, then we need sperm," Olivia explained as if Emily was unsure of the finer workings of baby production. Despite already having had a child.

She quickly swallowed her food and looked around the large dining room, hoping that none of the guests were able to overhear Olivia's words. Being at the head table meant that many people were occasionally glancing at them and raising a wine glass in salutation.

"Not now," Emily whispered as she smiled at Olivia's uncle who was smiling at them. She raised her own glass in thanks.

"Well, I have to ask Simon tonight. We won't see him again before he flies home," Olivia explained.

Emily spun her head to face Olivia. "Simon?"

"Yes. He's a friend, he'd be happy to do it. And we know he's already made a baby, so he's obviously fertile." Olivia picked up her wine glass and took a sip.

Emily's mouth opened and closed. This was not something they'd discussed. Not something she'd expected to discuss. And certainly not at her wedding reception.

"We need to talk about this in more detail before we make any rash decisions. And, I don't mean talk about it right now," Emily said firmly, hoping to end Olivia's interest in the conversation quickly.

Olivia slowly nodded and returned to her own meal. Emily watched her process the exchange. She knew it would go one of two ways, either Olivia would understand that now was not the right time, or—

"I'm not suggesting I sleep with him, just that he provides his sperm. Not tonight, that would be odd," she said. "But we need to speak with him. To sow the seed, so to speak. He'll put it in a little plastic pot—"

"Olivia!" Emily hissed. "Now is really not the time or the place to talk about this. Simon might not want to do it, or Sophie might not want him to do it. If you ask them on your wedding day, it will be hard for them to say no. Hell, I don't even know if I want him to do it."

Olivia looked confused. "But, we're supposed to be having a baby."

"Not in the next two days," Emily said. "We can talk about this later. It doesn't all have to be now." Emily brushed a strand of hair behind Olivia's ear.

She knew that Olivia was suddenly wondering about the next stage in her life. When Olivia had stepped down from being managing director at Applewood Financial, she'd thrown herself into decorating the house. And then into planning the wedding. And then the honeymoon.

In Olivia's mind, the wedding was practically over, and she was itching to get onto the next thing. Emily had known that the subject would be approaching at some point, but she'd still hoped that sperm wouldn't be a topic of discussion over the fish course.

"I promise we will talk about it soon, just not tonight. I want to be absolutely sure that we can't make a baby ourselves before we get outside help." Emily waggled her eyebrows suggestively.

Olivia frowned. "We can't make—"

Emily stared at her pointedly.

"Oh, oh!" Olivia suddenly understood. "Yes, of course, you're right. We should try ourselves, just to be sure."

Emily smiled and returned to her meal. She glanced up and saw Simon smiling at her. She quickly looked back to her plate, feeling her cheeks heat as she did.

CHAPTER FOUR

Olivia sipped her coffee. She stood in front of the large hotel window and looked out at the ocean. The dark blue waters glistened in the sunlight. The early morning joggers were already up and running along the beach.

She sighed.

"Are you sad?" Henry asked.

She turned to look at Henry, who was eyeing her suspiciously.

"No, why would I be sad?" she asked.

"Because you keep sighing." Henry pointed to the ever-present toy giraffe on the dining table. "Tiny says you're sad."

"Well, Tiny is wrong, I'm extremely happy." Olivia walked over to the table.

It wasn't entirely true. She felt like she *should* feel extremely happy. But, in reality, she was struggling with the big questions that Emily assured her could wait until they were back from their honeymoon.

Questions like, when they would investigate having a baby? What would the future look like? What was the timetable for the next few months?

Olivia's life had always been set to an exacting schedule. She knew what would happen the next day; she even knew what would happen the next month. Things were organised and followed a certain pattern.

Until recently.

Now, not a lot made sense. Big questions were met with no firm answer. She supposed this was something she'd need to get used to. Even if the very thought of not knowing caused a slight sweat to form at her brow.

She looked at Henry. "I'm just thinking about the day. I believe we're going shopping. That will be nice, won't it?"

"But Mommy said we were going to the beach again today." Henry pulled the crust off a piece of toast and started to eat it.

"I thought we were going shopping?" Olivia frowned.

She was certain that Emily had decided to have a day away from the beach, her pale skin beginning to complain at the strength of the sun.

"No, she said we're going to the beach," Henry repeated.

Olivia sipped her coffee. She eyed the closed bedroom door over the rim of the cup. She'd promised Emily an extra hour in bed, but now she was conflicted. Did she get Henry ready for a day at the beach or a day shopping?

She turned to regard Henry, who was telling Tiny about the enormous sand castle he was going to build at the beach.

She placed her empty coffee mug in the dishwasher in the open-plan kitchen of their hotel suite.

"You can watch ten minutes of television," she told Henry as she walked past him.

She'd barely finished the sentence before Henry was scooping up Tiny and his plastic breakfast plate and running to the living area.

She quietly crept into the master bedroom, closing the door behind her. The room was dark, a small streak of sunlight hitting the wall where the curtains had been hastily drawn.

Emily lay spread-eagle on the bed, the sound of her gentle breathing piercing the silence.

A memory of the night before flashed through Olivia's mind, and she felt her cheeks flush. They'd been on honeymoon for four days. In some ways, she wished it would never end. Spending time with Emily and Henry was a blessing. They'd watched movies, played at the beach, and played tourist around the local area. It was pure bliss.

Except for something niggling at the back of her mind. An anxious feeling. As with all vacations, she felt eager to get home and get back into the swing of work. Not that work existed for her anymore. Since she had been ousted from her own company, work was something that other people did.

And so, she found her mind drifting during movies, or while staring at the cresting waves of the sea, wondering what life would look like when she got home. She had to remind herself not to wish away the vacation in search of stability and order.

Things were looking very different indeed.

She was married; she was a mother to Henry. And she was unemployed, living off her considerable savings while Emily forged her new writing career.

After years of a very strict schedule, Olivia found herself adhering to other people's. Waking early to get Henry ready in the morning and allowing Emily to sleep in, a luxury Emily hadn't often experienced.

She loved being a source of assistance and strength to Emily. She wanted Emily to know she could rely on her, to know that they were a team. It gave her an enormous sense of pride and satisfaction to be the rock that Emily leaned on. Especially as Emily was a strong and independent woman who had almost never accepted support from anyone in the past.

She sat on the edge of the bed, not really wanting to wake Emily but knowing that she needed clarification on the day's plans before preparing Henry for the day.

"Emily," she whispered, reaching out and softly running her fingers through long blond locks.

Emily's eyes fluttered open, and she lifted her head a little to regard Olivia.

"Everythin' okay?" she mumbled.

"Yes, I'm sorry to wake you," Olivia said. "What are we doing today? I thought we were going shopping, but Henry says we're going to the beach?"

Emily chuckled and turned over to lie on her back. She pulled the sheet up to cover herself.

"Henry's lying," Emily informed her.

Olivia released an irritated breath through her nose. She couldn't believe he had managed to con her again.

Emily reached her hand out and massaged Olivia's knee through her jeans.

"Don't worry."

Olivia shook her head. "I don't understand why he's suddenly lying to me."

"He lies to me as well," Emily said. "And to Lucy, and Irene… anyone who will listen. It's a phase."

"When does this phase end?" Olivia asked.

"Soon," Emily said. "I'll speak to him again. He just knows you're a soft touch."

Olivia jumped to her feet. "I'm not a soft touch," she complained.

Emily laughed. "You are. You'd give him the world, and he knows it. You're the weak link in the chain, sorry."

Olivia bent down and picked up Emily's clothes from the floor, discarded eagerly the night before.

"I really don't see where this behaviour came from," Olivia grumbled.

Emily sat up in bed and rubbed her eyes. "He's young, he's learning social skills. Like all other children, he stumbled on the fact that sometimes you can get exactly what you want by lying. He's exploiting that knowledge."

"He doesn't exploit you," Olivia said. She folded Emily's clothes and placed them on the top of the chest of drawers.

"He tries. But I'm a human lie detector, so I see through his fibs."

Olivia shook her head again. "I'm not enjoying this stage of his development."

Emily chuckled. "I don't think anyone does. Do you know what you have to do now?"

Olivia regarded her. "No, what?"

"Punish him."

Olivia blanched. "P-punish him?"

"Yep. I'm not talking about hot pokers or anything, but you need to do something. He lied to you, and you need to demonstrate to him that, firstly, you caught him in a lie. And, secondly, you need to punish him. If you don't, you'll always be the soft touch."

Olivia sat in the chair in the corner of the room. She knew being a parent would have difficult moments, but the idea of punishing Henry horrified her. So far, Emily had taken the lead on anything like that.

"We agreed that we would be equal partners in Henry's life," Emily said. "You can't always think of him as my son. He thinks of you as a second mother now."

"He calls me Olivia."

"Only because you haven't encouraged him to call you something else. If you wanted him to call you 'Mom,' then he would. He adores you."

Olivia's heart soared at the very thought. She did consider Henry her son, but she was always wary of stepping on Emily's toes. She didn't want Emily to feel like she was being replaced. And there was something so real about being called "Mom." The weight of the responsibility was heavy; she knew she would be ready for it when it came. But she wasn't sure if she wanted to assist in its early arrival.

"What kind of punishment?" she asked.

Emily shrugged. "What do you think is appropriate?"

Olivia stood behind the sofa and listened to the magical sound of Henry's giggles. She narrowed her eyes. He sat in his giraffe-emblazoned pyjamas, happily watching morning cartoons.

She knew the happy scene in front of her was about to dramatically change. And she would be the cause of that change. It seemed so grossly unfair that Henry had caused the situation, and her actions, actions required to fix the situation and make him a better person, were about to cause tears and heartbreak. For everyone.

"Henry," she said slowly.

He turned and looked at her with a big grin on his face. She loved that smile. The dimples. The big cheeks that she hoped he'd never grow into.

Henry's grin faded, and a puzzled expression replaced it as the silence continued.

"Henry," she started again. She dug deep and found some strength. "Did Mommy really say that we were going to the beach today?"

Henry quickly nodded his head.

It was a mistake.

The bold-faced lie right to her face caused Olivia to see red. Her sweet, innocent little boy had just lied to her.

"I know that's not true," Olivia said calmly.

"Yes, it is," he said firmly.

"You're lying to me, and we've already told you that's wrong. So, no television for one week."

Henry's mouth dropped open in horror. He stared at her for a moment, ascertaining the truth of her statement. His eyes filled with tears, and he let out a pained cry. He stumbled to his feet and ran from the living room towards the master bedroom.

Olivia felt any residual anger at being lied to leave her. Anguish replaced it in a split second. Who knew that being a parent could be such an emotional rollercoaster? She found herself rooted to the spot, staring blankly at the doorway Henry had vanished through. She had made him cry, for the first time. And he'd run to Emily to dry his tears. She felt like a monster.

Emily appeared in the doorway, buttoning up her top, all thoughts of some extra rest gone. Henry walked beside her, his face bright red and his breath coming in heavy pants as he tried to explain how he had been wronged.

"Why did she do that?" Emily asked Henry. She offered Olivia a sympathetic smile.

"I…don't…know…" Henry wheezed in between tears.

"I think you do," Emily said as she crossed to the kitchen.

"No," Henry said.

Emily poured herself a cup of coffee from the carafe. "Are you sure? Because I heard that you told a lie. And if you told a lie, then I think you should be punished. We don't tell lies, do we?"

Henry backhanded a few tears and shook his head. His cheeks were bright red with the exertion. Olivia worried that all the blood in his body was currently in his head. Surely that couldn't be healthy?

But Emily stood tall, slowly sipping her coffee and looking down at him with a neutral expression.

Olivia was impressed that Emily didn't crumble and scoop him up into a hug. But then she supposed it was that kind of behaviour that would prevent Henry from ever learning.

"Maybe you should say something to Olivia?" Emily suggested. She tilted her head in her Olivia's direction.

Olivia held her breath and stood a little straighter. She was sure that Henry would hate her forever. She'd punished him and made him cry. How would he ever forgive her? She would have to comfort herself that she was helping to raise a good person, even if that good person resented her cruelty.

Henry started walking towards Olivia. The action quickly turned into a sprint and he fell into her legs at speed, nearly knocking her over.

"I'm sorry, Olivia. I'm sorry I lied!" he cried through his tears. "Please don't hate me."

Olivia pushed aside any notion of stoically standing by. Instead, she fell to her knees and pulled him into a hug.

"I could never hate you," she promised him. "Never."

Henry sobbed onto her shoulder, and Olivia gripped him tightly. She looked up to see Emily looking at her. Emily raised her eyebrow meaningfully. Olivia let out a sigh. This was the bit she hated, the follow-through. Emily had explained again and again the importance of the follow-through.

She swallowed. "I love you very much," she said. "But you're still not allowed to watch television for one week. And you need to remember to not lie to me."

Henry's head nodded against her shoulder.

"Okay, let's put this behind us and have a great day," Emily said. "Henry, go to your room and get some clothes out for shopping, all right? I'll be in soon to help you get ready."

Henry pulled away and dashed towards his bedroom.

Olivia got to her feet and looked at Emily. "That was hard."

"It was. But it's the right thing to do. He'll forget about all of this within the next fifteen minutes."

"I won't," Olivia said.

Emily walked over and placed a soft kiss on her lips. "Being a parent is hard. But you're very good at it."

"Why do people put themselves through this? I'm going to feel guilty about this moment for days, *weeks*, to come. Henry is probably not going to remember it by dinner. And he caused the problem," Olivia grumbled.

"Are you sure you want to have another one?" Emily asked seriously.

Olivia thought about the question for a few moments. She did want another child. She wanted Henry to have a sibling to play with, and she wanted to grow their family. She didn't feel like they needed another baby to be a family, but somehow, it felt right.

"The pros substantially outweigh the cons."

"Spoken like a true mathematician," Emily replied with a smile.

Olivia barked a laugh. "Is that what I am?"

"Of course."

Olivia shrugged. "I don't feel like one. I don't feel like much of anything at the moment. It's a strange time," she admitted.

"It's one of the things you are. Even if you aren't working. A doctor is still a doctor even when they're unemployed. You're still a finance wizard even though you're not working." Emily walked back to the kitchen and opened the cupboard to fetch a bowl. "Are you sure you don't want to go back to work?"

"Of course, we agreed that I'd stay with Henry and the baby while you build up your new career," Olivia said.

"Just because I'm starting a new career doesn't mean that you can't work if you want to. I know that work is important to you. And I like the suits." Emily winked.

Olivia laughed but shook her head. "No, we made an agreement. It's important that one of us remains with the children. Especially if you're going to be flying back and forth to London."

Olivia had made a promise to Emily, and it was one she intended to keep. She didn't want Emily to have to worry about things. They were a team now; she would stay home while Emily learned her new craft. She wasn't about to go back on a promise she made two days before their wedding. Even if she was struggling to see what her future looked like now.

"You could come with me sometimes. Lucy would happily take Henry for a few days if you wanted to come and see the theatre," Emily suggested.

Olivia vehemently shook her head. "I told you, I'm not ready to get on one of those death traps." The memory of the crash was still vivid in her mind. Her ankle throbbed with a phantom pain.

"You have to get back on the horse eventually. Are you going to stay in New York and surrounding areas, doomed to only travel in cars and trains, for the rest of your life?" Emily asked.

"As I believe I proved when planning this honeymoon, this country has a perfectly nice railroad network."

"It does," Emily said, "but it doesn't take you to Europe. And what if Henry wants to go to…I don't know…Disney?"

"The train—" Olivia began.

"…Land."

Olivia brought up the mental image of the railway map and pondered routes from New York to California. It wouldn't be easy, or fast.

"Not to mention that I don't want Henry to be frightened of planes. Especially as I'm going to be using them so often," Emily continued. "Think about it. Please?"

Olivia swallowed and nodded.

Emily leaned closer and placed a chaste kiss on Olivia's cheek. "Thank you." She returned her attention to preparing her breakfast.

Olivia wondered how on earth she got so lucky. She may have been unsure of some things, like her suddenly non-existent career path, but she knew choosing Emily as a life partner was the best decision of her life.

Now she just needed to ensure she lived up to Emily's expectations.

❖

Olivia arranged the stack of napkins so they sat at the correct angle to the table. The noise of the busy food court at the shopping mall made it difficult to focus on anything, and she mentally willed Emily to hurry in her return.

Sensory overload, Emily had called it. Noisy, Olivia had corrected her. She wasn't ready to start labelling situations that frustrated her; she knew where that path led.

"When we get home, can I paint?" Henry asked.

"Home to the hotel or home?" Olivia asked.

Sending the concierge out for children's painting supplies had been somewhat frowned upon by Emily on the second day of their stay. Even if they were staying at a luxury resort and, as far as Olivia was concerned, that's what the concierge was there for. Besides, the man didn't complain the first two times she sent him out. Although, maybe the third time to get a better shade of yellow had been pushing it.

"Home," Henry clarified. He reached forward and pushed the straws so they were precisely angled to the napkins. He'd taken to helping Olivia arrange table settings exactly, happy to help position every item perfectly.

"Then, yes."

"Will you paint with me?"

Olivia gave him a sideways glance. Henry seemed to have completely forgotten about his earlier tantrum. It surprised her that just a few hours had passed, and he was acting like it never happened. She knew he'd forget eventually, but it had happened so quickly.

He'd taken her hand as they arrived at the mall and animatedly pointed out the grand water fountain. And since then, he'd been chatting like normal.

Maybe disciplining him wouldn't be as difficult as she feared. Perhaps she could continue to punish him when necessary and not be fearful that he would hate her for the rest of his life. Maybe children really were as resilient as Emily suggested.

Not to mention forgetful.

"I will," she said.

"Can we do it after we get a kitten?"

Manipulative little sh—

Emily lowered a tray to the table. "Okay, three different meals for three people," she said. She placed a chicken salad with no dressing in front of Olivia.

"Ick," Henry said as he peered at the food.

"Pasta for Henry." Emily placed a bowl of pasta in tomato sauce in front of him.

"Ick," Olivia said with a smile. She speared a piece of her lettuce and placed it on top of the mountain of pasta shapes.

Henry accepted the greenery without complaint. He picked up his fork and tucked into his meal.

"What have you two been doing?" Emily sat down and unpacked her sandwich.

"Olivia said she's going to paint with me."

"When we get home," Olivia hurriedly added.

Emily looked at Henry with a shocked expression. "You're already planning what you're going to do when we get home? We're on vacation for another three days. Don't wish it away."

"But you won't be there." Henry grumpily chewed on another piece of pasta.

"Mommy has to work," Olivia reminded him. She knew Emily was dreading flying to London at the end of their honeymoon. Of course she was happy for the opportunity, but being away from Henry for work was something she had thought would remain in her past.

"Work, work, work," Henry grumbled. He stared at his bowl and moved the pasta around.

"If I don't work, then you'll have to get a job," Emily said as she took a sip of her coffee.

Henry's eyes snapped up.

"Actually, that's a great idea." Emily's eyes shone with excitement. She turned to Olivia. "You and I should stay home and paint, we can send Henry to work."

Before Olivia could answer, she continued, "He can't do anything that involves reaching for things. Or anything that involves driving…have you learned how to drive yet, Henry?"

Henry shook his head, eyes wide.

"I think you could get a job cleaning toilets. You have little hands. You could reach around the bend. I think you'd be good at it."

Henry shook his head faster. "But…"

"Oh, phew, I'm glad that's been arranged. Now I don't have to go to London." She took a hearty bite of her sandwich.

Henry looked at Olivia with a face of sheer panic. Olivia looked back at him with confusion. She wondered if Emily had been in the sun for too long and was suffering heat stroke.

Henry turned back to Emily. "Mommy, I don't want to clean toilets."

Emily's face fell. "No?"

"No," Henry practically begged.

Emily let out a sigh. "Okay. Then I suppose I'll have to go to work instead. It's a good thing I didn't cancel my flight."

Henry nodded, relief evident on his face.

"Oh well, you'll be okay with Olivia while I'm gone, won't you?"

"Yes, we're going to paint," Henry explained.

"Good, make sure you sign your own paintings so I can have a look when I get home. I don't want to mix up who painted what."

Henry giggled at the ridiculous idea.

"Eat your food," Emily told him. She smiled and gently ruffled his hair.

Olivia realised that Emily had just turned a potential tantrum around with a few well-placed sentences. Emily's exceptional motherhood skills awed her once more. She hoped that she would be able to be half the mother Emily was.

She speared a piece of cucumber and chewed it.

Although, she did basically manipulate him, she mused. Her eyes flicked up to Emily who was engrossed in eating her sandwich. *So* that's *where he gets it.*

A woman walked past with a sleeping baby in her arms. Olivia watched her with interest. The woman approached a table with a man and an older woman. She picked up a baby bottle from the table and expertly shifted the baby into a feeding position. Olivia memorised the movement, knowing that she would need it in the future.

Having a baby had seemed like a genius idea when she'd suggested it. She loved the idea of doing her bit to complete their family, adding another child to the mix. A sibling for Henry to play with.

But once the euphoria of the decision had worn off, fear had crept in. Getting pregnant, having a baby, and nurturing it all seemed like difficult mountains to climb. Emily said that they would deal with them one at a time, together.

She felt a warm hand cover her still one that she'd unknowingly rested on the table. She turned to see Emily looking at her.

"I can hear you stressing," she said softly.

Olivia smiled and turned her hand over, grasping Emily's. "Sorry, I can't switch it off."

"I know. Just remember to talk to me."

Olivia nodded. "I will. When I have the right words, I will."

Emily smiled and removed her hand. "I'll be here."

CHAPTER FIVE

Emily checked her bag for her passport and boarding pass for the third time in the last thirty minutes. Her breath was strained, and her heart beat a little faster at the prospect of travelling. Which was strange considering her previous career working as airline cabin crew.

When she'd initially planned to come to London on the very last day of her honeymoon, she hadn't fully grasped how heartbreaking it would be.

She'd just spent a full week with her new family, her new wife and co-parent, and she didn't want to get back to reality. Even if reality was the job of her dreams. She supposed she couldn't really complain, being a playwright was something many people would kill for. But the timing couldn't have been worse.

The distance would undoubtedly be worth it in the end. Seeing her play performed live on stage and having the opportunity to learn on the job were opportunities that no one could turn down.

She let out a sigh.

"Are you sad?"

Henry looked up from his colouring book to eye her suspiciously.

"Yes," she replied honestly. "I'm going to miss you and Olivia very, very much."

Henry nodded his understanding. "I won't miss you."

Emily stared at him in surprise and laughed. "You won't?"

"No, Olivia said that we're going to have so much fun that we won't have time to miss you," Henry explained. "Sorry."

"Oh, I see." Emily smiled, her gaze drifting to where Olivia stood in the middle of the airport terminal building having an animated telephone conversation with Simon.

"Well, I'll miss you," Emily continued. "And you'll be starting school, which is exciting. So, you have to remember everything that happens and tell me all about it."

Henry carried on colouring and slowly nodded. She knew he was still sad about her going to London for the week but didn't know how to express it. Which she was selfishly pleased about, because she didn't think she could cope with Henry getting upset at her departure.

She looked at her watch. There was half an hour until she needed to go through security.

"Honestly, you'd think that I still worked there," Olivia huffed as she sat down with them.

"Yes, you would," Emily replied with a knowing smile.

"He calls me!" Olivia said.

"Because you email him twenty times a day, and it's easier to call you rather than spend two hours replying to your emails."

Olivia huffed again and shook her head. Emily smirked; she knew she was right.

Olivia's idea of leaving her previous job behind was a little different from most. She wondered whether Olivia would ever be able to let go of Applewoods. Olivia continued to promise that she was stepping away, even if it was taking time. But Emily knew that Olivia was struggling with it.

She knew it was hard for Olivia, being forced out of a company that she had been running for so many years. A company that her father had established. But office politics and backstabbing meant that the only way to ensure the company survived was for Olivia to no longer be a part of it.

Despite the enormous pain it had caused Olivia, she was mindful of the employees who needed Applewoods to stay afloat. And so she'd stepped aside, leaving her former assistant in her place. Luckily, Simon had shadowed Olivia for long enough to know how to run the business.

Emily hadn't said too much about what would come next. Olivia had funds to take her time before diving into a new career. And Emily didn't feel like it was her place to rush Olivia into action. If she wanted to take some time off, then Emily would, of course, support her.

The problem was that Olivia seemed bored. The endless phone calls to Simon proved that she was having trouble letting go. Olivia was keen to deny the obvious, frequently claiming that Simon couldn't do without her. And any time that Emily suggested that Olivia might be bored, Olivia couldn't refute it quickly enough.

Emily couldn't quite get to the bottom of the subject. Figuring out Olivia's thought process wasn't the easiest thing in the world. She knew that eventually Olivia would figure it out and then, hopefully, come to Emily with her conclusion.

"Thank you for coming to the airport. You didn't have to," Emily said. She knew Olivia's fear of flying extended to the entire air industry. Being in the terminal had put her on edge immediately.

"It's what married couples do." Olivia gestured with her head to a few couples who were saying goodbye to each other.

"Some, not all," Emily said. She lowered her voice so Henry wouldn't hear. "You don't have to be here. If you want to head home?"

Olivia looked interested in the idea, and Emily decided that it was up to her to put it into action.

"In fact, I was thinking of going through security and doing some shopping."

"Oh," Olivia said. Her brow furrowed as she caught up to the idea. But there was an undeniable hopefulness in her tone.

"Are you sure you're okay with everything for Henry's first day?" Emily asked.

Olivia nodded. She took her iPad out of her bag and unlocked it. "I have everything written down."

She handed the iPad to Emily. Emily felt her eyebrows raise at what she saw.

There was a schedule for the night before as well as the morning itself. It included everything from teeth brushing to checking shoes to ensure they were not too tight. Then there was a packing list for Henry's bag, a list of contact telephone numbers, times, names of classmates, teachers, and more. Olivia was more prepared than Emily would have been.

She handed the iPad back. "You seem to have everything ready." She knew not to mock Olivia's over-preparedness.

Olivia regarded the list. "I think so. I've been working on it for a few weeks."

Emily turned to Henry. "Henry, be a good boy while I'm gone and make sure you do everything that Olivia tells you, okay?"

Henry put down his crayon, sensing that it was finally time to say goodbye. He nodded. "Bye, Mommy."

She leaned into a big cuddle and kissed his hair. "Have fun at school, and I'll call you every day," she murmured, trying to keep the tears back. She didn't want to make a big deal about her leaving.

"I will." Henry pulled back from the hug and picked up his crayon again.

She stood up. Olivia did the same, and they embraced.

"I'm going to miss you," Olivia admitted.

"I'm going to miss you, too, but we have to remember that we've done this before."

"No, we haven't," Olivia said.

Emily chuckled. "Maybe not exactly this, but we've been apart. And everything worked out."

"It did," Olivia said. "I'll call you."

"You better. I'll text and email as much as I can, as well. This will get easier." She wasn't sure who she was trying to convince.

"It will," Olivia repeated.

Emily stood back from the hug and threw the strap of her bag over her shoulder. She looked towards the security gate and then back to Olivia.

"I'm so proud of you," Olivia said. "Now, go and show them how good you are."

Emily sucked in a deep breath and nodded sharply. She kissed Olivia on the cheek and ruffled Henry's hair and walked towards the gates.

❖

Emily shifted uncomfortably in the airline seat. She looked around the first-class cabin, wondering if the other occupants were looking at her and wondering why she was there. Did they assume she had been given a free upgrade?

She turned to look back out the window. She wasn't made for a life of luxury; she felt ridiculous. She wished she hadn't allowed Olivia to book her ticket; she hadn't realised that she was in first-class until the very last moment. As she stepped on board the plane, the cabin crew had gestured her to the left and Emily's heart had sunk.

She should have realised. Of course, Olivia would want her to have the best, not thinking about how uncomfortable it could make her. There was no price on the boarding pass, but Emily could just imagine the figure. It made her head swim that someone would spend that amount on travel. She now knew why Nicole had told Emily that Olivia was dealing with her first flight to London, clearly, this was Olivia's way of looking after her. If she couldn't be there herself, then she'd ensure that Emily was looked after in a way that Olivia thought was enjoyable and relaxing.

She sunk further into the leather, wishing for the seven-hour flight to be over as soon as possible.

A member of the cabin crew stood beside her. Emily looked up, feeling suddenly very small and insignificant in her seat. The woman looked immaculate, makeup done to perfection and not a single hair out of place.

Emily knew she looked a mess. She'd rushed to the gate having spent a little longer than expected in the airport shop.

The woman held out a menu. "Can I get you some champagne now, Mrs. White?"

Emily shook her head. "No, I'm fine. Thank you."

"We'll be taking orders for dinner in a few moments." The woman walked away.

She wondered why she was so nervous. She'd been that woman, dressed up to the nines and working the first-class deck.

She never looked down on any of the passengers, quite the opposite. She always felt that they would look at her as if she was below them. Now she was on the other side and she still felt the same, like the cabin crew were judging her. She wondered why, no matter what side of the transaction she was on, she felt inferior.

"Ridiculous," she mumbled to herself. She'd definitely speak to Olivia about never booking first class again.

It wasn't just the atmosphere, it was the cost. She didn't like Olivia spending her money on frivolities. Especially when they were ones that she didn't enjoy.

Money. She let out a small sigh and looked out the window.

The enormous wealth gap was something they had talked about, but something Olivia had yet to fully grasp.

Olivia had money, and she liked to share it. And while Emily allowed her to an extent, she was still far from comfortable with the idea.

Olivia's savings account made Emily's eyes water. Inheritance money from her parents, as well as half a lifetime of managing a successful company, had presented a lot of zeros.

Money was always going to be something Emily struggled with. Spending the majority of her life not having any and being in unimaginable debt was bound to create issues around the subject. As much as Olivia tried to say that money didn't matter, to Emily, it did.

She'd silently promised herself that she would pay Olivia back and then some. Before she fell asleep at night she would dream of being able to reimburse Olivia for the debts she paid, as well as surprising her with expensive gifts like jewellery.

Whether she found fame and fortune writing in the theatre, or she worked like a machine for the next thirty years, she was determined to pay Olivia back. She couldn't spend her life being reliant on her; she needed to stand on her own two feet.

The money she'd made from the script sales had gone some way towards her feeling like an equal. She'd paid for some of the furniture in the house, as well as contributing to the honeymoon. Olivia had seemed quite confused by Emily's insistence on paying for certain things. Especially as they shared a central bank account for most living expenses.

Emily looked around the cabin. She decided that it would be the last first-class flight she would take until she could afford to pay for one herself. Then maybe she would feel like she deserved to be there.

She let out another sigh and reached forward for the paperwork she had shoved into the magazine rack earlier. She flipped through her handwritten notes, prepping herself for her first day at the theatre.

Up until then, she had worked from home, occasionally going to meetings in England with Nicole. But now she was actively working on a production. And that meant being at the London office and the theatre every workday. Now everything felt a lot more real.

The irony that she was now in Olivia's position was not lost on her. Not long after Olivia had stopped her exhausting weekly commute from New York to London, Emily was starting hers.

Although she drew the line at sleeping on the plane and then going straight into a full day of work. No, she was leaving a day early to check into her hotel and get a proper night of sleep. She couldn't imagine going straight to the office on Monday, meeting her colleagues, and diving into work, having stepped off a seven-hour flight just hours earlier.

She smiled to herself, remembering Olivia's rigid schedule aboard the flight. Requiring her meal as soon as possible before slipping into her pyjamas and going straight to sleep.

She recalled standing beside Olivia and enquiring about her meal. Olivia delicately wiping her mouth with the corner of her linen napkin and saying it was wonderful.

They'd come a long way.

She shook the memories away and refocused on the work in front of her. If she had to be away from her family, she was going to make every second count.

Chapter Six

Olivia looked at the never-ending traffic and let out a long breath. She pressed a couple of buttons on the steering wheel, and the radio sprung to life. She'd learned from experience that Henry would start complaining of boredom if he sat in traffic for too long without a distraction.

She'd only been separated from Emily for an hour and she already felt like an essential part of her was missing. Once the airport had swallowed up Emily, Olivia's mood had soured.

"When are you going to have a baby?"

She turned to regard Henry in his booster seat beside her. Henry was usually in the back, playing games or reading. She'd moved him up to the front in case he was missing his mother. She realised a little too late that Henry was going to utilise the opportunity to quiz her.

"I don't know," she answered honestly.

"Tomorrow?"

"I don't know."

"Next week?"

She turned her attention back to the road.

"Will it be a boy or a girl?" Henry continued. "Or a fish?"

"Definitely a fish," Olivia said.

She'd learned to not be so literal with everything Henry said. Emily had even encouraged her to sometimes engage in his ridiculous statements.

"Will your belly be made of glass? Like a goldfish bowl? Will I see it swimming around?"

Olivia quashed down a feeling of disgust at the very idea. Henry was off on a tangent, and she knew she had to pull him back to reality.

"Are you looking forward to school?"

Henry shrugged. "Yeah," he replied half-heartedly.

"You'll make lots of new friends," she repeated what she'd heard Emily say the day before.

"I don't want new friends."

Olivia didn't know what to say to that. She felt the same. New friends were awkward and irritating. Learning what they liked and didn't like. Cultivating the friendship, taking time to see them when you'd rather be doing something else. And then often realising that they really weren't the kind of friends you wanted anyway and spending the next few months nicely turning down every opportunity to meet.

Friends were exhausting. New friends were akin to some horrific challenge from one of those ghastly reality TV shows.

"There's a playground at your school," Olivia said.

"Really?" Henry perked up.

"Yes, it has a slide." She wondered if she should be spending time instilling the values of the playground equipment rather than the learning activities. "And a library."

"Lucy said we should get a cat."

Olivia looked at him and raised her eyebrow. "When did you speak to Lucy?"

"After the wedding. She said we should get a cat."

"I thought you wanted a kitten?"

"I thought about it, and now I want a cat."

A car horn sounded. Olivia crawled the car forward the few feet that were so important to the driver behind her. She turned back to Henry.

"Why a cat and not a kitten? You were adamant about getting a kitten."

"Lucy says that we should get a cat because there are already too many cats in the world that don't have families. And we're a family. And kittens become cats anyway," he explained as if Olivia had no idea of the connection between kittens and cats.

"Why bring another kitten into the world when there are already so many cats in need of a good home?" Henry asked, clearly repeating Lucy's speech verbatim.

The thought touched a nerve, and Olivia felt her body run cold. It wasn't much of a leap to reach the same conclusion when it came to babies. Were they being selfish thinking about having a baby when there were already children in the world who needed a loving family? Would Olivia be the right type of personality to adopt? Would the authorities even allow her to?

"Olivia?" Henry shook her from her thoughts.

"I'll discuss it with your mother." She turned back to face the road. She imagined that adoption required some kind of medical and psychological evaluations. What would happen if her quirks prevented them from being able to adopt? What would Emily think of her then?

"Olivia?"

"Yes?" She itched to turn the radio up to distract Henry. She was having a crisis, and she couldn't focus on that and Henry's cat discussion at the same time.

"If we got a cat, could I name it?"

"Absolutely."

"Olivia?"

She let out a small sigh. "Yes, Henry?"

"When are you going back to work?"

She looked at him. "I-I'm not."

"Why?"

"Because your mommy and I agreed that I would stay home and look after you while Mommy works in London." Olivia nervously licked her lips, hoping that would be the end of the conversation.

She recalled how she had strolled around the living room with a glass of red wine in her hand, explaining to Emily that it really was the absolute best thing for her to stay home and tend to the house while Emily focused on her career. Emily had seemed so relieved and grateful that Olivia would do such a thing.

She had felt pride swell within her that she was able to help Emily. Olivia had come to understand that writing was Emily's passion, and Emily had a once-in-a-lifetime opportunity laid out in front of her.

To Olivia, it seemed impossible for Emily to be able to take the work opportunity while caring for Henry. Emily had even stated that she was considering whether or not to continue working with Nicole, claiming that the time away from her family would be hard to take.

And so, Olivia had stepped up and offered to take hold of everything. She would look after the house, care for Henry, and carry the next child.

Emily had only been gone for a few hours and already Olivia was wondering what she had done. The idea of not working was supposed to be one that filled people with joy. People did all they could to get to retirement age as early as possible, keen to throw off the shackles of employment. But Olivia already felt tense at the prospect of no longer working.

"Forever?" Henry asked.

Olivia felt the panic rise again.

She slowly nodded. "Yes, forever."

"And I can have a cat?" Henry asked, seizing upon Olivia's accepting mood.

"I'll discuss it with your mother," Olivia repeated. "We have to make big decisions as a family."

"Can I name the new baby?"

"Probably not."

"Why not?" Henry groused.

"Because you called a giraffe 'Tiny.'"

"But that's a great name!"

"Shall we tune to your station?" Olivia was already reaching for the radio knob before Henry could reply.

Classical music faded away and pop music started to play. Henry danced along to the familiar tunes.

Olivia breathed out a relieved sigh and slumped a little into the driver's seat.

"I wonder how many cats there are in New York who need a new home?" Henry asked.

Olivia rested her head on the side window with a thud.

"I bet it's a million," he concluded.

CHAPTER SEVEN

A re you nervous?" Nicole asked.

Emily hurried to match to Nicole's pace as they walked along the busy London street together. Nicole weaved in and out of people like a professional and Emily did her best to keep up and not get lost in the crowd.

"Terrified," Emily admitted.

"Good. That's normal."

Nicole turned down a side street, and Emily scrambled to catch up with her. Luckily, the side street was much quieter. Emily easily caught up and they started walking side by side.

They'd met for a quick breakfast at Emily's hotel before walking to the office together. Emily was regretting the second croissant as her stomach started to twist and turn with nerves.

"The team is excellent," Nicole explained. "Obviously. Seeing as I hired them all."

Emily chuckled.

"First there's Carl. He'll be your co-writer. He's an exceptional writer, he knows our styles and requirements, so he'll be able to lead you in the right direction. You'll learn a lot from him, but he isn't your boss. You're a team." Nicole threw her a meaningful look.

Emily nodded. "Team, got it."

"Don't sit back and let others take all the glory. Just because you're new doesn't mean you're not as good as they are."

Nicole had been throwing pep talks into most of their conversations over the last few months. From the day Emily had first shown her the scripts she had written to Nicole becoming her agent, Nicole had been very keen to bolster Emily's flagging self-confidence.

"Absolutely," Emily said.

"So, you'll be sharing an office with Carl. Then there's Martin, the stage manager, and Hannah, the set designer. At this point, you'll mainly be working with them. Until we move to live production in two weeks, that is. Then there will a whole company of people for you to meet."

"Carl, Martin, and Hannah. Got it."

"Every Monday, Wednesday, and Friday we have a morning update meeting. We all sit down and catch up, usually bemoan how little time we have, that kind of thing. I'll be at each meeting, but outside that, I'm afraid I'm in and out of the office."

Nicole turned her head to look up and down the street. She took Emily by the elbow and pulled her across the road, weaving in between black cabs.

Emily allowed herself to be dragged along. Nicole had been a lifeline during the scary transition from unemployed and almost destitute to scriptwriter. In the back of her mind, she knew she was living a rags-to-riches story that she would one day have to write. She just wanted to get a little further into the riches part before she put pen to paper. At the moment, the whole thing still felt surreal, like a bubble about to burst in her hands.

"Here we are," Nicole said.

In front of them was a door, coated in black paint that was sun-bleached and lightly peeling. Emily looked up at the rest of the facade. The building was in serious need of some maintenance. The old wooden windows needed replacing and the brickwork was occasionally visible in between gaps in the plasterwork.

"I did tell you that there's no money in theatre, right?" Nicole stage-whispered to her.

Emily laughed nervously.

"It's fine inside," Nicole said. "And it's close to the theatre. I'll show you that this afternoon. Ready to meet the team?"

Emily nodded. "As I'll ever be."

"And how, precisely, am I supposed to bring back that set for the final act? By then, we've already put two others in front of it. The space is tiny, I can't get that set back out without moving everything in front of it. Or removing a wall. Your choice."

Martin Faraday crossed his legs and turned to the side. He leaned heavily on the back of his plastic chair and looked away.

Emily tried to control her expression, but she could feel a smirk beginning to form. Martin was the perfect drama queen. He was exactly what she had expected to find in the theatre. Mid-forties, scruffy, and oh-so-artistically dramatic. He'd already dropped around thirty "darlings" into the short conversation and constantly huffed or turned his face away from the group in dismay at not hearing what he wanted to.

Emily turned to regard Nicole, awaiting her response to Martin's latest complaint. Nicole was as calm and collected as Emily imagined, batting away each of Martin's grievances with faultless logic and simple solutions.

It had only been half an hour since she had first entered the building, and they were already straight down to work. They had all been introduced, smiles and handshakes were exchanged, and tea and coffee in cups and saucers had been distributed. They'd gathered in a large and empty room, pulling plastic chairs with metal frames into a circle to start the meeting.

Contrary to Nicole's statement, the inside of the building was as old as the outside. It had worn brick walls that had been covered over the course of many years with layer upon layer of white paint. The ceilings were high, and the single-glazed windows protected little from the elements. Emily had already written a note to herself to bring warmer clothes next time. The wind was unforgiving.

"You're not packing up the hospital scene next to my landscape," Hannah said. Hannah was in her early thirties and had long, brown hair that was tied up in a messy bun. "If that gets damaged, we'll never have time to repair before the next night."

Martin spun in his chair and pointed towards Hannah. "You name one time that my guys have damaged one of your sets, one time," he demanded.

"I'm just saying…" Hannah huffed.

Nicole held her hands up. "Okay, stand down, both of you."

Martin lowered his accusatory finger and Nicole lowered her hands.

"I suppose we could move the scene to a new location, but we have to come up with a reason for the children to be out of school?" Nicole mused as she studied the script.

"A sports day," Emily quickly said. "Then we can use the exterior and that should be in position two, if I'm not mistaken? Easy to get out in time for the final act?"

Martin smiled. He turned to Nicole. "I like her. We're keeping her."

Nicole turned to Carl. "What do you think, Carl?"

Emily turned to him. He'd been quiet since she'd arrived, offering her a quick handshake and a tight, silent smile.

He looked at the script in his lap and chewed on the end of a mangled pencil, his heavy framed glasses almost covering his deep frown.

Emily felt herself holding her breath as everyone awaited Carl's input. She found herself second-guessing her suggestion. Maybe it wasn't a good idea, maybe she'd just thrown a wrench in the works? She didn't want to get off to a bad start with the man she was going to be spending most of her time with.

Carl slammed the pencil down onto the papers and looked up. A smile crossed his face, and he nodded.

"Yep. Sounds good, I think we can make that work." He smiled at Emily. "Great idea."

Emily slumped a little in relief. "Thanks."

"Well, that's one problem dealt with," Martin drawled. "I don't want to bring anyone down, but need I remind you that we open in three weeks and we have yet to build the trap for the *genius* who suggested that an actor can vanish during a two-second power outage."

Carl looked at Emily and rolled his eyes jokingly.

"It never ends," he whispered with a wink.

CHAPTER EIGHT

Olivia paced the hallway as she looked intently at her watch. They were already three minutes behind schedule.

"Henry!" she shouted up the stairs.

"Coming," he called back.

She picked up his backpack and checked the contents. Her heart clenched as she felt the lightness of the bag. It reminded her that Henry was far too young and far too small to be going to school, getting on the school bus, spending the day with strangers that she hadn't personally vetted. And all he had to get him through the day were the measly contents of his bag. How would he survive the onslaught of school with some pens, paper, and snacks? It seemed ridiculous.

Henry appeared by her side. "Ready," he said. He looked excited, but that didn't stop the butterflies in her stomach.

She eyed him critically, checking his clothes, shoes, and jacket were all going to be appropriate for the day ahead. She felt like she was throwing a baby bird out of the nest and hoping he'd learn to fly on the way down.

"Can we wait for the bus outside?"

Olivia shuddered at the thought of the bus. She'd been online the previous night, reading the horror stories other parents told. But, of course, the bus was one of the things Henry was most excited about.

She zipped up his bag and looked at her watch again.

"Did you brush your teeth?"

He nodded.

"And you're wearing underwear today?"

He nodded again.

"Do you need the bathroom?"

He shook his head.

"Why are Mommy's old work clothes in your bedroom?"

Olivia recalled the hurried farewell before Henry had woken up on Sunday morning. Emily waking her up in her old Crown Airlines outfit that had quickly been discarded. Olivia couldn't bring herself to put it away, so she'd left it on the chair by the wardrobe, hoping for a repeat performance soon.

She felt heat rise in her cheeks.

"I-I was clearing out the wardrobe," she lied.

"Are you going to throw it away now that Mommy doesn't need it anymore? Because she's not working on the airplane anymore, is she?"

She opened her mouth to reply when the light from the hallway window changed hue.

"The bus!" Henry shouted.

She let out a sigh of relief.

He grabbed the bag out of her hand and ran towards the door. Olivia quickly followed, not ready to let him vanish just yet.

In hindsight, Olivia suspected that getting onto the bus and questioning the driver about his credentials was probably not the best move. He hadn't seemed pleased. Henry's first day of school was only an hour old, and she was already in a state of sheer panic.

In truth, she had been for the past month. She was certain that schools had incorrectly calculated the correct age to take children into their clutches. Surely, Henry was too young?

Maybe home schooling would be a good idea? She was positive she knew more than the children who were apparently qualified to be teachers these days. She made a mental note to broach the subject with Emily. It would also help with the absolute boredom she knew awaited her on days that Henry was at school.

She'd been standing in front of the open fridge for a while, enjoying the cool air on her face. She stared at its contents. She wanted something, but she couldn't figure out what it was. Her eyes drifted from the milk cartons to the various juices that lined the shelf.

With a sigh, she picked up the bottle of white wine from the door and slammed the fridge closed. She picked up a water tumbler and poured half a glass of wine into it. She drank two large gulps without a second's thought.

Suddenly, she looked at the tumbler with wide eyes, slowly lowering it to the counter and taking a few steps away. She looked around the kitchen, self-conscious that someone might have seen her transgression.

She quickly walked away, grabbing her phone from the side table as she stalked towards her office. She closed the door behind her, wanting to put more distance between her and the evil drink.

Pacing the room, she selected a contact and held the phone to her ear.

"Good morning," Nicole answered quickly. "How are you?"

"I'm a drunk," Olivia said.

"'I'm well, thank you, Nicole, how are you?'" Nicole joked.

"Is Emily there? Don't tell Emily I'm a drunk. Don't tell her you're speaking to me."

"Emily is out to lunch. What's going on?"

"I just drank wine," Olivia whispered tersely.

"You swine."

"It's not even nine a.m." Olivia paused by the window and looked outside. "I just put Henry on the bus to school and now I'm drinking wine. Out of a tumbler."

"A tumbler? Heathen."

"Nicole, I'm being serious."

"Sending your child off to his first day of school is stressful," Nicole said.

"I'm an alcoholic," Olivia decided. "I'll have to seek help."

"You're not an alcoholic, you were stressed."

"A tumbler, Nicole," Olivia said.

"When was the last time you drank alcohol?"

Olivia leaned against the window frame and furrowed her brow in thought. "Last…Saturday?"

"And did you down vodka from the bottle last Saturday?"

"No, of course not." Olivia continued her pacing.

"Did you, perhaps, have a glass of wine with dinner?"

"Two," Olivia confessed.

"Look, I'll be blunt. You're not an alcoholic. The fact that you reached for alcohol at a time of stress isn't great news, but it's certainly nothing to worry about."

"How can I even think that I'm going to be a suitable mother?" Olivia wondered aloud. She sat on the edge of her desk, head bowed.

"It's my understanding that most mothers turn to alcohol. Have you not seen internet memes?" Nicole replied. "Alcohol is a coping mechanism for many. It relaxes them. As long as you know when it's too much, or the wrong time, which you clearly did because you called me, then it's fine."

Olivia sighed.

"You're worried about Henry. You're stressed, and you drank some wine. How much did you drink anyway?"

"Two—*large*—mouthfuls," Olivia said.

Nicole laughed loudly. "Oh, lord, I thought you were going to say two glasses. Olivia, it's fine, you're fine, Henry's fine. Just go and do whatever it is you do these days and don't panic about it."

"Don't tell Emily," Olivia said, getting the feeling that Nicole was about to end the call.

"I won't tell Emily anything, I promise," Nicole said. "Now, I have to go and do some work. I'll speak to you later."

The line went dead, and Olivia sank further against her desk. She stared at the phone for a moment before looking around her office.

Go and do whatever it is you do these days, she repeated in her mind. She wasn't quite sure what that was. Since stepping away from Applewoods, she'd become more focused on other things, her garden, the wedding, Henry's first day of school.

Her garden had been tended to perfection; all her projects had been put into motion. She couldn't make the vegetable garden grow any quicker, nor could she tend plants that had yet to properly take root.

The wedding was over. Henry's first day of school was here.

She shivered involuntarily.

Suddenly things seemed very cold and lonely. She scrolled through her contacts before selecting a name that used to appear much higher in the "recently called" list.

She put her phone to her ear and waited.

"Hey, boss," Simon said.

Olivia chuckled. "Not anymore."

"How are you?"

Olivia paused. She wasn't sure how to answer. "Fine," she decided upon. "You?"

"Yeah, good." He didn't sound certain.

"Are you sure?" she asked, wondering if she had managed to correctly read his tone.

Simon let out a sigh. "Just…stressing. Sophie had a scan yesterday. Everything's fine, but it made it more real, you know?"

Olivia didn't know. She remained silent, hoping Simon would continue.

"Now I'm thinking about the nursery, the crib, the stroller, the clothes, food…there's so much stuff. Sophie says we'll deal with it, and we have plenty of time. But we don't, there's so much stuff to do. We're bringing a baby into the world, and I don't even know if I'll be a good dad."

"You'll be a wonderful father," Olivia told him sincerely. Everything else sounded terrifying, but that point she was sure of.

"But a good dad needs to have enough bed sheets, onesies, little tiny socks. This baby is going to be born in winter. Do I need extra blankets? What if I overheat the baby? Babies can't tell you when they're hot. I'm terrified I'm going to boil the baby. I'm pretty sure you get sent to a special prison for that."

Olivia nodded her head, enrapt in his fear. It was true, babies couldn't tell you anything. Olivia had been terrified of damaging

Henry when she first met him, convinced she'd say the wrong thing. She'd relied on the fact that Henry could speak and be reasoned with. But babies didn't speak. She swallowed. She didn't even know at what age babies learned to speak. Was that something she should know?

"And then I looked at the prices, whoa! I look at things and think, 'This baby is going to only use that for three months but it costs a bomb,'" Simon continued, although Olivia barely heard him.

Olivia felt panic pull at the collar of her blouse. She reached up and undid an extra button.

"I shouldn't be bothering you with all of this," Simon mumbled.

Olivia wondered how long she had silently worried and left Simon to ramble on.

"You're not bothering me, we're friends," she explained. She decided to leave out the fact that he had sent her spiralling into a panic of her own. Was she ready to have a baby? She was grateful she didn't have one on the way.

"We are. Anyway, enough about me, why did you call?" Simon asked.

Olivia sighed. "I'm a drunkard."

"No, you're not," he said.

Simon didn't beat around the bush. It was one of the things that Olivia loved about him. He said what he thought and that clarity often relaxed her.

"I just drank wine. In the morning!"

"Gonna do it again?"

"No!"

"Well, there you go then. Call me when it becomes a habit."

She considered arguing the point but knew that Simon wasn't going to back down. He'd tell her she was being ridiculous, and maybe she was.

"I saw an article that said a baby's first year can cost over nine thousand pounds," Simon said.

"What?" Olivia said. "That's preposterous. On what?"

"Everything!" Simon cried. "I had no idea babies needed so much stuff. I'll make a list for you."

"For me?"

"Well, yeah, you'll need the same when you and Emily have another. You're still planning on doing that, right?"

Olivia swallowed nervously. They hadn't spoken about it much, focusing on getting Emily's career up and running before moving on to the next life-changing hurdle.

"Probably," she replied half-heartedly.

Simon paused. "This might not be my place to say, but, do you want to talk about it?"

"I…" She trailed off. "We're waiting to see what happens with Emily's work."

"Ah, I see. So, what are you doing in the meantime?"

"Finishing up with the house. We still haven't finished decorating and furnishing," she lied. She'd sorted those details out within two weeks of moving in. "Busy, busy."

"I painted the nursery at the weekend. Well, it's called the nursery now. Used to be the box room where I kept my PlayStation. But, apparently, the baby needs a place to sleep, so I moved the PlayStation to the living room."

"What a gesture," Olivia joked. "Simon, may I ask you something personal?"

"Sure."

"Are you worried that the baby will inherit some of your traits?"

Simon chuckled. "Wow, I've missed working with you."

Olivia didn't know how that was relevant and silently waited for the answer to her question.

"I suppose," Simon finally replied. "I don't put much thought into it. Luckily, I'm healthy, so I don't need to worry about the baby inheriting an illness. Maybe they'll need glasses like I do. Maybe they'll get really thin hair when they hit twenty-five like I did. I don't know. What's done is done. Hopefully they'll be just like Sophie."

"I hope they'll be just like both of you," Olivia replied honestly.

"Just without my big ears," Simon joked. "Sorry, I just noticed the time. I have a meeting so I have to go. I'll catch up with you later, okay?"

"Absolutely," Olivia said.

They exchanged their goodbyes, and Olivia hung up the phone. She tapped the edge of the phone to her lip as she pondered what to do. She'd already promised Emily that she'd not interrupt her during her first day at her new job.

"It's so quiet in here," she mumbled as she looked around the room. "Too quiet."

CHAPTER NINE

Emily leaned back in her chair and tilted her neck slowly from side to side. She hadn't ever had a job where she spent hours at a desk, staring at a screen. She thought she would enjoy the rest, but she was finding that she felt cooped up instead. Not to mention that her neck and shoulders were definitely complaining about their suddenly sedentary lifestyle.

She stood and walked over to the window as she had grown accustomed to doing recently. The writers' room was small, just two desks facing each other in the middle of the room. Several large whiteboards filled the walls behind each desk.

Windows overlooked the street below. The scene wasn't much to look at, but it made a difference from staring at the words on the screen.

The door opened behind her, and she turned to see Carl walk in. He wore his oversized dark green, quilted jacket, which had pieces of paper flowing out of its large pockets.

"Hi," he said.

"Hi, how's it going?"

He nodded and hung his coat up on a nail that he frequently used as a makeshift coatrack.

It had only been a couple of days, but Emily already felt she had a good handle on Carl's personality. He was weird. Maybe weird was a little strong, he'd certainly be called eccentric if he had money. But she didn't think he did, and so weird was more suitable.

He pulled out his office chair and sat down.

"Nicole said she can't make dinner tonight. She said she'd call you," Carl said suddenly.

"Oh, okay." Emily smiled. "Thanks for letting me know."

"And Martin is still not happy about the first hospital scene."

Emily frowned. "What now?"

Carl pulled his keychain from his pocket and slowly worked his way through the large bunch of keys. "Dunno. He was shouting."

Emily watched as he located his desk key and unlocked the drawer. He pulled out his laptop and placed it on the desktop, meticulously wiping the top with his shirtsleeve.

"So…what are we going to do?" Emily pressed.

Carl shrugged. "Wait for the meeting with Nicole tomorrow."

Emily didn't like that idea. She was working on that scene right now. If there was a problem, then she needed to know before the run-through the next afternoon.

"Maybe I'll call him," Emily said as she walked back to her desk.

"No." Carl's head snapped up. "No, um, I'll call him. I don't want you to have to deal with his bad mood. Sorry, I should have dealt with it while I was there, but he was being, well, Martin."

Emily chuckled. "Yes, Martin is special."

"I'll call him. In fact, I'll pop out and do it now. I was going to get a drink anyway. Can I get you a tea? Or a latte? You like lattes, don't you?"

Emily nodded. "I do, a latte would be lovely."

Carl stared at her for a few seconds.

"Everything okay?" Emily asked again.

He shook his head as if to clear the mental cobwebs. "Yes. Yes, sorry, I…I was thinking about something."

He grabbed his phone out of his pocket and gestured towards the door.

"I'll be back soon," he said.

He turned and opened the door, nearly walking into Hannah as he did.

"Sorry," he mumbled and stepped around her before rushing from the room.

Hannah rolled her eyes and shook her head at his behaviour. She stepped in and closed the door behind her.

"Carl's being his usual bizarre self, I see?"

Emily smiled. She was glad to hear that she wasn't the only person who thought Carl a little odd, but she wasn't about to openly talk about him behind his back.

"Coffee run," she explained. "And making a call."

Hannah walked over to the window and looked out. "Oh yes, you don't get any signal in here, do you?"

"No, something to do with the roof?"

Carl had explained it to Emily during her very brief introduction to her new office, but it had quickly tapered off into a ramble about the building's previous use as a school.

Hannah turned around and thrust her hands into her pockets.

"Cold, too!"

Emily laughed. "Yeah, it's an interesting place to work."

"You'll be out of here soon, working in the theatre. Then you'll be craving a solid desk," Hannah said.

"I don't know, Carl seems to think we're a week behind."

Hannah sat on the edge of Emily's desk. "Carl isn't known for his optimism…Oh, is that your little boy?" She pointed to a picture of Henry with Olivia on Emily's desk.

"Yes, Henry." Emily looked at the image fondly.

"And your…sister?"

"Wife," Emily corrected her gently. She hated the coming-out conversation. It was necessary as she didn't want to start her new work friendships with lies. But she was also aware that some people reacted poorly to the news.

"Ah, sorry, I didn't want to presume. Some people are offended if you suggest they might be gay," Hannah said with another eye roll.

Emily let out a small sigh of relief.

"So, are they here in England?" Hannah asked.

"No, they're home in New York. I'm commuting."

"Wow, that's some commute! Nicole did mention that you held some of the rights to the play. Is that how you got this job? Sorry if I'm being nosey, just seems like a hell of a commute."

"It's fine, I don't mind," Emily said. "Yes, I have a deal with Nicole. I've given up some of my royalties, and in return I'm working in the industry to get more experience. I wish I didn't have to travel, but it is what it is."

Hannah blew out a breath. "Wow, I don't think I could cope with that commute. Wouldn't it be easier to move the family over here?"

Emily chuckled. "Oh, Olivia won't travel."

"No?" Hannah asked in surprise. "You're going to be apart a lot, aren't you?"

"Yes, but we'll make it work," Emily said.

"Sorry, I'm being so nosey," Hannah said.

"Oh, it's no problem." Emily smiled. She liked Hannah, she was open and talkative. Emily had noted that the stereotype of British people being quiet and reserved was often true. She'd often felt like a brash American when she'd been outspoken or inquisitive.

"The reason I stopped by was to invite you to team drinks, if you have time. The rest of my team will be there, so you can meet all the designers. Martin's team will be there. It will be fun, and you can network. Networking is really important in theatre. When there's a deadline on and you need something doing fast, you'll be glad you had drinks with them the week before."

Emily knew what she meant. It was always a good idea to befriend people so they felt more like helping you out when you needed them.

"Sounds great, when is it?" She reached for her phone to open her calendar.

"Thursday, straight after work. It's at the Hogshead, just around the corner. I could pick you up and show you the way, if you like?"

Emily quickly nodded. "Yes, please. I'm struggling to find my way around London. All these narrow streets, I like my grid system back home."

Hannah laughed. She walked behind Emily's chair and tapped her shoulder. "Don't worry, Cinderella. I'll get you to the ball."

"Thanks, and thanks for the invite. I'm looking forward to it." Emily added the reminder to her calendar.

"No problem. Us girls have to stick together," Hannah replied. She looked at her watch and sighed. "Better get back to the theatre. See you tomorrow!"

Hannah left, and Emily was alone in the cold, cramped room again. Being a scriptwriter certainly wasn't a glamorous job. She felt homesick, despite the calls and texts to Olivia and Henry.

She sighed and forced herself to focus on her laptop screen, shaking her mouse to wake the device up. She reminded herself that she'd be home in a couple more days, even if only for a short while.

Chapter Ten

Olivia tilted her head to the side and regarded the television advertisement with interest. The device really did replace all her current chopping utensils with one easy-to-use, easy-to-clean unit. And the free recipe book that came with it would no doubt be useful. The free shipping was also very convenient, although she wasn't quite sure where they had come up with the original cost of shipping the small device.

The advert dipped into a gloomy black-and-white scene, and the actress struggled to chop a mountain of carrots.

Olivia's eyes narrowed.

Why is she chopping so many carrots?

The actress cut her finger and rushed to the sink.

She must be making at least ten carrot cakes.

Her phone vibrated on the sofa cushion beside her, and she jumped in shock. She snatched up the phone and slid her finger along the screen to answer the call.

"Olivia Lewis," she greeted.

"Mrs. Lewis, it's Miss Costa, Henry's teacher."

Olivia jumped to her feet and was already heading towards the door.

"I was just wondering if I could have a few moments of your time after school one day this week?" Miss Costa continued.

Olivia stopped dead with one arm already tucked into her coat.

"Y-yes, of course," Olivia replied. "May I ask what this is about?"

"Oh, it's nothing serious," Miss Costa said. "Just a quick discussion about Henry's progress."

Olivia felt her eyebrows knit together. She wasn't sure if this was usual or not. The teacher certainly sounded unconcerned.

"If this week doesn't work, then next week would be fine, too. It could be the morning if the afternoon isn't suitable?"

Olivia realised she had remained silent too long while her mind caught up with the unexpected invitation.

"T-this afternoon is fine," Olivia said.

"Great. I'll keep Henry after class, and we'll wait for you. I look forward to seeing you."

The line went dead. Olivia lowered the phone and looked down at the blank screen. She unhooked her arm from her coat and took a deep breath to calm her racing heart.

She walked back into the living room and turned off the television. Any notion of investing in a Slice Dice Pro would have to be parked for the meantime.

She placed her phone on the coffee table and started to pace. Her only frame of reference for parents being called into schools was from television, and she hadn't watched that much television in her life. Emily was attempting to get her interested in some of her favourite shows, but it wasn't going well.

In most shows, parents seemed to be called in when the child had been fighting. But that didn't appear to be the case this time. Besides, Henry would never fight anyone.

She pivoted once she reached the end of the room and turned to walk back across its length.

The teacher seemed very calm. It was unlikely that Henry was in trouble. He wasn't ill or they would have informed her immediately.

"Henry's progress," she muttered to herself. She looked up at the mirror. "What the hell does that mean?" she asked her reflection. She shook her head and began to walk to the other side of the room again.

Maybe he's a genius? Olivia recalled the previous morning when she had stopped him from washing his nose hairs with her expensive shampoo. *Or not.*

She stopped in the middle of the large and silent room and heaved a long sigh.

"This won't do," she muttered to herself. "It's like a graveyard in here…"

CHAPTER ELEVEN

Emily sat in the back row of the theatre with piles of paper on the chairs next to her and by her feet. She had her phone shouldered against her ear as she listened to Olivia's soft tones.

"The whole house?" Emily asked.

"Yes, you can control it from an app," Olivia replied. "Actually, I think there's very little that can't be controlled from an app these days."

"Hmm, so, how much does this cost?" Emily asked. Not that it mattered. Olivia was free to spend her money on whatever she pleased. But Emily couldn't rid herself of the worry about money.

"Not a lot. And then Henry can listen to whatever he likes in his room, I can listen to my music in my office, and you can listen to those Backstreet Boys you're so fond of," Olivia teased her.

Emily rolled her eyes. "I mentioned *one time* that I used to like them, years ago."

"You forget I helped you unpack when you moved in," Olivia joked. "If I'm not mistaken there were quite a few albums in those boxes."

"If you want to go down that path, we could discuss the contents of the box in the bottom of your wardrobe," Emily suggested.

"Well, no, no, we don't have to… I mean, I was only joking," Olivia stammered.

Emily smiled. She could picture the adorable blush on Olivia's tanned cheeks.

"It's okay, I'm only teasing you," Emily said. "So, what else has been going on?"

"Um, well...nothing much. I did look online at a...well, no, nothing much..." Olivia drifted off.

Emily shifted to press the phone closer to her ear. She waited for a moment to see if Olivia would continue, but nothing further was forthcoming.

"What is it?" Emily asked.

"We should talk about it when you're home."

Emily shifted uncomfortably. "That doesn't sound good."

"It's nothing bad," Olivia attempted to reassure her.

"Well, I'm going to worry about it now," Emily said.

She suddenly felt every single one of the miles between them. She wanted to see Olivia, to look her in the eye and be sure that she was okay. To be able to soothe away the worry lines that she knew were forming on her forehead.

She noticed Hannah walking past and offered her a tight smile. Hannah smiled back and hurried towards the stage to give Emily some privacy.

"I...I wanted to talk to you about adoption," Olivia blurted out.

"Oh." Emily froze. She hadn't expected that. "Adoption," she repeated.

"Yes. I-instead of having a child biologically."

"Do you not want to carry a child?" Emily asked. She recalled that, when they had looked at a website about pregnancy and giving birth, Olivia had looked decidedly green. "Because I don't want you to feel obligated to do that. I can carry another child, as long as you don't mind more stretch marks and saggy breasts."

The sound manager walked past at that moment, clearly overhearing the conversation. Emily felt her cheeks heat up.

"You're beautiful, you always will be," Olivia said. "But no, it's not that."

Emily waited for Olivia to continue but was greeted by more silence.

"Then what is it?" Emily asked.

"Oh, well, it's the fact that there are so many children out there who already need a family," Olivia answered quickly.

Almost a little too quickly for Emily's liking.

She'd started to identify the telltale signs of when Olivia had prepared a statement in advance. Often it was because it was a complicated matter and she wanted to make sure she got her point across. But sometimes because she was lying and there was something hidden beneath the surface.

"Should we be having a baby when there are children who don't have a family?" Olivia continued.

"That's a tough question," Emily admitted. "There's no easy answer."

"It seems like a good idea," Olivia said.

"In principle, yes," Emily said. "But adopting isn't that easy. We'll have to go through lots of checks, financial, psychological, and more. Then we wait to be approved. And if we get approved, then we have to wait for the right child who will work with our lifestyle. It could take a very long time."

Olivia sighed. "I…just…"

Emily waited. Olivia's speech pattern always slowed as she became more stressed or confused. Emily had learned that it was best to give her time to say what she was trying to process.

"There are…so many children in the world who need families."

"There are," Emily said. "And, as I say, in principle, it's a good idea. I don't know if I'm ready to go through that process. Or even if we'll be successful. But then again, whatever we choose is going to be hard. Having a child when you're in a relationship with a woman is damn difficult. It would be easier if one of us could produce sperm."

Another member of the backstage crew walked by and looked at Emily curiously. She smiled politely at him and then turned away.

Olivia was right, we should have discussed this at home.

"Straight couples can decide to have a baby, or even accidentally have one. Same-sex couples have to plan it, spend money on it, justify it." Emily let out a deep sigh.

"You sound like you're having doubts?" Olivia asked.

"No, I'm not having second thoughts. I want to have another child with you. I just don't know if I'm ready for someone to interview me about how to be a mother."

"I understand," Olivia said. "It isn't something I relish either. But think about it. I have been reading up on adoption."

Of course you have.

"And I have some links to send you."

Of course you do. She smiled fondly to herself. She really missed her.

She felt like she was being watched and wondered which member of the production crew was going to overhear her bizarre phone call next. She looked up to see Nicole standing over her with an apologetic expression.

"I'm sorry but I have to go. I'll call you later," Emily promised.

"Okay, I'll send you those links."

"You do that. I love you."

"I love you, too," Olivia said.

Emily hung up and let out another sigh. She closed her eyes and leaned her head back.

"Trouble in paradise?" She heard Nicole pick up some papers from the chair next to her and sit down.

She opened her eyes and looked at Nicole. "Not trouble exactly. Olivia wants to consider adoption."

Nicole chuckled. "That'll be fun," she joked.

"Exactly." Emily was relieved that Nicole appeared to share her reservations. "I'm all for adopting, I think it's a great thing. I know there are children in the world who need to be adopted, and I think people who do adopt are incredible, I really do."

"You don't know if it's for you. That's fair enough."

"Is it?" Emily started to wonder.

"Of course. Adoption is something that you don't just fall into. There's a lot of soul-searching before you even apply. And then the application process is long and difficult. While two teenagers can create life behind the bike shed at school without society raising an eyebrow, a couple wishing to adopt has to jump through hoops of fire." Nicole brushed some lint from her skirt. "Why's Olivia thinking about adoption anyway?"

"No idea," Emily said.

"Maybe she doesn't want to ruin her figure."

"Well, she did nearly lose her lunch when she read about what pregnancy does to the body," Emily said. "But we got over that. At least, I thought we did."

"Is everything okay?" Nicole asked.

Emily looked up at her. "I…I'm struggling a little. Being away from them. I thought I'd be okay, I thought I'd slip back into my old routine, but I haven't. Knowing they are both home and I'm here, it's hard. And just then, I wanted to be with her. Having a serious conversation over the phone is hard. It's all hard."

Nicole nodded. "I can imagine it is." She paused for a moment. "What do you want to do?"

"I don't want to lose this opportunity," Emily said quickly.

Nicole smiled and soothingly squeezed Emily's knee. "Good, but I don't want you to be depressed either. Why don't you see how things go? Maybe you'll slip back into it, maybe you won't. Either way, keep me in the loop."

"I will. I'm sure it's because spending so much time at home has spoiled me. I'll get used to it, don't worry."

"I'll try not to, but I did just discover you. I can't lose you again so soon." Nicole stood up and looked towards the stage.

"I thought we agreed on the second backdrop?" she shouted to Martin.

"This is the second backdrop," Martin called back.

"I may be getting old, but my eyesight hasn't gone yet!" She turned to Emily and rolled her eyes. "I need you to stay. You're the only person who doesn't seem determined to drive me into an early grave."

"It's early yet," Emily joked.

Nicole laughed. "Oh." She reached into her inner jacket pocket. "This came for you." She handed Emily a sealed envelope, her first name handwritten on the front.

"For me?" Emily took the envelope.

"Yes, the box office took it."

Emily looked at the envelope and quickly ripped it open.

"There's no other backdrop on the van," Martin called from the stage.

"Absolute incompetence," Nicole muttered under her breath.

A piece of thick paper fell from the envelope into Emily's lap. She picked it up and examined it. It was a ticket, in the stalls for that evening for the musical showing just up the road.

She held it up for Nicole to see.

Nicole frowned and took the ticket from Emily.

"It's a great production," Nicole said.

"I didn't book a ticket," Emily said. "You didn't request this?"

Nicole shook her head. "I wouldn't send you a ticket to a rival production. We have our own perfectly good musical on."

"Then who's sent me a ticket?"

"It must be an error," Nicole said. "I'll take it back to the box office. Maybe it's for another Emily?" She picked up the envelope and put the ticket back in. "I'll return it to the box office. I'm sure someone will pick it up. Anyway, do you have the updated script for this next scene?"

Emily reached for the papers on the floor and picked up the reworked scene.

"Marvellous, we need to get that to Martin. And you need to speak to him about the last scene. There's a problem with lighting."

"I thought he fixed that?" Emily asked.

"So did I, but he had a question. You'll need to talk to him."

"I'll catch up with him now. You were right when you said it was hectic before a new show opened."

Nicole laughed. "You think this is hectic? Wait for opening night!"

Olivia walked down the corridor of the school, weaving her way past children who were all eagerly trying to leave. She remembered the way to Henry's classroom from the parent orientation night.

She'd yet to meet Miss Costa, but Henry had described her as the teacher from *Matilda* so she had high hopes for his academic future.

She turned the corner and approached the open door. Her eyes were immediately drawn to Henry. He sat at a desk, his brow knit in concentration and his cheek sucked into his mouth. He looked well and healthy, and Olivia breathed out the sigh of relief that she had been holding in ever since she'd spoken to Miss Costa that morning.

"Mrs. Lewis?"

Olivia looked towards the front of the classroom. A young woman with long, brown hair and glasses approached her with her hand out.

Olivia shook her hand.

"Miss Costa," Olivia said politely.

"Please, Miss Costa is what my students call me. My name is Natalie."

"Olivia," she returned in kind.

"Olivia!" Henry's voice boomed, having just noticed her arrival.

Olivia walked over to his desk and bent down to kiss his hair.

"How's your day going, Henry?"

"I got another star," he said, ignoring her question. "And I'm going to get a badge tomorrow when I do my alphabet."

Olivia smiled. Henry had taken to education well. He enjoyed the process of learning and was academically minded. In his short time in school, he had already amassed several badges, stars, and certificates, which he collected with pride.

"Is Tiny home alone?" Henry asked her with a puzzled frown.

"He's in the car," Olivia said.

Tiny wasn't allowed in school, much to Henry's disappointment. It had been a shock to suddenly spend large portions of time away from Tiny, but Henry seemed to console himself in the knowledge that Olivia would look after him.

"Henry, would you like to go outside and play on the playground while your mother and I speak?" Natalie said.

Henry quickly packed up his bag and threw it over his shoulder before rushing past Olivia and disappearing into the corridor.

Natalie gestured to the window where the playground apparatus could be seen.

"We can keep an eye on him while we speak," she said as she pulled out a chair in front of her desk. She walked around the desk and sat down.

Olivia waited until she could see Henry arrive in the playground. A moment later he came into view. He ran towards the play area, dropping his bag and launching himself up the slide. It was a long way from the Henry she remembered in his hospital bed. She swallowed hard at the memory.

She turned to face Natalie and slowly lowered herself into the chair that had been pulled out for her. A familiar sense of dread crept up her neck. She wondered how it was that the memory of being disciplined in school could be so strong when everything else from childhood faded into nothing.

"Henry is wonderful," Natalie said. "He's making friends, engaging well with students and teachers."

Olivia nodded.

Of course he is. He's Henry.

Natalie seemed to pause for a moment. "He mentioned that his other mother had gone away?"

Olivia nodded again. "That's right. Yes."

"I'm sorry to hear that. You must both miss her terribly?"

"Yes," Olivia said, "but we're managing."

Natalie offered her a tight smile. "That's good, I'm glad. I know it must be very difficult for you."

"We have each other," Olivia explained. She drifted her gaze to look at Henry playing outside.

"Of course, and, as I say, Henry really is wonderful. But we have noticed that sometimes we struggle to get his attention. And when he is excited, he can forget what he was doing and start on another task."

Olivia turned to look back at Natalie. The conversation seemed to be veering away from how well Henry was doing.

"At first, we thought it was because he misses his mother, but there are educational markers that indicate it might be something else," Natalie continued.

Olivia swallowed again. She realised that Natalie had just been praising Henry's social skills to soften the blow that something was wrong.

"We'd like your permission to set up a meeting with Henry and our school counsellor."

"For what purpose?" Olivia quickly found her voice again.

"Just to ascertain if there is any particular reason why Henry struggles to focus."

"ADHD?" Olivia guessed.

Natalie looked uncomfortable. "Well, yes, that is one possibility."

"Autism?" Olivia continued.

"It would be difficult to say until we investigate further, but, yes, that is another possibility."

Natalie sat forward a little. "Mrs. Lewis, Olivia, we just want to provide Henry with the very best level of education that we can. If there is a diagnosis to be had, it's good that we get it as early as possible so that we can adapt his learning needs, if necessary."

"But...he's so young...how can you..." Olivia turned to look out the window. Henry was happily playing, oblivious to what was being said a few meters away.

"It's nothing to be worried about, we just want to make sure that Henry has all the support that he needs."

Olivia snapped her head back towards Natalie. She opened her mouth but struggled for any words to come out. She picked up her bag and shot up to her feet.

"I'll think this over," she said.

"Of course." Natalie stood up as well. She reached for an envelope on her desk and handed it to Olivia. "This contains all of the information you need. There's no hurry. We're bringing it to attention now so we can work together for what's best for Henry."

"Yes. Is there anything else?" Olivia needed to get out of there. Taking in sufficient oxygen was starting to be a struggle, and she had no desire to look weak in front of Henry's teacher.

Natalie shook her head.

"Thank you for your time," Olivia said formally. "I will…I will contact you shortly."

"Thank you for coming in," Natalie said. "Would you like me to show you out?"

Olivia shook her head. She turned on her heel and walked briskly out of the classroom.

Her eyes started to fill with tears. She blinked to clear her vision, aware that her heels clacked loudly in the school corridor, wanting to make sure that nothing sounded out of the ordinary. The last thing she needed now was to draw more attention to herself.

At breakneck speed, she went from feeling that the whole thing was a miscalculation and that Henry was fine, to firmly planting the blame upon herself. Henry had been a normal child when she met him. Now he was tumbling towards a behavioural diagnosis.

How would she explain this to Emily? She hadn't spoken to Emily about the meeting at the school, and now she had to tell her that she'd broken her son.

She exited the corridor and stood in the playground, sucking up large gulps of air.

Henry happily ran from apparatus to apparatus. She'd only been looking after him for less than a week and already she felt like a complete failure.

She took a deep breath and blinked away the moisture in her eyes.

"Henry," she called out softly.

He turned and looked over at her. His red cheeks and wide grin made her smile despite her heartbreak.

He picked up his bag and ran over to her. "Are we going home?"

"Yes, we are." Olivia held out her hand, and Henry grabbed onto it.

"Are you in trouble?" he asked as they started to walk across the playground. "Miss Costa puts Kevin in timeout when he's in trouble."

"Have you been in timeout?"

"No."

"Good."

They walked in silence. Olivia could practically feel Henry's eyes as he stared up at her.

"Have you been crying?" he finally asked as they approached the car.

"No, just...I've...been cutting onions." She opened the car door for him.

He rolled his eyes. "Wow, Mommy's right. You are *really* bad at lying."

CHAPTER TWELVE

The noise of the Hogshead Pub was overwhelming. Glasses chinked and a loud, constant rumble of conversations filled the large bar area. Hannah linked arms with Emily and guided her towards the back of the room where a group of people drank, chatted, and laughed.

"Hey, everyone," Hannah shouted over the din. "This is Emily, our fantastic new writer!"

Emily was taken aback by the spontaneous cheers and sounds of congratulations and welcome. Half-full glasses were raised in the air in greeting. She turned to Hannah and smiled.

"One big, happy family," Hannah said. She leaned in close to Emily's ear so she could hear her. "Let me introduce you to the people *worth* knowing."

Emily nodded. "Let's do it."

Hannah grinned as she navigated the crowd. Emily followed her closely, not wanting to lose her newly acquired guide.

She looked up to notice Carl perched at the end of the bar, nursing a pint of beer and looking straight at her. She offered him a warm smile, and he smiled back, his face lighting up upon seeing her.

After nearly a week of working with him, she hadn't changed her mind on him in the slightest. In fact, she was starting to enjoy her time in the theatre as it meant she was away from the small office she shared with him. At the start of the week, she thought she would just enjoy getting out of the cold, cramped space, but now she was more relieved to be away from Carl.

There was nothing wrong with him, nothing she could easily put into words. He just seemed to always be there, always looking at her, always following her. But it was impossible to have a conversation with him. As soon as she tried, he clammed up.

"Emily, this is John," Hannah said, pulling her from her thoughts.

Emily shook the cobwebs from her head and turned to face John. She smiled and held out her hand. "Hi!"

She tried to focus on what John was saying about his role in lighting, but she struggled as she felt Carl appear behind her. Hannah had headed to the bar to get them both drinks. Emily was stuck between giving her undivided attention to John and wanting to turn around to see why Carl was standing right behind her.

In the end, she managed to step to the side enough to force Carl to be included in the conversation. John regarded Carl warily and continued talking to Emily about the intricacies of lighting the stage. Usually she would have been fascinated, but the way Carl stood and stared at her was most off-putting.

Hannah rejoined the group and looked at Carl.

"Can we help you?" she asked.

"I…was just leaving," he said. He looked at Emily. "See you tomorrow."

He quickly turned and ducked through the crowd to leave the bar.

"Odd lad," John said.

"Yeah," Hannah said.

Emily watched Carl go. She almost felt sorry for him, but she had to admit that there was an underlying creepiness to his actions.

"Anyway, what was I saying about multiple spots?" John said. "Oh yes…"

Emily leaned heavily against the wall of the elevator and let out a long sigh. She had no idea how five hours had passed so quickly.

And she couldn't understand how the theatre production team was still alive after all the alcohol consumed within those five hours.

Everyone wanted to welcome her to the team by buying her a beverage. She'd never been offered so many drinks in her life. In fact, she'd switched to non-alcoholic drinks when she started to feel lightheaded after only half an hour in the pub. Nicole had turned up for a brief while and informed her that the team drinks at the Hogshead were a regular thing. Emily had no idea how anyone managed to function after spending so many hours propping up the bar.

Despite the flow of booze, the evening had been hugely successful. She'd met and spoken with almost every department of the company, from the unpaid technical interns learning the ropes to the office staff. Names and positions swam around her head despite her best efforts to keep them all in order, knowing they would be of use later.

The elevator came to a stop, letting her out onto the carpeted hallway heading towards her hotel room. She felt exhausted and wondered if she'd manage to get herself up in the morning after such a full evening of socialising.

"Mrs. White?"

Emily looked up with a frown. A member of the staff stood in front of her hotel room with an enormous bunch of flowers in his hands.

Emily slowly nodded. "Yes, that's me."

"I was going to leave these outside, due to the late hour." He nodded at the bouquet. "They just arrived by courier."

Emily was stunned. "Oh, they're beautiful." She swiped the electronic lock with her room key and pushed open the door.

"Can you put them on the table?" Emily asked as she kicked off her heels.

He stepped into the room and placed the flowers on the side table. The bouquet was presented in a large see-through bag of water with colourful ribbons tying it all together.

"Good night," the porter said as he let himself out of the room, closing the door behind him.

Emily bent down to sniff the bouquet. Floral scents filled her senses, luxurious and not too strong. Some bouquets were like an explosion of fragrance, but this was artistic and measured.

She smiled as she reached into her bag and picked up her phone. She flopped onto the bed as she dialled Olivia.

As always, the call took a little while to connect, and even though she was certain it was now done by satellite, Emily mentally pictured wires connecting across the UK and then the ocean before reaching New York.

When the call did connect, it only rang one and a half times before Olivia answered.

"Hello, darling," she said.

"Thank you," Emily replied sleepily. The bed was so soft that she could already feel herself starting to drift off. She'd known that lying down before washing her makeup off would be fatal, but her aching feet and swimming head had urged her.

"What for?" Olivia asked.

"You know what for." Emily chuckled.

"Do I?" Olivia asked.

"The flowers," Emily replied. She pulled herself into a sitting position, knowing that she was seriously about to drift off if she didn't take drastic action. She wondered when Olivia had ordered the flowers, if she'd forgotten all about them.

"I...I haven't sent any. Should I? I can speak with the florist who I used to use for—"

"You haven't sent any?" Emily interrupted.

"No," Olivia said.

Emily slid off the bed and walked over to the bouquet, wondering if the hotel had made a mistake and the blooms weren't for her after all.

"Would you like me to send you flowers?" Olivia asked, a hesitation in her tone.

"No, no," Emily said. "There's just some flowers here. I assumed they were from you."

She saw a small envelope wedged between the stems and shouldered the phone as she plucked it out.

"Who's sending you flowers?" Olivia asked, her tone becoming a little frosty.

"I don't know. I'm looking at the card now," Emily replied.

She opened the envelope, pulled out the thick card, and frowned.

"Well?" Olivia asked impatiently.

Emily chuckled. "It says it's from my secret admirer. I think this is meant for someone else."

"Secret admirer?" Olivia demanded. "Who?"

"Secret admirers don't sign their names. That's what makes them secret," Emily said. She dropped the card and the envelope to the table. "It must be for someone else. I don't have a secret admirer and there is no name or room number on the note. Maybe the courier got the address wrong. Maybe the hotel made a mistake."

"But—"

"No one even knows I'm staying here," Emily continued. "Only you and Nicole, and I think we can rule out Nicole."

Olivia remained quiet for a few moments. Emily understood all too well that the distance suddenly felt a whole lot more real.

"I've missed you," Emily whispered. "So, so much."

"I've missed you, too," Olivia replied.

"But I get to see you tomorrow," Emily said. She wouldn't admit it to Olivia, as she was trying to appear strong, but she had been counting down the hours to her flight home.

"I suppose I'll clear out a drawer for you. Maybe a bit of the wardrobe," Olivia joked.

"How generous." Emily chuckled and walked into the bathroom. She turned on the light and picked up a makeup removal pad.

"Henry saw your Crown uniform," Olivia said.

Emily smiled at the memory of her last morning in New York.

"Oh yes?" she asked.

"Yes, it was terribly embarrassing," Olivia added.

"You're the one who tore it off me and threw it on the floor," Emily replied.

"I picked it up," Olivia said. "But I left it on the chair. In case there was a repeat performance."

"Oh, I see. Is that a request?"

"This has been a very long week," Olivia confessed.

"I know." Emily started to feel guilty. She knew Olivia didn't want that, but it was impossible not to feel guilty. They were apart because of her. Because of her dream. "It will get better," she promised.

"It will," Olivia said. She cleared her throat. "Henry is here and would like to speak with you."

"Can you put me on speaker? I'm not ready to let you go just yet…"

CHAPTER THIRTEEN

Emily dropped her suitcase and fell to her knees in the arrivals terminal as Henry rushed into her arms. It had been just under a week since she'd seen him, but it had felt like a lifetime. She'd had to be apart from him before, but this time she was choosing to. It broke her heart.

"Mommy, school is amazing!" Henry cried. He pulled back. "I got a badge for my alphabet."

"Wow, that's great!"

Henry pulled a badge out of his pocket and handed it to her. "Miss Costa says I'm very good."

She examined the badge. "That's wonderful, Henry."

Olivia approached, wringing her hands nervously.

Emily stood and pulled her into a hug. "I missed you. So much," she whispered into Olivia's ear.

Olivia returned the hug. "I missed you, too."

"Mommy, do good boys get presents?" Henry asked, tugging on her jacket.

Emily leaned back a little and smiled at Olivia before turning to look down at Henry.

"What kind of present?"

"I want a cat."

"He wants a cat," Olivia repeated. "Instead of a kitten."

Emily frowned. She hated that she was missing out on things. When she left, Henry was adamant about getting a kitten, but somehow that had changed. And that left Emily unsettled. She didn't want to miss out on anything, no matter how small.

"Why do you want a cat, Henry?"

Olivia disengaged herself from the hug and pulled up the handle of Emily's suitcase. They started to walk towards the airport's car park.

"Because cats are like bigger kittens," Henry explained. "And cats have no family, and we could be a family for a cat."

"Why bring another kitten into the world, when there are so many cats needing homes?" Olivia added.

"But kittens are so cute," Emily said. The truth was, she hated kittens, but she wanted to steer Henry back towards the idea of getting one rather than a cat. "You can teach them things, while cats are stuck in their ways. And older cats might just sleep all day."

Henry's brow furrowed as he thought about it. "Maybe," he said.

Olivia looked at her with confusion, and Emily shook her head indicating that they'd have the conversation later, away from little ears.

"Olivia says I can name the cat," Henry said. He smothered a yawn behind his hand.

Emily smirked. Olivia would live to regret that promise. Henry's terrible naming skills were renowned. Tiny was one of the few that hadn't been vetoed.

"I see," Emily replied. "So, you enjoyed school?"

"Yes. I have lots of friends."

"Someone called Dean wants to come over to play," Olivia added. She sounded uncertain.

"That sounds like a great idea," Emily said. Most of Henry's current friends were much younger than he was. It wasn't a problem now, but it would be soon.

"So, I can really get a kitten?" Henry yawned again.

Emily made eye contact with Olivia. Olivia shrugged indicating that it was up to Emily.

"We'll talk about it," she said. "Are you tired?"

He slowly nodded and stopped dead in front of her, looking up with tired eyes.

In a move perfected over the years, she slung her bag high up onto her shoulder before bending down and picking him up. He wrapped his arms around her neck and fell heavily against her.

Olivia looked apologetic. "We've had a busy day."

"It's fine." Emily sniffed the back of his neck. She used to do the same when he was a baby, when he had a baby scent that comforted her. While that scent was now gone, he still smelled of home.

They continued walking. Emily hoped that Olivia had parked nearby. Henry was small for his age but catching up fast. She wasn't sure she could stomach watching him grow another half an inch every time she saw him between work trips.

She looked at Olivia who walked beside them stoically. She thought back to the nervous hand-wringing and wondered if that was just nerves from being at the airport. She suspected that it was something more.

"I suppose you want a puppy?" she joked to break the ice.

Olivia shook her head. "No, it would scare the cat...kitten, I mean."

"I was joking."

"Oh." Olivia nodded. "I see."

Emily frowned. Olivia was definitely distracted. She could practically see the cogs turning.

"How's the vegetable garden? Enough to feed the East Coast yet?"

Olivia smiled. "It's going well, still a ways to go before I set up my own supermarket."

Emily grinned at the joke. "Have you been in touch with Simon?"

"Yes, he's so nervous about the baby," Olivia said. "I told him that he'd be fine. Silly boy."

Emily chuckled. She loved it when Briticisms slipped from Olivia's lips so casually, a result of her extended time in the country.

"And school's been okay?"

"A-absolutely."

"And you've been okay?"

She saw Olivia tense up, clearly aware Emily had detected something was wrong.

"Y-yes," Olivia stammered.

Now Emily was worried. Hand-wringing and stuttering. It had been a while since Olivia had exhibited those symptoms. Something was bothering her. Emily needed to tread carefully and uncover what it was.

It only took five minutes to walk to the car, but, to Emily, it felt like thirty. Henry had fallen asleep in her arms. She'd forgotten how much heavier a deadweight could be.

Olivia unlocked the car and moved the booster seat from the front to the back before placing Emily's suitcase in the trunk.

Emily put Henry into the seat and fastened him in, placing a kiss on his forehead before taking a step back.

"I thought a cat would be a better idea than a kitten."

Emily jumped at Olivia's sudden and unexpected presence behind her. "Jesus, Olivia, you scared me."

Olivia took a step back. "I'm sorry, I just...I don't understand. What's the difference between getting a kitten or getting a cat?"

Emily closed the car door softly. "Henry's five—"

"Nearly six," Olivia interrupted.

"Nearly six," Emily said. "If he gets a cat, say a seven-year-old cat, and that cat lives for twelve years, it will die when he is ten. If he gets a kitten and it lives for twelve years, it will die when he is seventeen."

"You don't know when the cat will die," Olivia said.

"No, but based on the law of averages, a cat lives until it's about twelve. It might die at eight, or might live to be twenty. Either way, the younger the cat is when Henry gets it, the older Henry will be when it dies. I know Henry has to learn about death at some point, but I would really rather delay that if we could."

"I'd never thought of that," Olivia whispered. "You're right, of course."

She turned away and stalked towards the driver's door. Emily watched her go, wondering what was bothering her.

They both got in and fastened their seat belts.

"So, do we get him a kitten?" Olivia asked.

Emily considered it for a moment. "I think maybe we should. He's the right age to take on a bit more responsibility. And he does seem to have his heart set on one."

"I'll do some research," Olivia promised.

"So, everything's good? Other than the kitten drama?"

Olivia looked at her and nodded her head. "Perfect," she said.

Emily turned to check on Henry in the back of the car. "I think I should travel to and from the airport on my own," she said. "Henry's exhausted and you have to sit in traffic to get here. There's no point in us all suffering."

"But I don't mind," Olivia said.

"You hate being at the airport," Emily said. She'd seen Olivia's nervous swallow at the sound of a plane landing. "It will mean being apart for another hour, but it's better than dragging Henry all the way out here after a school day, and so close to his bedtime. I'd love to see you both as soon as possible, you know that. But this is probably for the best if we're going to be practical about it."

Olivia opened her mouth, presumably to argue, but thought better of it and closed it again. She nodded her agreement and put her hands on the steering wheel, preparing to drive them home.

"So, what's going on?" Emily asked as the car started. "And don't tell me nothing."

CHAPTER FOURTEEN

Olivia felt the air in the car become thin. She'd hoped at least to be able to get home before telling Emily. She wondered if this marriage would last even less time than her first.

"Olivia, you're worrying me," Emily said.

She gripped the steering wheel nervously, staring out at the dark car park. She knew she had to say what she was thinking quickly, get it out in the open, like pulling off a Band-Aid.

"I'm a bad influence on Henry," she stated. "I...I don't think I should be the one to look after him for a prolonged period of time."

"Is this about the wine?"

Olivia turned to face Emily. "Nicole told you?"

It wasn't the first time that Nicole had proved untrustworthy with information. She didn't know why she kept confiding in her. Although she had to admit that her leaks often led to positive outcomes. And sometimes she was on the receiving end of the information, so it had benefited her in the past.

"She mentioned that you were about to check yourself into Betty Ford. She was worried about you. Look, having a glass of wine, or two gulps, isn't an issue—"

"It's not that."

Emily looked panicked, and Olivia knew she couldn't put it off any longer.

"The school called me to come in and speak with them about Henry. T-they are concerned about him," Olivia explained. She took a deep breath. "Apparently, they check children for…disorders. They have some kind of a…preliminary test."

"Test for what?" Emily asked.

"Autism." Olivia felt the word drop like a stone between them. "Clearly, it's my influence. Maybe I'm catching or something. But I can't…I can't be the reason that Henry—"

"Hold it right there," Emily said. She held her hand up, silencing Olivia. "Firstly, you are not infecting Henry with anything. We don't even know if you're on the spectrum."

Olivia snorted a laugh. She might never have been officially tested, but she knew something was different about her. She might not admit it out loud, but she knew the truth. As much as she might like to ignore it and pretend it wasn't there, it was.

"Olivia," Emily said softly. She took her hand. "You haven't made Henry this way. If, *if,* Henry has autism, then he has autism. We'll do our best to get him what he needs. And he needs you. You're not infectious. You shouldn't think like that."

Tears started to roll down Olivia's face. "Maybe I haven't infected Henry, but what about the baby? If I carry a baby, then it will have my genes. It might be like I am."

"Good, I want nothing more than a little you." Emily pulled her closer, and they leaned into an awkward hug, the centre console a barrier between them. "It wouldn't matter to me, Olivia. You are who you are. I never want to change that. If you have our baby and it is like you, then I'll be ecstatic."

"Are you sure? I know I'm hard work," Olivia said.

"You are hard work," Emily said in a joking tone. "But you're worth every second."

Olivia sat back. She got a tissue out of her jacket pocket and started to wipe her eyes.

"I'm sorry," she whispered.

"What did the school say, exactly?" Emily asked.

Olivia reached across into the glove box and pulled out the letter that Natalie Costa had handed to her. She gave it to Emily.

"She said that there would be further tests needed, and we'd have to consent…I'm so sorry. I should have told you on the phone, but I didn't know what to say…"

Emily held up her hand to silence Olivia's rambling as she read the letter.

Olivia pulled down the sun visor and peered at her reflection in the tiny mirror. She wiped away her crumbling mascara and tried to fix her hair. She'd promised herself that she would keep it together, at least until they got home. Now she was falling apart in a public parking lot, making her feel like more of a disaster than she already did.

"So, he showed some development markers in class and they asked him to do a test," Emily recapped. "And that came back with a possibility that he might be on the spectrum and now they want to do more tests, right?"

"Yes," Olivia said.

"Okay." Emily folded up the letter and put it back into the glove box. "Well, I say that we let them do further tests. What do you think?"

"Me?" Olivia was floored that Emily was asking her.

"Yes, you. You're also his parent. And you have a little more experience with this kind of thing than I do." Emily looked at her, reading her in an instant. "I know you think you're to blame for this, but you're not."

Olivia shook her head and looked away. "He was fine when I met him, and now…"

"Now what?" Emily asked. "Neither of us has detected anything. Neither of us has seen a difference in him since we got together. It's not like you walked in, and he had a complete personality transplant."

Olivia turned back to face her. "But it's too much of a coincidence."

"Millions of people are on the spectrum," Emily said. "And diagnosis rates are shooting through the roof. Why do you think they are on the lookout for it in schools?"

Olivia shrugged.

"Do you think we should take the tests?" Emily asked again.

Olivia remembered her own schooling. She wondered if things would have been easier if someone had noticed her differences back then. She'd always considered a diagnosis as nothing more than a label, but if that label could help Henry succeed in school, in life, then surely it was an important label.

But then there was the part of Olivia that didn't want to know. If Henry was diagnosed, would she be next? Would some scientist want to know if she had indeed infected him? Would she be the key to the scientific discovery that autism was transferrable by touch?

"Olivia." She felt Emily's hand on her thigh. "I can see you panicking. Take deep breaths."

Olivia sucked in a lungful of air. The painful burn indicated that she'd been holding her breath. She nodded her head.

"He should have the tests. Maybe it will help," Olivia said.

Now wasn't the time for dramatics and ridiculousness. Now was the time for being practical.

Emily's hand softly brushed against her thigh. "We'll talk about it more at home."

"I'm okay," Olivia said. "I just worry. Henry…he…he does things. Things that I do. He straightens things. He's very precise about where the remote control goes."

"Olivia, he gets that from you. As in, he copies your behaviour. It might mean nothing. He might be copying the things that you do. It's not necessarily an indication of anything bigger."

Olivia considered that for a moment. She knew her obsessive behaviour was considered a behavioural disorder. She liked things just so, but knew that it was more than that. If she was unable to straighten an item on a table for some reason, it riled her.

Once she'd noticed Henry doing the same, she'd started to worry. But Emily was probably right. Henry was a sponge and did enjoy copying her and helping her with tasks.

"I hope that's the case," she said. "I worry. I don't want him to struggle like I have."

Emily smiled. "I know. Let's go home. I want to cuddle up on the sofa with my wife."

Olivia sucked in another breath. The talk had gone better than she'd expected. Emily wasn't angry, in fact it seemed she was quite the opposite. Sometimes it was hard to remember that she had married someone who understood her and actively worked with her. As she turned back to face the steering wheel, she glanced up at the rearview mirror and she caught a glimpse of Henry. She hoped that he would have the same luck in his life.

CHAPTER FIFTEEN

Henry entered the kitchen and looked from Emily to Olivia with a grumpy pout.

"Good morning," Emily greeted him.

It was good to see some things never changed. Henry was just as grumpy and disoriented in the mornings as ever. He stood in the doorway in his pyjamas, with one side of his hair stuck to his head and the other side in complete disarray. He held Tiny in one hand and let out a sigh.

Olivia got up from where she had been sitting at the breakfast table and pulled out a chair for him. She crossed the room and put some bread in the toaster.

Emily remained in her seat, eager to see how things played out. Olivia had explained that Henry was still not engaging with her first thing in the morning, but at least he had stopped running away altogether.

He ran across the room and nuzzled himself onto Emily's lap. She put her arms around him and hugged him to her.

"Do you want toast?" Emily whispered to him.

He slowly nodded his head against her chest.

"And juice?" she asked.

He nodded again.

She turned to speak to Olivia, but as always Olivia was a few steps ahead. She lowered a glass of orange juice to the table.

"What do you say?" Emily asked.

"Fanko," Henry mumbled.

Emily could tell that Henry was going to take longer than usual to wake up and start to interact, so she carried on her conversation with Olivia.

"Are you sure you don't want to come?"

Olivia shook her head. "I have the contractor coming about the shelves. And then the electric man about the speaker system."

Emily chuckled.

"What?" Olivia asked.

"Electric man," Emily said.

"Well, I'm sorry, but I'm not calling him an audio and visual engineering guru. No matter what he wants to print on his business card."

"Tell them to come back during the week?" Emily said.

"I can't. The contractor is about to have a month-long vacation, and he's the only person I trust to supply the same type of wood as my desk. Can you imagine having mismatched wood types?"

"No...I can't..."

"And Mr. Guru is busy, and I wanted to get his quote finalised as soon as possible. It's ridiculously quiet around here."

Emily looked around the kitchen. The dishwasher was whirring, the washing machine could be heard from the utility room, the coffee machine spluttered as it brewed its black magic. In the other room, she could hear the television.

"What are we doing today?" Henry asked. He looked up at her with half-closed eyes.

"We're going to see Tom and Lucy."

Henry's eyes started to widen in excitement. "Really?"

"Really."

Henry shuffled himself down from Emily's lap and sat on his own chair.

"Can I take my badges to show Lucy?"

"Absolutely, she'd love to see them."

Olivia placed a plate of freshly buttered and cut toast in front of Henry.

"Thank you," he said as he lifted a triangle.

"You're welcome," Olivia said. She sat down and looked at Emily. "I'll be fine on my own. You won't be that long anyway."

"I know," Emily said. "I miss you. I want to maximise this time together. But I'll be a big girl. I know I still have tonight." She winked at Olivia, enjoying how her cheeks started to colour at the insinuation.

"What's happening tonight?" Henry asked through a mouthful of toast.

❖

"Mommy, I'm a helicopter!" Henry cried.

Tom was gripping his hands and spinning him wildly around the garden.

"You break it, you bought it," Emily called out to Tom.

"He's fine," Tom said.

"Be careful with him," Lucy shouted. "You'll snap his arms off."

Tom rolled his eyes at them. He lowered Henry to the ground and started to chase him.

Lucy poured some more homemade lemonade into Emily's glass. Emily watched Henry and Tom playing in the garden and let out a contented hum. Henry had been eager to see Tom and Lucy and tell them all about starting school. She was happy to see him enjoying himself, even if the jet lag was causing her to feel a little sluggish.

In all her time in cabin crew, she never once suffered from jet lag. But now she was left wondering what day it was and why she felt exhausted in the afternoon. She guessed the real secret to avoiding jet lag was having such a packed flight schedule that jet lag was never able to find you.

"It's like old times," Lucy said.

"No, it's not. I was always working. I think I only ever sat in this garden twice the whole time I lived here," Emily said.

She leaned back and enjoyed the feel of the sun on her face.

"No, really?" Lucy asked. "I thought we did this a lot."

"We spoke about doing it a lot," Emily said. "But I was either working, or exhausted from working."

She shivered a little at the memories. Long night shifts, worries about Henry's health, mounting bills, and seemingly no way out. Things had changed beyond all recognition.

"Well, we're here now," Lucy said. "How is work? Is it exciting?"

"It's amazing," Emily confirmed. "I wish it was here in New York, but still amazing."

"Do you miss being home?" Lucy asked.

"Yeah, I feel like I'm in the same situation I was before. Just with more money, doing something I love, and not such a gruelling schedule." Emily sat up and looked at Lucy. "I just got married, like, a couple of weeks ago, and I've already spent a week away from my family. I swear Henry is bigger than when I left."

Lucy laughed. "He's having a growth spurt."

"He is. I always worried he'd resent me for working so much, but I could deal with it because I knew it wasn't a choice. I had to do it. But now, I do have a choice. And I'm choosing to spend time away from him, and I feel awful."

"Henry's a good boy. He understands. As well as he can at that age."

Emily shook her head. "I don't know if he does. He's getting older. He's asking more questions. And then there's Olivia. I feel bad that she's suddenly taken on the role of his primary carer. I wonder if I'm doing the right thing. Lucy, am I being too selfish?"

"You're not," Lucy said firmly. "You have an amazing opportunity, anyone would tell you that you'd be a fool not to take it. You have a skill, a talent that not everyone has. This is the chance to make a name for yourself, to build up a new career and make some money. And I'm sure Olivia is loving her new role with Henry."

Emily sipped at her lemonade but remained silent. She wasn't sure she wanted to venture into this conversation. Although, the gates had been opened now, so she doubted she could avoid it.

"Isn't she?" Lucy frowned.

"I'm not sure," Emily admitted. "She loves Henry, and she's great with him. But..." She blew out a breath and flopped back in her chair. "I don't know if she's happy."

Lucy chuckled. "Of course she's happy! Anyone who sees the three of you together could tell you that."

Emily sat up again and watched as Tom and Henry ran circles around the large oak tree at the bottom of the garden. She recalled the previous evening, cuddled up on the sofa with Olivia, talking about London and her new job. Olivia had been engaged and asking questions, but Emily noticed that her own commentary was missing. When Olivia used to talk about work, it was with a spark in her eye. Now that spark was gone. After a brief conversation about the contractor who was installing the household surround sound system, Olivia had become quiet. Like there was nothing else to say.

"I think that she feels that something is missing," Emily said softly. "When I met Olivia, her work was everything. But now she's retired, and I think she did it for me. Obviously, she was pushed out of Applewoods, but I thought she'd find something else to do. Then she suggested that she stay home while I go out to work. And now she throws herself into project after project, like she's trying to fill a void."

"Like the garden," Lucy said.

"Like the garden, and decorating the house, and a new baby," Emily added. "If she truly wanted to do those things then it wouldn't be a problem, but I get the impression that she's just trying to fill a hole."

"Have you talked to her about it?"

Emily snorted a laugh. "A little. It's hard with Olivia. Often, she doesn't know why she does things herself. It takes her a while to process what she's thinking, feeling, and why she is doing what she's doing. Sometimes she can't process it at all. I think something is starting to niggle at her. She was very quiet when she picked me up from the airport yesterday."

She decided not to venture into the whole possible diagnosis discussion. That could wait for another time when she had more information. And she didn't want to muddy the waters. She was positive that Henry's potential diagnosis and Olivia's listlessness were not connected.

"Maybe she'll be ready to talk about it soon?" Lucy asked hopefully.

"I hope so. I can't stand to see her unhappy."

"Do you think she's actually unhappy?"

Emily considered the question. "I don't know about unhappy, but she doesn't seem happy either. Maybe a little lost and trying to find her footing."

"Maybe she just needs time. You said yourself, you haven't been married long and there have been a lot of changes." Lucy smiled endearingly. "She'll settle soon, I'm sure of it."

Emily didn't share Lucy's optimism, but she returned the smile nonetheless. Lucy had always been the kind of person who was content to wait and see. But waiting and seeing had never been Emily's strong suit. She knew something was up, and now she was itching to fix it.

"Mommy!" Henry ran towards them. "Tom says he's going to get me!"

Emily held her arms out, and Henry barrelled into her. She pulled him up into her lap and wrapped her arms around him.

Tom slowly approached with his hands up. "I don't think I would have been able to catch you, Henry. You're too fast for me."

"I'm fast!" Henry said. He squirmed out of Emily's arms and started to run in the opposite direction. Tom jogged after him.

Emily chuckled as she watched them go.

"What's Olivia doing today?" Lucy asked.

Emily rolled her eyes. "She's meeting with a contractor to get an estimate for putting some shelves in her office. And someone else is installing a multi-room sound system that is supposedly essential."

"Having music playing is nice," Lucy said.

"It is, but we have a radio. And a CD player. A television. Laptops, iPads. A means to play music isn't something we're struggling with. And the shelves in her office aren't really essential either. Not that I'd stop her from doing what she wants...I just worry."

"Worry that she's struggling to let go of work?"

Emily nodded. "She's calling Simon less and less, but she wants to remodel her office. I'm not going to say no. It's her money after all."

"Sounds like she needs a project," Lucy suggested. "Something beyond the house, not a garden project. What's the situation with the baby? Are you still going down that route?"

Emily shrugged. "It's hard to say, we both know we need to discuss it more. There are so many options and the process isn't going to be a quick one. But I feel rushed and Olivia is bored. There's this huge disconnect. I feel like it was only yesterday that we got married. I've been so busy that everything feels like it's going a million miles an hour."

"Talk about jet lag," Lucy said with an understanding nod. "But Olivia doesn't have much going on so, for her, it's been ages."

"Exactly. And I'm trying to do both things at once, but I can't rush such an important decision and we have such limited time to speak. It's not really a conversation you can have over the phone." Emily shifted uneasily in her seat. "And then there's the fact that she is now talking about adopting a child."

Lucy's eyebrows rose. "Oh. That's…"

Emily nodded. "I know. And I also know that, as an ex-foster child, I should be all about adoption, giving a child a home and a second chance. But I can't help thinking it's a bad idea. Just the thought of the application process gives me nightmares. Justifying to a stranger that I'd be a good parent, when I'm hardly ever going to be home. And my financial history. And to be brutally honest, I don't know if I'd be a good parent to a troubled child. I don't feel properly equipped."

"I thought Olivia wanted to carry a baby herself?" Lucy asked hesitantly, obviously wondering if there was a deeper reason why she'd changed her mind.

"She does. She did," Emily said. "She started to talk about there being so many children in the world already who needed homes. But I think the truth of it is that she feels the baby may inherit some of her…traits."

Lucy looked at her with a frown before the inference suddenly dawned on her. "Oh, her…traits."

"Of course, I told her that I didn't care about that. I mean, I don't, really. If the baby grows up to have some kind of diagnosis, then it's not the end of the world. I'd love them all the same. Just as I love Olivia. But I think the pressure of that possibility is getting to her."

"Poor thing," Lucy said.

Emily closed her eyes and rested her head back again. She didn't expect married life to be easy. She knew they would encounter bumps along the way. But she had hoped to at least get the first month out of the way without any major issues.

"I've started a new yoga class. Maybe I could invite Olivia to that?" Lucy suggested.

Emily bit her lip to stop herself from grinning. She looked at Lucy and nodded. "Absolutely, she might like that."

She knew that Olivia wouldn't like it at all. But she figured it was up to Olivia to turn down the opportunity to socialise, not her. Maybe Olivia was bored enough to take up yoga. That would be a red flag in and of itself.

"Oh, yes, before I forget." Lucy reached into her pocket and pulled out a small silver key. She placed it on the patio table and slid it towards Emily. "We had a new lock installed. The old one was jamming up, and I knew it was just a matter of time before I was locked out of my own house."

Emily looked at the key in confusion.

"You may not live here anymore, but it feels wrong for you to not have a key," Lucy added.

Emily smiled. "That's so sweet, Luce."

She picked up her bag to find a place for the key. As she dug through its contents, she realised a week at a new job meant the bag had quickly filled up with various bits and pieces. She knew she needed to clear it out, but time spent with her family had been much more pressing.

She unloaded some items, receipts, gloves, her purse for pounds, her purse for dollars. At the bottom of the bag her fingers grazed some paper and she picked it up.

Her eyes widened as she saw the envelope. A plain white envelope with her name handwritten on the front. Identical to the envelope that Nicole had handed her in the theatre.

She tore it open and looked inside. A theatre ticket sat in the envelope, looking so innocent and so menacing all at once. It was to the same show, but for a different date. Her heart palpitated as she realised this was not the same ticket as before, but a new ticket.

She had no idea how it had gotten into her bag.

"What's wrong?" Lucy asked, picking up on Emily's panic.

"I…" Emily trailed off. She wasn't sure how to explain what was wrong.

She handed the envelope to Lucy. She got to her feet and paced the small patio as she searched her mind for any recollection of the envelope.

How did it get in my bag? Who's had access to my bag?

"A ticket to a show?" Lucy asked in confusion.

"Not long after I started, Nicole said there was a message for me at the theatre's box office. It was an envelope, just like that one, containing a ticket. I don't know who it was from. Nicole took it back to the box office."

"And now it's back in your bag?" Lucy asked.

"No, worse, this is a new ticket. The date is different."

Lucy turned the ticket over and examined it for more information.

"I don't know how it got in my bag. Someone must have put it there." Emily shuddered at the thought. She paused and hugged her middle. "Oh, God…and the flowers."

Lucy looked up at her. "What flowers?"

"A couple of nights ago, flowers were sent to my hotel room. I thought Olivia had sent them, but she hadn't. The card said it was from a secret admirer. I assumed they were for someone else and had been delivered to me by mistake."

"You think they're connected?" Lucy sat up in her chair.

Emily shrugged. "Seems too weird to not be, don't you think?"

Lucy nodded. "I think you need to tell someone."

"I can't tell Olivia, she'll panic. And I don't really know anything. Maybe the flowers really were for someone else, and I'm just being paranoid."

Lucy held up the envelope. "That doesn't explain this."

Emily flopped back into her chair. "I don't want to worry Olivia. Being so far apart is hard enough without worrying about this as well."

Lucy looked uncertain. "Well, then, you have to tell Nicole. At least so someone is aware of it. It's creepy, Em. Even if the flowers weren't for you, then how did this envelope get in your bag? If the first one was left at the box office and this one was in your bag, then this person knows where you work and has access to your bag without you noticing. It could be someone you work with."

Emily swallowed at the insinuation. "I...I work with a lot of people. The theatre is always full of people I don't recognise."

"All the more reason to let Nicole know." Lucy put the ticket back into the envelope and slid it over to Emily. "I get that you don't want to frighten Olivia, at least until you have more information. But please tell me that you'll speak to Nicole."

Emily picked up the envelope and looked at the handwriting. She didn't recognise it, and it was only her name, just a handful of letters. It was easy to disguise your handwriting for such a short missive.

"I'll talk to her before I fly back," Emily said.

CHAPTER SIXTEEN

O livia heard the front door click closed and hurried to go greet her family.

"Olivia! We brought dinner home!" Henry shouted out from the hallway.

She approached them with a quizzical look. "I thought I was cooking tonight?"

Emily kicked off her shoes and picked up the takeaway bag from the side table. She nuzzled up to Olivia's side and pressed a soft kiss to her cheek.

"Less time cooking, more time together doing *other* things," Emily whispered huskily in her ear.

Olivia felt her cheeks heat up.

Emily brushed past her and walked towards the kitchen.

"Olivia, where's Australia?" Henry asked.

She looked down at Henry and blinked. While she was used to Henry's constant questions and fast-paced topic changes, he still sometimes caught her off guard.

"It's…um…" Olivia paused. She wondered how to explain exactly where Australia was without some form of visual cue.

"Have you been to Australia?"

"Yes, a couple of times."

"Will I go to Australia?"

"Maybe." She'd quickly learned that "maybe" was a safe answer for most questions.

"I'm going to be a rocket ship when I grow up," Henry said with a wide smile before he turned and walked away.

Not for the first time, Olivia felt like she had been spun in circles by Henry's greeting. She shook her head and followed Emily into the kitchen.

"Henry wants to go to Australia," Olivia said.

Emily was placing plates on the work surface and looked up with a wry grin.

"Does he?"

"Yes, he's also going to be a rocket ship when he grows up."

Emily pouted. "Oh, just this morning he said he was going to be a mom, just like me."

Olivia chuckled. "It appears your time has passed."

"Usurped by a rocket ship," Emily sighed. "Story of my life."

Olivia checked behind her that Henry wasn't in sight before walking up behind Emily. She wrapped her arms around her and placed a soft kiss on her neck. The previous night had been wonderful, but Olivia still felt like she had a lot of catching up to do.

Emily sighed contentedly. "I've missed this."

"I've missed this, too," Olivia said. One of her hands drifted up Emily's stomach. "I've missed something else, too."

Emily giggled at the suggestion.

"I'm hungry," Henry said as he entered the kitchen.

Olivia jumped back as if burnt.

Emily laughed softly. "Why don't you set the table, Henry? We'll be in soon."

Henry narrowed his eyes and looked at Olivia, and then his mother. "Were you kissing?"

Chance would be a fine thing.

"Yes, and next the kissing monster might come for you," Emily told him. She raised her hands and started to stalk towards him.

Henry squealed and quickly barrelled out of the room.

Emily turned to face Olivia. "It's cute how you still jump a foot in the air when Henry catches us," she said with a grin.

Olivia threw a towel at her.

❖

Emily stood in front of her wardrobe, wondering what to pack for the upcoming week. The freezing cold of the office was a stark contrast to the airless theatre. The answer could only be what everyone suggests when packing for the unknown: layers.

Her phone rang, and she dashed back to the bed to answer the call she had been expecting.

"Hi, Nicole. Thanks for calling me back."

"No problem, I just got in and thought I'd contact you now. You sounded a little tense in your voicemail."

Emily grimaced. She'd been trying to go for light and airy, but the situation was obviously already affecting her.

"Yeah, well, um…I think something might be up," Emily tried to explain.

Suddenly she felt like she was making a big deal out of nothing. She glanced at the clock on the wall and realised what time it was in London and felt extra guilty about bothering Nicole.

"Are you unwell?" Nicole asked. "You were a little sniffly last week. Has that blown up into a cold?"

Emily sat on the edge of the bed. "No, no, that was dust in the air. Um. No, you remember the envelope? The one with the ticket that you gave me?"

"Oh, yes," Nicole recalled.

Emily bit her lip. Telling Nicole that something might be wrong seemed like a huge step, especially as she was going to ask her boss, and Olivia's best friend, to keep it a secret. A real secret. Not a Nicole secret.

"I got another envelope. I found it on the bottom of my bag this afternoon. It had my name handwritten on the front, and inside was another ticket, a new one. For this Thursday."

Nicole remained silent, and Emily felt her heart plunge. Now that it was out there, it seemed ridiculous.

"A-and then there's the flowers. Well, maybe, I'm not sure," Emily continued.

"What flowers?" Nicole asked.

"Um, the other night, after the happy hour, there were flowers delivered to my hotel room. I thought they were from Olivia, but she said she didn't send any. The card didn't say anything, it was signed from a secret admirer. I assumed they were for someone else, you know, delivered to me by mist—"

"Okay, cancel your hotel room for the upcoming week," Nicole cut her off. "I'm going to book you something myself under another name. Only you, Olivia, and I will know where you are staying."

Emily felt a weight rise from her shoulders. She hadn't realised until that moment how worried she was. Having someone else take her worries seriously was such a relief.

"Thanks, Nicole."

"Not a problem. I'm sure it's nothing, but there's no need to take a risk. We'll get to the bottom of it, I'm sure. But for now, we'll take every precaution."

Emily walked over to the bedroom door and gently clicked it closed.

"One more thing," she murmured. "Could you keep this from Olivia? I…I just don't want her worrying. It's such a long way, and I know I'd be in pieces if something was happening here. I don't want to worry her when it's probably nothing."

"I understand. I know how…unreasonable Olivia can be. She'd probably chain you to the bed and wouldn't let you fly out again."

Emily glanced at the white negligée she'd laid out on the bed for later that evening. She mused that being chained to the bed wouldn't be such a hardship, considering she'd missed her newly wedded wife so much the previous week.

"Yes," Emily said. "I think it's best to not say anything, for now."

"Agreed. I'll sort you out with a new hotel in the morning, and I'll phone you with the details. Do you still have the envelope and the ticket?"

"Yes."

"Good, bring it with you, and we'll do some detective work of our own. I'm sure it's not as nefarious as it first seems. Don't worry, Emily. We'll get to the bottom of this."

Emily breathed out a sigh of relief. "Thank you, I thought I was being silly. I'm sure it's nothing but…well, it's pretty scary when I think about it."

"I can imagine!" Nicole said. "Try to put it out of your mind. Enjoy your time with Olivia and Henry, and we'll deal with this when you get back here."

"I'll do my best," Emily said. "Sorry to bother you so late."

"Oh, this isn't late," Nicole reassured her. "Now, as your boss, I order you to worry about this no more. Spend some quality time with Olivia. She already semi-hates me for taking you away."

Emily chuckled. "She doesn't. But I will take up your suggestion."

Nicole laughed. "Goodnight, darling."

"'Night, Nicole."

Emily hung up. Now she just had to get the strange events out of her mind and enjoy the evening.

As her mind whirled with questions, she knew that would be easier said than done.

CHAPTER SEVENTEEN

"Bout it's not fair," Henry said.

"Henry," Olivia warned him. She looked at Emily, hoping that she'd be able to stop the imminent tantrum.

Unfortunately, Emily was frozen to the spot, staring down at Henry, where he had placed himself on the floor, squarely between Emily and the front door. She rested her hand on the extendable handle of her suitcase and looked helplessly down at him.

"It's not fair," Henry repeated. "You were away last week."

"And I told you that I'd be away this week, too," Emily explained gently.

She took her hand from the suitcase and crouched down in front of him. Olivia took a step back to give mother and son a little more privacy, though she remained nearby in case she needed to mediate.

"I wish I didn't have to be away from you, Henry," Emily said. "I love you very much, you know that."

Henry screwed his face up and turned away from Emily to face the door.

"The last thing I want is to leave," Emily said. "But I have to go to London for a couple more weeks. I have to be there to make sure that my play is ready so lots of people can pay lots of money to go and see it."

"I hate your play," Henry mumbled.

"Henry," Olivia warned him again.

"It's okay," Emily said. "I know why you hate my play. Sometimes, I hate it too because it means that we're apart. But then I also love it because it's something I've wanted to do for a very long time. And it's important to me."

Henry peeked his head over his shoulder. "I don't like you going away."

"I don't like going away. But I have to. And I'll be back on Friday night and we'll spend the whole weekend together."

Henry's watery eyes blinked, and a couple of fat tears ran down his red cheeks.

"Promise?" he asked.

"I promise," Emily said.

She held out her arms, and Henry fell into the embrace.

Olivia let out the breath she had been holding since it became clear that Henry wasn't happy with Emily's departure. Olivia knew how hard it was for Emily to leave them, especially Henry.

The fact that Emily could leave just went to show how important the scriptwriting was to her. Olivia knew that Emily had found her dream.

She looked at Emily and Henry on the floor of the hallway and understood just how much Emily wanted the job of her dreams to work out. Suddenly the cold bed and the lonely house during the week weren't as bad. Not when she knew that it was all in aid of Emily's dream.

Olivia looked at her wristwatch. Soft tones of classical music sounded from the speaker system she'd had installed. It was the first day of the second week of Henry's new school routine. It had taken a little while to develop the right schedule, but she'd managed it.

"Henry," she called softly.

A moment later Henry appeared at the top of the stairs.

"I'm ready," he said as he hopped down each step one at a time, holding onto the handrail as he went.

She walked towards the hallway and picked up his rucksack and jacket. Everything slid into place perfectly, and she ushered him out of the door with a kiss on his cheek.

Once she had safely seen him off, she closed the door.

She smiled to herself in the knowledge that she'd cracked the whole getting ready for school procedure.

She walked into the kitchen and started to unload the dishwasher. As she did, she calculated approximately how many more days of school Henry would have in his lifetime.

She always found mathematic problems soothing. However, this one appeared to be giving her palpitations. She focused on the music playing throughout the house and quickly finished emptying the dishwasher.

When she finished, she closed the appliance and wiped her hands on a tea towel. She placed the towel back on its hook and looked around the kitchen to ensure everything was in place.

She looked at her wristwatch again.

Henry had been gone for six minutes.

She unlocked the back door and walked into the garden, taking a deep breath and enjoying the fresh morning air. Strolling up and down the various paths, she occasionally bent down to pluck an errant weed. There weren't many. She'd been outside the previous evening doing the same thing after Emily had left for the airport.

They'd agreed that Emily would travel to and from the airport herself. Olivia wanted to see her off from the airport but had agreed that the traffic was too much for her and Henry.

Emily had also changed her bookings to economy seats, much to Olivia's confusion. When Olivia had discovered that Nicole was booking Emily into economy seats for the journeys back and forth, she'd quickly paid the difference for the upgrade to first-class.

Why anyone would willingly choose to downgrade themselves to the bowels of the aircraft was beyond her, but Emily was strong-willed and knew what she wanted.

Olivia wished for such clarity in her own mind. She should be happy, living a life that many people dreamed of. No boss, no responsibilities beyond home and family. She had time to start hobbies, she could learn an instrument or read entire collections of classic works.

Instead she stood in her back garden, three tiny weeds clutched in her hand while she wondered how on earth she was going to fill the next few hours, never mind the next few days until Emily returned.

As soon as Henry left the house, it was as if all the light and energy left with him. The same was true of Emily, as if Olivia's world was operated with two dimmable light bulbs.

"It takes time," she reminded herself. Time to settle into a new pattern. New was something that Olivia had never been fond of. There was a good reason why she had lived by her schedule for so many years.

She thought back to her beloved schedule. She enjoyed being busy. The business world was something she understood, something she was passionate about. She'd come to understand that her work-life balance was ridiculously tipped in favour of work. But now it seemed like the scales had been reversed.

There was no way she could have balance now. She'd made a commitment to Emily that she would remain home and watch over Henry. Now she was a stay-at-home mother, a homemaker. But she didn't feel equipped to be those things. She was sure there were things she ought to be doing, but she didn't know what they were.

But she wouldn't worry Emily about such things. She would figure them out for herself eventually. Her entire reason for taking on the role of homemaker was to allow Emily to spread her wings and do something she enjoyed.

Emily had been a veritable superwoman during the first few years of Henry's life. She'd worked several jobs at any one time, she'd always given Henry what his medical condition required no matter how difficult or expensive. And Henry was a well-adjusted boy, no worse for wear. Olivia knew that was down to Emily's exceptional abilities at doing whatever it took, and pushing her own needs to one side.

Now Olivia wanted to allow Emily to do things for herself. Even if that meant pushing her own needs aside.

She strolled to the patio furniture and sat on a chair and looked over the immaculate garden. She pictured Henry playing there, maybe with a sibling.

Emily had seemed quite against the idea of adoption. And after reading some of the horror stories, Olivia could understand why. The hoops that people were required to jump through to become approved were an eye-opener. The possibility that you might not get approved would be something that could easily eat away at someone. And even if approval did come, waiting for the right child to fit in with your life was another obstacle.

Olivia liked the idea of adopting a child. But she knew she liked it for all the wrong reasons. She wouldn't be the type of person who would be able to attend to the complicated needs of a child who had suffered during their early years. While she knew she could lavish them with love and material goods, she also knew that she didn't have the right skill set to help them with difficult psychological issues. It was only last week that Henry climbed into the washing machine during an impromptu game of hide and seek.

She liked the idea of adoption because it removed the possibility that she could be to blame for a child being like her. A child who carried her defective genes and became a fish out of water in society, just as Olivia had often felt.

But Emily had spoken at length of how much she adored Olivia's unique personality. And Olivia knew that she would never want to fix herself, should such an option become available. She knew that in some ways, her differences made life difficult, but in others it gave her an edge, an insight that others lacked.

Adopting a child just because she didn't want her biological child to potentially be like her was the wrong reason to adopt.

She made a mental note to set up a monthly donation to a few of the adoption organisations she had spoken to during her investigations. While adoption wasn't for her, she knew their work was essential and they deserved the funding they needed.

She let out a long sigh and looked down at the weeds she still held in her hand.

❖

Olivia stood in the corridor and watched through the glass panel of the door as Natalie Costa finished up the day with her class. The tall, slim woman exuded energy and drama, walking up and down the rows of desks and reading aloud from the book in her hands. The children giggled and gasped at the story.

"May I help you?"

Olivia turned to see a male teacher approaching her. "I have an appointment with Miss Costa," Olivia replied. "Regarding Henry White."

The man nodded solemnly. "Oh, yes, I heard about Henry. My apologies."

Olivia frowned. She hadn't expected the news of his potential diagnosis to be common knowledge, nor a cause of such sympathy. She glanced at the floor, eager to break eye contact.

"If there's anything we can do, then please don't hesitate to let us know." The man turned and walked away.

Olivia glanced up and watched his retreat. Something seemed wrong, as if he already knew of the diagnosis, as if Henry was about to be sent to the gallows. She spun to look through the glass door again and focused her attention on him. He was smiling, engaged in the story being told. No sign of whatever horrors the supposed teachers had apparently unearthed within him.

A few moments passed and the bell signalling the end of the day sounded. Mayhem followed. Children of all ages spewed out of doors and filled the hallway. The sudden switch from the quiet murmuring of classes being taught behind closed doors to loud chatter was deafening and disorientating.

Olivia took a step into Henry's classroom, away from the masses.

"Olivia!" She felt Henry's arms around her waist as he cuddled against her. "This is my mommy."

She blinked and looked down at him in confusion. He'd never referred to her as his mother before, and now he was introducing her to a group of children from his class.

"Hello, children," Olivia said quietly as she looked at the pairs of eyes staring up at her.

The group of children murmured and oohed and ahhed.

"Children, it's rude to stare."

Olivia looked up and locked eyes with Natalie Costa, relieved to be rescued.

"Sorry, Miss Costa," the children said in a frighteningly synchronistic buzz. They dispersed, and she was left with Henry clutching hold of her.

"Henry, maybe you'd like to go to the playground while I speak with your mother?"

Henry nodded and released his hands from Olivia's waist. Olivia watched him go with a heavy heart, knowing that he was clueless that they were speaking about him and his development.

"Would you like to sit down?" Natalie said.

Olivia was about to shake her head when she remembered Emily's words about taking a seat even when she didn't want to. Apparently, standing would only make an uncomfortable situation more so.

"Thank you," she said.

They walked to the desk at the front of the class and both sat down. Natalie looked out the window at Henry playing on the climbing apparatus.

"Henry really is remarkable, very resilient."

"He is," Olivia said.

"He was saying this morning how much he missed his mother, his other mother," Natalie explained.

Olivia nodded. "She only recently left us," she said. She thought of Emily's face as she'd said goodbye to catch her flight the evening before. It felt like a lifetime ago.

"Of course, I'm sure with time it will be easier for him. For both of you."

"I hope so, for Henry's sake. Although I doubt it will become easier for me, the house is so very quiet without her," Olivia admitted, almost surprising herself at her admission.

Natalie stood and pulled her chair around the table to sit beside Olivia. She reached out and took Olivia's hand.

"It will get better," she said.

Olivia looked at their interlocked hands and frowned. Natalie was clearly one of those touchy-feely people Olivia rarely understood. She squeezed Natalie's hand carefully before removing hers from the grasp.

"You need to stay busy," Natalie said.

"I'm recently retired," Olivia explained. Retired was the easiest way to explain it. Between jobs sounded strange, especially when she had no current plans to return to work.

"Wow." Natalie sat back in her chair and looked at Olivia. "Forgive me, but you seem very young to have retired."

Olivia smiled. "I owned the company. There was a change of ownership. Now I'm focused on Henry, with Emily being away he really needs me."

"It must be lonely while Henry is at school."

Olivia felt her smile fade. "It is."

"May I ask what your company did?"

"It's an accounting firm."

"Oh, that explains Henry's math skills. He really is exceptional for his age," Natalie said.

Olivia beamed happily. She leaned a little closer. "Let me tell you, it wasn't always that way. He hated math. And Emily, well, her math skills weren't up to much. I spent a lot of time with him, changed his perception of the subject. He was just fearful of it. Once we broke down that barrier, the rest was easy."

Natalie looked at her for a moment. "That's a real talent," she said. "One I'd love to have in my class. We have a volunteering program here. Would you be interested in speaking with the class? Trying to break down that barrier for all of them?"

Olivia blinked. "A w-whole class? Oh, I don't know. I'm not very good with children."

"I beg to differ," Natalie said. "Henry proves otherwise."

Olivia turned to watch Henry swinging from the monkey bars. She hadn't thought her actions with Henry were out of the ordinary. He feared something she understood and she'd helped him to conquer that.

"We need more engaged parents," Natalie added. "People who have a skill set, who can help the kids at a young age. We need to get to them before these fears take root. And, you said yourself, the house is quiet. This would enable to you get out of the house, but still be there when Henry needs you."

Olivia knit her brow and considered the offer. It seemed like a good suggestion, but she was still not sure. Standing up and speaking in front of a room filled with children struck fear into her heart.

Of course, she was used to public speaking. To adults. Children were a very different matter. A terrifying prospect.

Her terror must have been clear on her face. Natalie grasped her hand again and squeezed it.

"It's okay, you wouldn't be on your own. I'd be right here with you," Natalie said. "We can speak beforehand. I can explain how everything works and even some basic teaching techniques if you like."

Olivia thought of her days from the previous week. They had been long and dull. Maybe volunteering would be a way to fill some of those hours. And she'd be closer to Henry. If he did receive a diagnosis, then she would be able to monitor him, ensure that he was being provided the best education possible.

"I think you're right," Olivia said. "I need to get on with my life. I can't just sit at home." She turned to face Natalie and squeezed her hand. "Thank you, Natalie."

Natalie beamed happily. "Thank you. It will be great for the kids."

Olivia shuddered a little. "If I can get the courage to stand up in front of them. I think an introduction to some teacher training would be most appreciated."

She remembered Emily's suggestion about making friends with some of the children's parents. Emily had said it was a great way to socialise with more people. Olivia thought about how proud Emily would be if Olivia managed to make some friends while she was away. Of course, Olivia had friends. But Emily thought most of them were better classified as business colleagues. She was forever pushing her to be more sociable and mix with more people.

She looked at Natalie. The young woman seemed nice. A perfect candidate for a new friend.

"Maybe you could come to dinner?" Olivia suggested.

Natalie's eyebrows raised. "Dinner…sounds lovely."

"Wonderful." Olivia mentally brought up her weekly planner. Not that she needed to. Nothing was happening until Friday evening when Emily got home. "How about Thursday?"

"Thursday is good," Natalie said.

"Do you prefer red or white wine?" Olivia asked. She'd cooked beef for Lucy a few weeks ago only to be told that red wine made her feel queasy. She didn't want to have to serve white wine with beef again.

Natalie smiled. "Oh, um, either is fine. Would you like me to bring anything?"

"Just yourself," Olivia replied. She smiled with pride. She'd just managed to make a new potential friend, and without any input from Emily.

Natalie gestured towards Henry. "Will Henry be okay with this?"

"Oh yes, Henry keeps telling me I need to make new friends," she replied. Since starting school, Henry had suddenly become very popular and was enjoying being the centre of attention. He'd gone from not caring about making new friends to telling everyone that it was the best thing to do.

Natalie licked her lips and nodded. "Good, that sounds perfect."

"Excellent, it will be great to entertain again. It's been a while. I might be a bit rusty," Olivia said. With Emily being away during the week, Olivia's evening meals often consisted of watching Henry cover his face with some form of pasta sauce.

"As long as it's not…too soon?" Natalie asked.

Olivia brought up her mental calendar again. There was plenty of time to prepare for a dinner between now and Thursday.

"No, I think it's perfect timing," Olivia replied.

Natalie smiled. Olivia noticed her cheeks were starting to redden slightly and wondered if maybe they should open a window.

Before she had a chance to say anything, Natalie coughed lightly. She shook her head as if to clear some cobwebs. "Anyway, you came here to talk about Henry. Have you made a decision on the further tests?"

"Yes, I-I think it's for the best. If we can help him, then we should." Olivia let out a nervous breath.

"Great, I'll get that scheduled. I can book a meeting for you with Mr. Palmer. He deals with the tests, so he can explain everything to you."

Olivia felt a flash of fear. She had only just gotten used to Natalie; she didn't want to have to speak to someone else. "Oh, I thought we could discuss it? I'd prefer if it was you."

Natalie ducked her head slightly. "We can certainly arrange that."

"Wonderful."

CHAPTER EIGHTEEN

Emily jumped at the knock on her hotel room door. She looked at her watch and frowned. Nicole had said she'd be there at half past seven and it was twenty past.

She tiptoed to the door and looked through the peephole. A sigh of relief passed her lips when she saw Nicole standing in the hallway with a cardboard container with two steaming hot coffees.

She opened the door and smiled. "Morning."

"Hello, how is the new room?"

"Perfect, flowerless," Emily replied. "Come in."

Nicole walked in and placed the coffee cups on a table near the television.

"I spoke to the old hotel reception; the flowers were definitely for you. The receptionist remembers someone calling and asking to confirm your room number for a delivery. As you had no other deliveries, and neither did anyone else that evening, it seems the flowers were for you."

Emily sunk onto the edge of the bed.

"But," Nicole injected a chipper tone into her voice, "no one knows you are here. And it's not like they sent you a horse's head. It was just some flowers, nothing too sinister. Obviously, the way they went about sending them wasn't great. I'm increasing security at the theatre. You'll be working there all week. I've not said anything to anyone, so I suggest we just carry on as usual and pretend that nothing is going on. That way we're more likely to spot something out of the ordinary."

Emily appreciated Nicole's attempts at downplaying the situation. Up until that moment she had convinced herself that the flowers were simply a mistake, a mix-up with room numbers. But now that categorically wasn't the case. Now she had someone sending her theatre tickets, putting an envelope directly into the bag that she kept with her at all times. And that person had known her hotel room, had even referred to themselves as her secret admirer.

"Who do you think it is?" Emily asked.

Nicole pulled out a chair and sat down. "I was going to ask you the same thing. Clearly someone has taken a liking to you. Have you noticed anything?"

She'd been asking herself that question all weekend. The flight had been a long and sleepless one as she replayed all her interactions with her new colleagues. She didn't have an answer, but she did have a suspicion. One that she was nervous to voice.

Carl had done nothing wrong exactly. He was just different. Maybe he was trying to be attentive. Maybe it was more. But Emily didn't want to put his career at risk. She knew that false accusations were very dangerous things. Even when someone was proved innocent, the accusations lingered like a bad smell. She wouldn't do that to Carl, not without some more evidence.

"I don't know," Emily said. "I've met a lot of people; I really couldn't say."

Nicole nodded. "Well, now we'll have two pairs of eyes on this. We'll figure it out together. If there is anything untoward happening, I want you to tell me immediately."

Emily nodded. As independent as she liked to be, the whole situation had her rattled. She had no intention of dealing with it alone.

"Sorry to be a bother," Emily said.

"You're not the bother," Nicole said firmly. "Someone is bothering you. Don't feel guilty about this, Emily."

She smiled tentatively. "I'll try."

"How are things aside from this?" Nicole asked, trying to change the subject to lighter things.

Emily was happy to oblige.

"Really well," she said. "I'm learning so much. I see the connection between a lot of things now. I realise I've written things that have a good plot, but would be impossible to put on a stage. Every day I'm having new ideas or thinking about how to rework old ones. It's really exciting."

"That's fantastic, and exactly what I was trying to explain to you before. It's one of those things where you don't know what you don't know. But working in a practical environment gives you the opportunity to learn."

Nicole sat forward and sipped her coffee. "I'm keeping my ears open for any new opportunities, hopefully something in New York. With your new experience you should be able to apply for a few roles. The market is slowing down a bit, but that's the theatre for you, peaks and troughs throughout the year. I'll keep listening out for any good fits, and we'll have a chat about it nearer the time."

Emily nodded eagerly. Now that she'd had a taste of the work, she didn't want to let it go. While she didn't like the time spent away from her family, she had to admit that the week had flown by.

"Right, shall we put on a play?" Nicole asked. She held Emily's coffee out to her.

Emily took the cup. "Absolutely, let's do it."

Chapter Nineteen

"Where are we going?" Henry asked.

"We're going to pick something up," Olivia explained. They'd been driving for twenty minutes and were nearly at the address Olivia had been given.

"What are we picking up?"

"A present for you."

Henry gasped in excitement, and Olivia couldn't help but smile.

"Is it a dinosaur?" he asked.

"No." She rolled her eyes. Sometimes she wondered where Henry got these ideas.

"An alien?"

"No." Olivia shook her head. "What do you really, really want? What did you tell me this morning you needed or else you would die?"

Henry remained silent. She glanced at him, surprised to see him deep in thought. She turned her attention back to the road and shook her head in dismay. For someone so hell-bent on getting a kitten, Henry was fairly slow on the uptake.

"A KITTEN!" he suddenly screeched.

She winced, both at the pitch and the volume. "Yes, a kitten."

Henry screamed happily and kicked his feet in excitement.

"All right, Henry. You have to be very quiet when we get the kitten or you'll scare him."

"Him? It's a boy?" he asked, eagerness in his voice.

"Yes, it's a boy. But you must be quiet. He's very little and you don't want to frighten him, do you?"

"I'll be *super* quiet," Henry promised.

Olivia briefly wondered what else she could convince him would be imperative for the kitten's sake.

"I have a name for him," Henry said. "You did promise that I could name the kitten."

Olivia searched her memory and slowly nodded. "I did. What do you want to call him?"

Henry didn't hesitate. "Captain McFluffypants the Seventh."

"Um...are you...are you sure? How about something shorter? Or something—"

"You did promise, Olivia," he said matter-of-factly.

Olivia suddenly understood Emily's smothered smile when she had told her that she'd agreed to Henry's request for naming rights.

"Are you sure? You'd have to call him that. When he's outside, you'd have to shout that into the neighbourhood."

"That will be his official name," Henry explained. "I'd just call him McFluffypants for short."

"For short?" Olivia asked.

"You *promised*," Henry repeated.

Olivia rolled her eyes. "Yes, I guess I did." She was going to throttle Emily when she saw her next. She already knew how this would play out. Emily would be in London, Henry at school and she'd be left calling the runaway kitten's name through the neighbourhood. Worse still, registering the animal at the veterinary clinic.

"Why did you come to school today?" Henry asked.

She and Emily had agreed not to tell Henry about the tests, in case his knowledge of them somehow changed the results. She didn't like the idea of lying to him, but she knew it was required.

"I might be helping out at your school in the future," Olivia explained, grateful for the excuse.

"How?"

"I'm not sure yet, I'm going to discuss it with Na—Miss Costa."

She looked at the GPS screen and saw that they were approaching the house where she was about to adopt and unfortunately christen a new pet. The first pet that Henry had ever had. The first pet that she had ever had.

"Is Miss Costa going to be your boss?" Henry asked through a giggle.

"Not at all," Olivia replied. "We'd be...working together. Like a team. She is coming over for dinner on Thursday."

"Why?"

"So we can talk about me helping at your school."

"She can pet Captain McFluffypants the Seventh, but only if she is good," he said.

"Why is he the seventh?"

"Why not?"

Olivia gripped the steering wheel a little tighter and took a deep breath.

Olivia sipped at her coffee and watched Henry's face with interest. The kitten had been home for twenty minutes. Twenty minutes of running around, exploring, and scratching everything in sight.

Olivia had already purchased and unpacked a scratching post, a bed, and some food bowls. The kitten happily ignored the scratching post but fell in love with the soft bed as soon as he climbed in.

He fell into a deep sleep, no doubt exhausted from the twenty minutes of insane activity.

Henry lay on the floor beside the cat bed. His face was almost touching the kitten's. Olivia could see that Henry was taking everything in; he was examining every centimetre of his new pet. Watching the kitten's breathing, staring at the long whiskers on either side of its face.

But Olivia had experienced Henry watching her as she slept and knew it to be unpleasant.

"Henry, why don't you let him sleep? You could go and play in your room for a while?" Olivia said.

"My room is boring," Henry said with a sigh. He flopped onto his back and stared at the ceiling.

Olivia looked at the clock on the wall. There was a little time before she needed to start preparing dinner.

"Maybe we could play something together?" she suggested.

Henry jumped to his feet. "Yes! I want to play airplane!"

Olivia looked at him with uncertainty. "Airplane?"

"Yes, it's fun," he said.

He grabbed her hand and pulled her to her feet. She carefully held her mug of coffee, expecting that she'd need a caffeine boost shortly. Especially if the game involved thinking about airplanes.

"We need to go to the dining room," he said.

"Okay." She allowed herself to be led into the other room. She had no idea what playing airplane involved. Since Henry had been at school, he had discovered a few new games that were, apparently, huge amounts of fun. Olivia wasn't quite so sure. Most of the games seemed to have no rules, and some even seemed to be made up as they played.

Emily said it was Henry's creativity developing. Olivia disliked the lack of reasoning.

In the dining room, Henry pulled the chairs away from the table and lined them up in rows of twos.

He pointed to one of the chairs and Olivia took her seat.

"You're flying to Australia," Henry said.

"That will take a long time," Olivia told him. "I have to start dinner in half an hour."

Henry rolled his eyes. "It's pretend, Olivia."

"I see. Will you be the pilot?" she asked.

"No, Tiny is the pilot." Henry ran from the room and returned a couple of moments later and put Tiny on the floor in front of the chairs.

"Okay…go," Henry commanded.

Olivia sat on the dining chair with the mug of coffee in her hand, wondering what she should do next.

"You're not very good at this," Henry said.

"What am I supposed to be doing?"

"Flying," he said.

Olivia looked around the dining room. "I'm not sure how to do that."

"You have to pretend you're on an airplane. You're not pretending."

That was true. She wasn't pretending. The very idea was causing panic to rise inside her, and she was desperately trying to remind herself that she was safe on the ground.

"I-I don't really like flying anymore, Henry," she said carefully.

They'd agreed to not say too much about Olivia being on the plane that had crashed for fear of giving Henry his own fear of flying.

"Why?" Henry asked as he sat on the seat beside her.

She reached over and placed her mug on the dining room table.

"Because I'm scared," she said honestly.

He slowly nodded. He took her hand in both of his and held it tightly.

"You don't have to be scared, Olivia. You have me. And I'll make sure you don't feel scared."

She looked down at his tiny hands wrapped around hers. She felt her eyes well up a little at the sweet gesture.

"Thank you, Henry." She squeezed his hands gently.

"It's all very safe," Henry said. "I'll talk you through the whole thing."

Olivia suddenly realised that Henry was repeating to her what Emily had told him when he took his first flight to London. She remembered how small and scared he had looked in the enormous first-class chair across the aisle from her own.

"Airplanes are the safest way to travel," he explained.

CHAPTER TWENTY

Emily hurried down the street, casting a few worried glances over her shoulder. She was convinced that someone was following her, but in a busy city like London, it was impossible to tell for certain. In her heart, she was sure that it was paranoia. Not that the knowledge helped to calm her much.

So far, there had been nothing unusual about her working week. No theatre tickets, no flowers, nothing. But an oppressive cloud of concern hung over her like a damp sheet.

Her phone rang, and she pulled it out of her pocket. She smiled as she looked at the caller ID.

"Hello?"

"Mommy, I have a kitten!" Henry screeched loudly.

"Wow, a kitten?" Emily played along. She'd already had a long text-based conversation with Olivia about the new addition to the family.

"He's amazing."

"I bet he is," Emily said. "What colour is he?"

"He's white with black ears, and his name is Captain McFluffypants the Seventh."

Emily bit her lip to keep the laugh from bubbling out. "Cool name, Henry!"

"I'm going to go and play with him now, bye." Henry rushed out.

She heard a few moments of muffled discussion and some rustling of the phone being handed over.

"How do we make him change the name?" Olivia asked without preamble. "I have an appointment with the veterinary clinic tomorrow, and I can't tell them that's the kitten's name. I'll be carted off to some hospital with padded walls."

Emily laughed. "I'm sorry, darling, not a lot we can do about it now."

"I know London is a long way and sometimes the connection is bad, but did you actually hear what Henry has named this poor animal?" Olivia asked.

"I did hear. I think it's nice. Does he have fluffy pants?" Emily asked through giggles.

"No, and I highly doubt he's a captain either."

"Just tell the clinic that his name is Fluffy, Henry will never know. It's not like he's ever going to take the cat for his booster shots. It can be his paperwork name, to save you from death by embarrassment."

"I feel like you set me up," Olivia said good-humouredly.

"No, you got yourself into the mess, I just didn't get you out of it," Emily said.

Olivia chuckled, and Emily's heart clenched at the familiar deep sound. She wanted to be there. Wanted to see Olivia's face, to stroke her cheek. Not for the first time she cursed that the two loves of her life were on separate continents. Work and home, so far apart. It was like the universe was playing a joke on her.

"Are you meeting Simon this evening?" Olivia broke the silence.

"Yes, I'm just on my way to meet him now. I'll say hello from you."

"But I haven't said hello."

"I know, but I'll still tell him that you have."

"Why?"

Emily rolled her eyes. "Because it's something that people do."

"Seems odd," Olivia said. "Anyway, have a lovely time. Text me to let me know you got back to the hotel safely."

"I will, I'll speak to you tomorrow. I love you."

"I love you, too," Olivia replied.

Emily hung up and looked once more over her shoulder. She shook her head at her own ridiculousness.

"Calm down," she muttered to herself.

She looked down at her phone again and selected the map icon. She was only a couple of minutes away from the coffee shop where they had planned to meet. With a final glance over her shoulder, she picked up her pace.

❖

"Simon!" She stood up from the table she had snagged at the back of the café and waved.

Simon saw her and hurried over, a wide smile on his face and his arms out in preparation for the hug.

"It's been ages," he said.

She pulled him into a hug. "It's been three weeks," she said.

"Ages," he said.

They pulled apart and sat down. The waitress was by their side immediately and they both ordered hot drinks.

"Olivia says hello," Emily told him.

"Does she, though?" Simon chuckled.

"Well, no, she doesn't understand why someone would say hello for someone else. So, I'm saying hello on behalf of Olivia because that's what people do."

He laughed out loud. "Now that's more like it."

"I'm learning," she said with a wink. Simon had been the person to first convince her to try to understand Olivia's unique ways. Without Simon's guidance and interference, they'd never have gotten together, so Emily would always be grateful for the role he played in their relationship.

"So, enjoying London?" he asked.

She pouted.

"Not enjoying London?" he tried again.

She sighed. "I am, and I'm not."

"Goldilocks," he joked. "This country's too warm and that country's too cold."

"Something like that. More like, this country has the job of my dreams and that country has the loves of my life."

"Sounds hard." He looked at her sympathetically.

"It is. I didn't think it would be this hard. I've done the awful commute, the terrible work hours, the being away from family. But somehow this is worse, because this is a choice."

Emily leaned back as the waitress lowered the drinks to the table. Though she was pleased for the prompt service, she was also frustrated by the interruption. Simon was the one person she felt she could speak to about these things. He knew all the players, he'd been there through the ups and the downs, and she trusted his opinion. If anyone was going to tell her what she needed, whether she wanted to hear it or not, it would be him.

It had been hard to arrange a time when they were both free. The theatre was taking up most of Emily's time, and Simon seemed swamped with work, too. When they'd finally found an hour when they could meet, they grabbed at the chance.

"Olivia and Henry don't begrudge you taking this job, doing what you love," he said.

"I know," Emily said. "But I feel guilty."

He picked up a teaspoon and stirred his drink, looking at the swirls sadly. "I know that feeling," he mumbled.

Emily pushed her cup and saucer to one side and snagged his free hand with hers.

"What's up?" she asked.

He shook his head. "It's fine, just…work stuff."

"Hey, I can't be the only one having a meltdown," she joked. "What's up?"

Simon turned his hand and grasped hers for a moment before pulling back to remove his glasses and rub his face.

"Being the boss sucks," he said simply.

Emily was floored to hear that Simon was unhappy at work. Olivia had laid a path for him to be in charge. During the handover, they had spoken frequently, and Emily hadn't heard anything to suggest that Simon wasn't happy.

"Don't tell Olivia," he said seriously, "but I never wanted to be in charge." Simon put his chin in his hand and let out a long sigh. "I thought it would be okay. I thought I'd figure it out. And the salary increase with a baby on the way is really nice."

"But it's not what you want?"

"No. And the baby is coming and I'm already struggling to find time to go out and eat lunch. What am I going to do when I'm a dad as well? The baby won't recognise me." He sat up. "I remember Olivia working all hours, but she had me. I brought her lunch, dinner sometimes. I got her coffee and water. I sent her home. I don't have a me."

"Can you get a you?" Emily asked.

He sat up and put his glasses on. "Nah. I'm pretty unique," he said.

"How about an inferior version, just to take some of the pressure off?"

He shook his head. "I'd still be stuck with the problem that I'm never home."

"Why don't you just say it's not what you want and take a step back?"

He shook his head. "After all the hell Olivia went through to set up this deal? Olivia gave up her dream job, stepped down, and put me in her place. If she hadn't done that, then Applewoods would have gone under and loads of people would have lost their jobs. I can't turn around now and whine that it's too much. I don't want to let people down."

"You wouldn't be letting people down."

"I feel like I'm letting Olivia down. She needed me to make this work. And I can technically do the job, I wish that I wasn't. It's not me. I'm not a manager. But I feel like I'm stuck with it now."

"You have to look after yourself," Emily told him seriously. "Simon, you have to come first. Life is too short to be doing things you don't want to do. Family has to come first."

She took a sip of her drink.

Simon stared at her.

"What?" she asked, once she had swallowed the hot liquid.

"Sorry, I'm wondering if you're the same woman who was just saying that she's miserable being so far away from her own family." He smiled.

She lowered the cup into the saucer. "I hadn't even thought of that," she said. "I'm sorry, I must sound like such a hypocrite."

"Not at all. I think we both would have given each other similar advice, without being able to apply it to ourselves. But, seriously, don't tell Olivia."

She shook her head. "I won't. But you probably should."

"I know. I'm thinking of the best way to say it. And maybe a solution for it. You know things are always better presented when you know a solution. Throwing a spanner in the works is a lot easier if you know how to fix it after."

"Olivia is an expert in corporate restructuring," Emily reminded him. "And, trust me, she needs something to do."

"Maybe she'd come back?" Simon mused.

Emily chuckled. "Firstly, Marcus would never have her. You'd lose your biggest client if Olivia even stepped foot in the office again. Secondly, she's not getting on a plane."

"True," Simon said. "Maybe I could hire a replacement who looks like me and she'd never have to know?"

Emily laughed. "Oh, yeah, that would totally work."

He took his glasses off and offered them to her. "Can you do a British accent?"

She ignored the proffered spectacles and picked up her cup instead. "I already have a job that keeps me more than busy."

"What are you going to do?" Simon asked.

She sipped her drink and offered a light shrug. "No idea."

"Ah, you're in the early stages. Stage two, you know there is a problem, but you're not quite sure whether you'll bother dealing with it." He nodded sagely and put his glasses back on. "I'm in stage four. I know there's a problem and I know I need to deal with it, but I'm too much of a coward to bother."

"What's stage three?" Emily asked.

"Knowing there is a problem and feeling guilty about it, but hiding it from your partner." He looked at her knowingly.

"I'm not hiding it exactly," Emily said. "More…unable to find the time to talk about it."

"You talk, like, eight times a day."

"More like five," she said. "But it's in spurts. You can't have a meaningful conversation when the stage manager is staring at you because you said the words 'saggy breasts' too loudly."

"Tell me about it…" He shook his head. "If I had a penny…"

She laughed loudly, not caring that the other customers were looking at her. This was what she needed. Support and distraction. Ridiculous conversation and laughter. She needed to forget about distance and possible stalkers.

She knew she'd have to deal with things eventually, but it felt so nice to have a night away from it all. Even if she knew she'd have to deal with it soon, now she could take a breath.

"You don't have to walk me back to the hotel," Emily said half-heartedly.

Even so, they walked arm in arm along the cobbled street leading to the hotel. Nicole had found one that was near the theatre but off the beaten track.

Emily was constantly surprised by the contrasts within London. One moment she was walking along a busy road with hundreds of people vying for space. A few seconds later she could be on a road that came straight out of a Dickens novel. Cobbled streets, tall, Victorian buildings, and not a soul in sight.

Despite feeling that her new hotel was safe and away from any unwanted flower deliveries, she was pleased to have Simon walking with her down the quiet street. Not that she wanted to admit that to him.

"It's fine," Simon assured her. "Besides, the streets of London are rough at night. You need a man."

She burst out laughing. "And when is this man going to arrive?"

He tried to look offended, but his grin was too wide. "Hey, I'll have you know I went to the gym last month."

"Wow, I thought I could see muscles through your work shirt. But I thought it was one of those padded Superman costumes kids wear for Halloween," she joked.

"Nah, that's at the cleaners. This is all me. I'm buff now. Here to protect fair maidens."

"Was there alcohol in your coffee? Because you're not buff, I'm not a fair maiden, and these streets are safer than New York."

"Maybe it's just an excuse because I've missed you," he said honestly.

She leaned against his side. "I've missed you, too. We'll have to make sure we put some time aside to see each other more often before I get a job in New York. I really had fun tonight."

"Me too. We'll make sure we set something up soon."

They approached the hotel entrance, and Simon looked up at the signage.

"Nice. Not *Olivia nice*, but nicer than that place in King's Cross."

"Don't remind me of that place." She shivered at the memory. "Don't remind me of that time at all. And it may not be Olivia nice, but it's good enough for me."

He gave her a wink. "Well, if you don't mind roughing it."

They exchanged a farewell hug and said their goodbyes. Ever the gentleman, Simon waited outside as she walked into the lobby. Once she got into the elevator, he waved before turning and leaving.

Her mind was full of their conversation. Simon's fear of being a father and his dislike for his new job made her wonder if she should break her promise and confide in Olivia. She knew that Olivia would solve the work problem in a flash. Most of Simon's issue was feeling beholden to Olivia, but Olivia would never want to see him unhappy.

She shook her head as she stabbed the elevator button. She couldn't tell Olivia even though she knew it was the right thing to do. Simon wanted to keep it between them, and she had to respect that. He'd sort things out in his own time. Just as she would manage to sort out her problems in her own time.

She pulled out her key card and walked down the softly lit corridor to her room.

She passed the key card over the sensor and a green light glowed on the panel, granting her access. She opened the door and turned on the light with her elbow as her hands were full.

It was then that she stepped onto a piece of paper. She frowned and looked down at it in confusion. She bent down to pick up the note that had clearly been pushed under the door while she was out.

She walked into the room and allowed the door to close behind her. She unfolded the note and instantly felt her stomach churn. It wasn't a note from the hotel as she had been expecting.

Did you like my flowers? I can't wait to see you at the theatre on Thursday, so we can finally be together. Don't be scared. We are perfect for each other and you will see that soon.

She stumbled back into the room, the note dropping from her fingers to the floor, sitting with heavy menace on the soft carpet. She reached into her pocket and called Simon, hoping that he hadn't already gone underground to get the train home.

After a couple of rings, he answered.

"Simon, I...can you come back to the hotel? T-there's this... this note. And I don't know what to do. I'm—"

"What's your room number?" Simon asked.

"It's 402."

"I'll be there in a couple of minutes. Don't go anywhere."

She had no intention of leaving. She could barely keep herself upright, never mind figure out how to open the door and leave.

Her safe haven wasn't safe at all. Whoever it was knew where she was staying, again. The person might even still be in the hotel.

She clutched her phone in her hand and held her breath, waiting for Simon to arrive.

CHAPTER TWENTY-ONE

Emily sat in the soft armchair and wrapped her hands around the mug of tea that Sophie handed her.

"I'm so sorry to be a nuisance," Emily told Sophie as she sat on the sofa opposite Emily.

"You're not being a nuisance. When Simon told me what happened, I insisted that you stay here. You can't stay in a hotel where someone is sliding notes under your door." Sophie shuddered at the thought. "No, you can stay here as long as you need."

"It will just be tonight. I'll change my hotel first thing tomorrow," Emily said. She already felt guilty about putting them out, as well as having to tell Nicole that the hotel switch had been ineffective.

Simon came in and sat next to Sophie. "The guest bed is made up. Would you like a wake-up call? Continental breakfast?"

Emily smiled at the attempted joke. She appreciated it even if it wasn't enough to make her laugh just yet. She was still shaking from the note. She felt violated and afraid. Someone knew where she was staying. Someone had stood outside her hotel room door.

"Simon said you'd had flowers delivered to you last week. Do you have any idea who it might be?" Sophie asked.

As Simon escorted her to his home, she told him what had been happening. She was no longer able to pretend that the flowers were a mistaken delivery, or a one-off event. She'd been clinging on to the possibility, but tonight had ripped that notion away from her.

Emily shook her head. "No, that's the frustrating thing," she said. "I really don't know. It must be someone at my new job, but I really don't know who. Well, I mean…I have theories…but nothing to accuse anyone."

Simon looked at her curiously. "You didn't mention you had a theory before."

She blushed and looked down at her cup. She'd told Simon she had no idea who her stalker might be, but at the back of her mind she still wondered about her co-writer, Carl.

"There's this guy at work," Emily said. "He's a bit…strange. But it might not be him and I don't want to say anything to Nicole because those kinds of allegations don't go away. He might be innocent."

"He might not be," Simon said. "If you have a suspicion, then you should probably tell someone."

Emily shook her head. "I can't, I mean, I feel so guilty."

Sophie let out a sigh. "Men," she said.

"Hey," Simon huffed. "We're not all bad."

"More men become stalkers than women," Sophie said. "And then it's us poor women who end up feeling guilty about the trouble *we're* causing." She shook her head at Simon before turning to face Emily. "This isn't your fault. It's the fault of whoever this stalker guy is. You need to tell someone whom you suspect before something happens, and they find you in a basement somewhere."

Emily felt her eyebrows raise.

"Whoa, whoa, no one is finding anyone in a basement." Simon held his hands up. "You're watching too much of the crime channel."

"If you weren't working until nine each night, then I wouldn't be watching the crime channel," Sophie said.

"We have eight hundred channels, I'm sure you could find something else to watch no matter what time I got home," Simon replied with a grin. "You just like all the gruesome murders."

Sophie swatted his arm. "Shh, you." She looked at Emily. "I'm sure you won't be locked up in a basement, but you have to be careful. You never know what people will do. What does Olivia say about all of this?"

Simon stiffened, and Emily bit her lip nervously.

"Olivia doesn't know?" Sophie guessed.

Emily shook her head. "Up until tonight I wasn't one hundred percent sure I had a stalker. And I don't want to worry her. She's miles away. She's too scared to fly after the crash. It would be awful for her. Since she's not working now, she has a lot of time to think. This would drive her crazy."

"But now that you know, you'll tell her...right?" Sophie said.

Simon joined Sophie in looking at her meaningfully.

Emily sighed. She knew she had to tell Olivia, but she didn't want to. It was another layer of guilt. The guilt of causing Olivia stress and concern.

"I will," Emily said. "But in person."

"That's a good plan," Simon said. "I know Olivia and she'll—"

"Freak out," Emily finished.

"Well, yeah." He nodded.

"I'd freak out if that was happening to you," Sophie said, clinging to Simon's arm. She looked at Emily. "What are you going to do?"

"I'll talk to Nicole. And change hotels, again." Emily worried her lip. She didn't know what else she could do. She still didn't feel like she could push Carl to the top of the suspect list with no evidence.

"What about this ticket on Thursday?" Simon asked.

"Nicole has it." Emily sipped the hot drink. "I assume she's planning to go and see who shows up." She saw Sophie's concerned look. "Or maybe she'll send someone else."

The truth was, she had no idea what Nicole's plans for the ticket were. She'd buried her head in the sand, but she couldn't do that any longer. Neither of these actions was a mistake. Someone was stalking her, someone she knew.

She sipped her tea again. She didn't want to show them just how shaken she was by the turn of events. She was desperate for answers but knew that she wouldn't get any tonight.

"I'm exhausted. I think I'm going to head to bed," Emily said.

She loved Simon and Sophie dearly, but right now she wanted to be alone. She needed to process what had happened and plan what she was going to do next.

"No problem." Simon got to his feet. "I put your suitcase up in the room."

"Second on the left," Sophie added as she stood, too.

Emily put the mug on the table and swept them both into a big hug. "Thank you, I really appreciate this."

"We're happy to have you here," Sophie said.

They said goodnight, and Emily located her room upstairs. She softly closed the door behind her and sat on the edge of the bed.

The last hour had gone by in a blur. True to his word, Simon hadn't taken two minutes to dash back to the hotel. In that time, Emily had stood still as stone in the hotel room, staring at the note, and willing it to deliver more answers. It hadn't.

Upon his arrival, Simon had quickly read the note and then told Emily in no uncertain terms that she would stay with him and Sophie that evening. She hadn't argued, too frightened to do so.

Simon found her half-packed suitcase and quickly gathered her belongings. It only took him a couple more minutes to zip up the case and hold the door open for her. They'd left, Simon with an arm protectively around her shoulder. Not for the first time that evening, she was relieved that she had met up with him that night.

She looked around the spare room. It was nicely decorated in light pastels and felt safe and comforting. She felt the soft bedding beneath her fingers and let her shoulders slump. She reminded herself that she was safe.

Now that she didn't have to be on constant alert, she took out her phone. She typed out a quick goodnight message to Olivia, claiming she was back at the hotel and was going to bed.

Three dots appeared, indicating that Olivia was composing a message.

While she waited, Emily took the note out of her pocket. The small slip of paper seemed heavy in her hand. She wondered what the person would have done if she had been in the room. Did they intend to speak to her? Was the note a hurried afterthought?

Her phone pinged, and she looked at the message.

Olivia said that she and Henry were well; Henry was about to have a bath and watch cartoons before bed. She ended by saying that she loved her and missed her.

Emily felt guilty as she tapped out that she loved and missed them, too. She put her phone on the bedside table and read the note one more time.

She shuddered at the tone of the letter. Possessive, romantic, creepy. Whoever it was, they were clearly quite delusional. She shoved the note into the side pocket of her suitcase, wanting to it to be out of sight.

After a moment, she zipped the side pocket closed to add another layer of separation between her and the intimidating message.

CHAPTER TWENTY-TWO

I don't want to go to bed!" Henry argued.

"I'm very much aware of that fact," Olivia replied in a quiet tone. "But I must talk with Na—with Miss Costa, and it is practically your bedtime."

"I want to show Miss Costa my multiplication." Henry clutched a math worksheet to his little chest.

"You can show it to her tomorrow," Olivia said. "Now, go and get ready for bed. I'll be up in a moment."

Henry turned around and thudded his feet as he walked up the stairs. Olivia folded her arms and watched him go until she was satisfied that he was doing as he was told.

Once he was out of sight and making a din in another part of the house, she walked back to the dining room.

"I'm so sorry, he's usually much better behaved," Olivia said.

Natalie Costa sat at the dining table, twisting the stem of a half-full wine glass and smiling warmly.

"Oh, it's fine. Children have their moments, angels one minutes and demons the next."

"Yes, I guess you know all about the mood swings. More wine?" Olivia went to pick up the bottle from the ice bucket.

"I better not." Natalie shook her head. "I'm driving."

Olivia lowered the wine bottle and nodded her understanding.

"Of course."

She stood by her chair, not sure what to do next. There was a strange atmosphere in the room that she couldn't put her finger on. It wasn't the first time that she had been unable to identify an undercurrent in a situation, and this familiar discomfort made her uneasy.

Her usual strategy was to ask Emily, or just wait to see what happened. Most times all became clear.

Natalie patted the seat beside her. "Come and sit down."

Olivia frowned. Her seat at dinner had been opposite Natalie. She considered that it was probably to make reading the paperwork easier. Although she wasn't sure where the paperwork was. Natalie had brought a small clutch bag, and the short dress she wore surely didn't have any pockets.

Maybe she's just going to talk me through the process, Olivia thought as she took the seat.

"The way you are with Henry is nothing short of remarkable," Natalie said. "It must be hard with Emily being gone."

"It is," Olivia said. "But we make it through. It's just about taking each week as it comes."

"That's a wonderful way to look at it."

Olivia considered that it was the only way to look at it. Each week she struggled through, but then at the weekend Emily returned and they could be a family together. She reminded herself of her "one week at a time" mantra every weekday.

"I don't think I could be as strong as you," Natalie said. She picked Olivia's hand up from where she had rested it on the table and placed her own hand atop it.

Olivia swallowed. She wasn't particularly comfortable with touching strangers, but she supposed she needed to suck it up if they were to transition from strangers to friends. She gently squeezed Natalie's hand and held it loosely.

"If I appear strong, it's for Henry's sake. He needs normality."

Natalie looked almost dumbstruck, and a smile started to grace her lips.

Henry appeared in the doorway with a confused look on his face.

"Oh, Henry, you're ready." Olivia got to her feet and pulled her hand away from Natalie's. "Say goodnight to Miss Costa."

"Goodnight, Miss Costa," Henry repeated dully.

"Goodnight, Henry. I look forward to seeing your math work tomorrow."

Henry offered her a small grin before turning towards the stairs.

"I'm just going to read him a story and tuck him in," Olivia said. "Please, go into the living room and make yourself comfortable." She started to walk away when she suddenly remembered. "Oh, the heat is malfunctioning, so it may be a little warm in there."

Natalie licked her lips. "Oh. So...maybe I should take my cardigan off?"

Olivia nodded and quickly walked out of the room. She hated that the heating unit in the living room was still on the fritz. She made a mental note to call the contractor first thing in the morning.

Henry waited for her at the bottom of the stairs with a miserable expression on his face, no doubt unhappy at being sent to bed a whole fifteen minutes earlier than usual.

"Why were you holding her hand?" Henry asked as Olivia approached the stairs.

"Because we're friends." Olivia put a hand on his back and gestured towards the stairs.

"No, you're not."

"Well, maybe we will be."

"And why is she wearing a little dress? She never wears that at school."

"Some people wear different clothes at work than they do at home."

"And she smells weird."

"She's wearing perfume."

"I don't like her being here," Henry whispered as they walked into his bedroom.

"Well, then it's a marvellous thing that you're going to bed," Olivia told him as she closed the door behind them. Henry's face fell, and Olivia felt her heart clench.

"I'm sorry," she said. "She won't come back here. We're just talking about my helping out at your school. I need to know what I need to do, so Miss Costa is explaining that to me. It's just one night and then she'll be gone. And Mommy will be home tomorrow."

Henry nodded and walked over to his bed. "Can McFluffypants sleep with me tonight?"

"No, it's a school night. Maybe, and I mean *maybe*, tomorrow." Olivia made a mental note to ensure that Henry's door was properly closed. The kitten slept all day and came to life at night, racing around the house and mewling loudly. The first night the little fur ball had woken Henry up at least four times, and he had been exhausted the next day. Now the kitten remained downstairs in the utility room at night.

"What story would you like?" she asked to change the subject.

Henry reached under his pillow and pulled out a stack of five books that he had clearly chosen earlier.

Olivia smiled. "You know the rules, just one."

Henry rolled his eyes in a way that reminded her so much of Emily. He looked at the books in his lap as if the decision was going to be the most difficult he had ever faced.

Olivia walked back downstairs and into the open-plan living room. Natalie had indeed made herself comfortable. Her heels were removed and placed by the side of the sofa while her cardigan was draped over the back. The main light was off, and the candles on the fireplace had been lit.

"I hope you don't mind," Natalie asked. "I just love candles. The glow is so mesmerising, isn't it?"

"Definitely," Olivia said.

Natalie approached her and handed her a glass of wine. "I topped you up. Just because I'm driving doesn't mean you don't get to enjoy yourself."

"Thank you." Olivia took the glass.

"Is Henry okay?" Natalie walked over to the sofa and sat down.

"Yes. He wants his new kitten to sleep with him, but doesn't understand that the kitten won't sleep through the night like he does."

"Would this be Captain McFluffypants the Seventh?" Natalie asked.

"The one and only." Olivia sat on the opposite sofa. "Of course, I had nothing to do with the name."

"Of course." Natalie chuckled.

"He is excited about the idea of me helping out at school," Olivia said, hoping to steer the conversation a little. For some reason the subject had yet to creep up. She presumed that Natalie didn't wish to talk too much about work, but the evening was running away.

"That's wonderful. He does talk about you often, so I know the other kids will be excited as well."

"So, um, what does it involve?" Olivia asked. She took a sip of wine.

"The children are very young, so we don't need to be too structured with a lesson plan. It's really something I'd leave up to you. I mean, I don't know what your teaching methods have been for Henry, but clearly they work."

"L-leave it up to me?" A mental image of children swinging from light fixtures and brawling in the classroom while she stood helpless at the front flashed through her mind.

Natalie crossed the room and sat beside her. "I'll be there with you, don't worry. I'll just leave the teaching to you. Henry's math skills and understanding of numbers are extraordinary. And each time he solves an equation he proudly tells everyone that you taught him how to. It's so…"

"Numerical?" Olivia guessed.

"Heartwarming," Natalie breathed.

Suddenly she was leaning in closer, so Olivia backed up a little.

"H-he's a good boy," Olivia said.

"He told me that you're very shy," Natalie said, edging closer.

"S-shy?" Olivia asked as her back came up against the arm of the sofa.

"Mm-hmm," Natalie hummed in agreement.

A loud *thwack* sounded through the living room.

The shock of the sound, along with her retreat from Natalie, caused Olivia to fall to the ground. She got to her knees and looked over the coffee table to see Emily standing in the doorway, having just dropped her suitcase to the ground.

"Sorry to interrupt," Emily said.

She looked towards Natalie, who was suddenly on her feet.

"Hi, we've not met, I'm Emily. Olivia's wife."

CHAPTER TWENTY-THREE

"W-wife?" the young woman choked out. She looked from Emily to Olivia and then back again. "B-but...you're dead!"

Emily watched as Olivia got to her feet and stared at the young woman in horror.

"Dead? What gave you that idea?!"

"You! And Henry! You said she was gone."

"To London," Olivia explained, eyes wide.

Emily wasn't quite sure what she had walked into. Obviously, there was a strange woman in her house putting some moves on her wife. Before she'd even heard about her apparent demise, she'd been sure that there would be a reasonable explanation for what she'd stumbled into.

Olivia had looked terrified as the young brunette started to approach her. Whatever was happening was definitely not Olivia's idea.

"Oh my God." The young woman put her head in her hands and sat on the sofa. "I'm mortified. I thought she was dead." She looked up at Emily. "I'm so sorry."

Emily laughed. It was all she could think to do in the midst of the crazy situation. She stepped forward and held out her hand. "Let's start again. Hi, I'm Emily White."

The woman sprung to her feet and shook her hand. "Natalie Costa."

Emily looked at Olivia with mock-horror. "Henry's teacher, Olivia! Really!"

"But…I…Emily, please…I…" Olivia fumbled.

"I'm kidding," Emily said. "It's okay. I can see there's been some wild misunderstanding here."

"I'm so sorry, Olivia," Natalie said. "I'm mortified. I completely misunderstood the situation. Henry said he was missing his mother. Said she was gone…we all just assumed. And then I saw you, and…"

"Don't worry, misunderstandings are rife in this family," Emily said.

"I'm so sorry you walked in on this. It was all my fault. Olivia was just being a perfect hostess, and I completely misread all the signs."

"Really, it's fine. I'm laughing about it already," Emily said. It was true. She was already thinking of all the ways she could mock Olivia.

Natalie snatched her cardigan from the back of the sofa and slipped her feet into her heels. "I should go."

"I'll walk you out," Emily said, seeing as Olivia stood like a statue in the middle of the room.

"The offer to volunteer with the children is still open, if you… if you feel like you can," Natalie said to Olivia before hurrying towards the hallway.

Emily followed her and opened the front door.

"Again, I'm so sorry. Really, I can't apologise enough. I can't imagine what you must think of me."

Emily shook her head. "I can see that it was all a huge misunderstanding. Nothing to apologise for. Obviously, if you could explain to the rest of Henry's class and the faculty that I'm not dead that would be great."

"Oh, I will, absolutely!" Natalie quickly exited the house, but stopped on the path and turned to face Emily. "Again, I'm so—"

Emily held up her hands. "It's fine. Well, it's not fine, but I understand that it was a mistake and I can totally see how it happened. We'll see each other at the next PTA meeting, and we'll laugh about it."

"I hope so," Natalie said, her cheeks a deep shade of red.

"Drive safe," Emily said with a soft smile before closing the door. She leaned her head on the doorframe and let out a small chuckle.

"I'm also sorry..."

She turned to see Olivia standing in the hallway, her fingers knotted together, and her face wrought with guilt.

"You have nothing to apologise for. She was the one attempting to mount you like a zoo animal. And I can't really blame her. I'd be the same if I saw someone like you on the market and thought I had a chance."

Olivia blushed and stared down at her feet. "I-I had no idea...I didn't..."

All thoughts of mocking her floated out of Emily's head. She stepped forward, pulling her into an embrace.

"Don't worry, I should have told you I was coming home early so that you could get your fangirls out of the house," she joked.

Olivia chuckled. "I don't have *fangirls*," she whispered into Emily's hair.

"Well, you would say that," Emily mumbled. "I'm sure there's a whole harem in here during the week."

"Only on Mondays," Olivia replied.

Emily laughed and gently slapped Olivia on the shoulder as she pulled back.

"Why are you home early? Not that I'm not pleased to see you," Olivia added.

Emily attempted to keep the smile on her face. "I'll tell you all about it once I get some coffee," she said.

"Oh, of course...I'll..." Olivia turned and walked towards the kitchen and Emily followed her.

She knew she had to have the conversation with Olivia, but she was hoping to put it off a few more moments. Nicole had insisted that Emily go home a day early while she contacted the authorities. It had been the right thing to do, but Emily knew it wouldn't go down well at all with Olivia.

In the kitchen, there were dirty dinner plates and various utensils and cookery stacked on the counter. Olivia set about putting the coffee maker on, and Emily leaned her back on a free square of work surface and folded her arms.

"Just a teensy, tiny question. Probably not even worth asking. But, why are you cooking a homemade meal for Henry's teacher?" Emily asked with a chuckle. She knew Olivia's tendency for getting herself into these kinds of situations.

Olivia reached into the cupboard and pulled out the good coffee, clearly trying to wiggle back into her good books. The action told Emily that Olivia was still a little uncertain of her reaction, expecting the worst.

Olivia started measuring the coffee into the filter in the top of the machine.

"She was coming over to discuss my volunteering in Henry's class. She was very impressed with Henry's mathematical abilities, and Henry told her that I had taught him. Apparently, they have volunteers come in to speak to the children, and she thought I might be a good candidate. We were supposed to be talking about that, and I thought she was being nice, so I was being nice in the hope that I'd make a new friend." Olivia turned and waved the measuring cup at Emily. "Which, frankly, is your fault. You're always telling me to make new friends. I tried and then, well, this happened."

Olivia picked up the coffee pot and walked over to the sink.

"Yes, completely my fault." Emily sat on a stool at the kitchen island.

"And I don't know where she got the idea that you were dead!" Olivia complained as she filled the pot. "I said I missed you. I didn't say I was grieving you. I said the weeks were long and lonely. The *weeks*. Indicating that the weekends were not."

She snapped the lid closed and stalked back over to the coffee maker, where she poured the water into the top.

"She didn't say that Henry was upset at the death of his mother. Just that he was strong and resilient, which he is. A-and I said that I needed to get on with my life as I'd recently retired to spend…more time with Henry."

Olivia lowered the jug, looking blankly at the wall as she thought on. "She said that Henry was upset that his mommy had gone away. And I...I asked her over to dinner." She lowered her head. "And asked if she preferred red or white wine." She spun around and stared at Emily. "Oh, dear God, I asked her on a date, didn't I?"

Emily held up her thumb and forefinger. "A little bit."

Olivia turned back to the coffee maker, slammed the lid down, and stabbed at the power button.

"But it was an easy mistake to make!" Emily said. "You couldn't have known that she thought 'gone away' meant 'gone to heaven.' You know how dramatic Henry can be." Emily held out her arms. "Come here."

Olivia grumpily crossed the kitchen and into Emily's open arms. "I screwed up."

"You had a misunderstanding, it's all over with now. She knows I'm not dead. She still wants you to volunteer, which I think is a great idea, by the way."

Olivia leaned back in Emily's arms. "You do?"

"I do. If you're lonely during the week, then it might be good to have something to occupy your time, especially when I'm away." Emily looked at her seriously. "Are you lonely?"

She felt Olivia go tense. It was a conversation that Emily had wanted to have ever since she started commuting. Now there was a reason to discuss it, and Emily was going to grab it.

"I..." Olivia trailed off.

Emily gently rubbed her sides. "It's okay. Whatever it is. You can say it."

Olivia took a deep breath and looked down at the space between them, avoiding Emily's eyes.

"I...I can't get settled." She met Emily's gaze. "I mean, there's something..."

"You feel that something is missing?" Emily asked after a few moments of silence.

Olivia nodded, relief flooding her face that Emily had caught on to what she meant.

"Olivia, I think you were a little hasty to give up work. I think you need something to occupy your mind. Being home alone while Henry is at school is enough to drive anyone to madness."

"But I promised you. I said we'd be a family."

Emily furrowed her brow. "We *are* a family. Being a family doesn't involve one of us being at home all the time. It involves both of us being happy. Because if you're not happy, then I'm not happy."

"I'm happy," Olivia hurried to reassure her.

"You're not," Emily replied. "Something is eating at you. Can you explain to me what it is?"

Olivia let out a small sigh and took a step back. Emily watched as Olivia started to pace the room. Whenever Olivia was trying to digest or explain something she was struggling with, she would pace, as if allowing the anxiety to flow through her feet and distribute itself through the ground like lightning.

"I...I promised you that I'd take a step back. When we were planning the wedding, I said that I'd stay home and let you explore a new career. And now I feel like I'm going back on that promise. Staying home is lonely. Doing it for years...I-I can't imagine it. I'm so sorry. I know I made a promise, but I don't know if I can keep it!"

Emily couldn't help it as a chuckle escape her lips.

"This isn't funny," Olivia said with indignation.

"I'm sorry, it's just...I thought you meant for a few weeks. We both knew that things were going to be stressful directly after the wedding. We knew I'd have to get back to London to work, and Henry was starting school. I thought you meant that you'd take things on for a few weeks until we were over that hump. But now I realise that you thought I meant forever."

Olivia wrapped her arms around her middle and looked at Emily. "You...didn't mean forever?"

Emily shook her head. "No. I know you love to work. I would never want to tie you to the house. Some people might want that, but I know it would be like torture for you."

Olivia let out a breath, one from deep inside her, that had been held in for weeks.

"I...thank goodness. I mean, I love Henry. I do. And I am happy to take on that responsibility until we are more established in our new pattern. But I thought we had agreed to forever! I was calculating how many weeks Henry had left until he graduated college."

Emily raised her hand to smother a grin.

"Don't you dare laugh," Olivia said.

Emily coughed and tried to retain a neutral expression. "I'm sorry, we should have been clearer. I should have been more specific. I just thought it was obvious. You're not a stay-at-home mom kind of person."

"What's that supposed to mean?" Olivia moved her hands to her hips.

"Really? You want me to remind you of the time I had to explain how the washing machine worked? Or the time I caught you ironing without plugging it in? And the fact you can't open a childproof bottle of bleach."

"I may not be a domestic goddess, but I learned. And I think I'm pretty good at it now," Olivia said proudly.

"You are," Emily said. "You are perfect. My little housewife. You know—"

"I told you, I'm not wearing that outfit." Olivia rolled her eyes.

"Spoilsport." Emily pouted for a moment. "Anyway, back to the matter at hand. I think volunteering might be a good idea. Or going back to work? Starting a new business? I think you need something to focus your energies on. Something that doesn't involve remodelling the house every couple of weeks."

"What about Henry?"

"He wouldn't be much good at starting a new business, but I could ask him."

Olivia rolled her eyes, but a slight smile was creeping onto her lips. "You know what I mean. Who will take care of Henry?"

"Well, my best friend is a registered childcare worker, as well as Henry's third most favourite person in the world. And even if Lucy couldn't take him for some reason, there are day care centres, nannies. We're not the only working family in this situation."

Olivia's brow furrowed as she took the information in. Emily thought it adorable how someone so intelligent and practical in most areas of life could miss out on some very obvious things in others.

"But…Henry…wouldn't it be better if he were with one of us?" Olivia asked.

Emily shrugged. "We can't see into the future, never mind various alternate versions of the future. It's one of the hardest things about being a parent. But I know that I grew up in various foster situations and Henry saw very little of me up until just a year ago. We seem to have turned out okay."

Olivia smiled. "That you did."

"I know the desire to ensure everything is perfect can be strong. But the truth is that life can be messy, things don't always go according to plan. You have to do the best you can. You may think that staying home with Henry is the best for him, but if you're not happy, then you will eventually become depressed and that will have a whole different set of repercussions."

"Everything is very complicated," Olivia groused. She walked over to the coffee machine and started to pour Emily a cup.

"It is," Emily said. "But hopefully the payoff is worth it."

Olivia walked over with the cup and saucer in her hand and a smile on her face. "Very worth it." She placed a kiss on Emily's lips and handed over the saucer. "I just wanted to help you, to play my part."

"You have helped me. You continue to help me. But it can't be at the cost of your own happiness, that's not how this works," Emily said. "We're a team."

"We are," Olivia said. Then, she realised something. "Oh, we've been so caught up in this that I forgot to ask. You didn't tell me why you're home early."

CHAPTER TWENTY-FOUR

Olivia paced furiously in front of the living room windows. Every now and then she turned to face Emily to say something, but the correct words would escape her, and she would continue pacing.

Emily had suggested that they move from the kitchen to the living room while she explained her early return. Olivia presumed the move was intended to soothe her, but no change of location could calm her now. She wouldn't be calm until she stood over the still and motionless body of Emily's tormentor.

She paused and blinked. She'd rarely had such violent thoughts. Clearing the image from her mind, she continued to pace. She needed to process what she had just heard. Someone was stalking her wife.

Her first reaction had been to declare that Emily wasn't to leave the house again until the matter was resolved. Luckily, she hadn't voiced that particular thought, knowing that Emily wouldn't have appreciated the sentiment one bit.

If she wasn't so livid and afraid, she would have mentally congratulated herself for holding back a thought that would have certainly been said aloud a mere year ago.

As she started to wear a track in the flooring, Emily sipped her coffee. Olivia had no idea how she could be so calm while she was out of her mind with worry.

"What do we do?" she suddenly asked.

She was used to organising things, seeking out solutions and implementing fixes. It had been her profession and her personal skill set. But now she had no idea what to do, what to say. All she knew was that she wanted it fixed.

"As I said," Emily repeated, "Nicole has called the police. Now we wait to see what they say."

"And no one turned up at the theatre?" Olivia asked.

"No. Nicole sent two of her friends, undercover, and the police also sent someone in plain clothes. No one saw anyone suspicious. Whoever it was could have changed their mind."

"Or seen the supposed undercover people and run off," Olivia added. "Incompetence."

"Maybe," Emily said. "Anyway, I wasn't there. Nicole sent me home long before that, told me to have a nice long weekend with my family and put it out of my mind. Which is what I intend to do."

"How can you be so calm?" Olivia asked. "There's a…a man, watching you."

"Olivia," Emily snapped. "That is not helping."

Olivia closed her eyes and took a deep breath. "I'm sorry," she mumbled.

"I may appear calm, but I'm pretty terrified about all of this. I'm trying to keep it together because freaking out isn't going to help anyone. I need to keep a level head."

Olivia opened her eyes and nodded. She turned to look out the window at the dimly lit street. She knew the odds of the stalker being in New York were very slim, but she scanned the shadows just in case. She was itching to go to her office and look at ways of improving the home security system. She'd seen an advertisement on panic rooms a while ago. Now she wondered if they needed one. Or a gun. She'd never liked the idea of guns, but if Emily was in danger then maybe she needed to investigate the matter. Or private security. Someone who looked like they could snap a man in half accompanying Emily around town would surely put off any stalker.

"Olivia," Emily said softly, trying to get a response out of her.

"I understand, I just…" Olivia trailed off. She had no idea what to say.

"You feel useless," Emily said.

"Yes, exactly. I-I…want to fix it."

"Of course you do, we all do. But we have to accept that, for the moment, we can't. But, do you know what you can do?"

Olivia turned to look at Emily with a raised eyebrow.

"You can make me forget about it for a few days. I'll have to go back on Sunday night, and then I will think about it again. But, for now, I have a weekend with you and Henry and I don't want to waste it thinking about…whoever it is. I don't want them to win by disrupting my life; I don't want to give them that power. So, I've told you all I know, but now I want to get on with our life. I want to feel normal for a couple of days."

Olivia bit down the first thought that came to mind and tossed a silent hurrah to herself for progress.

"O-kay." She hesitated. She wasn't sure how she was supposed to go back to normal after being told that some madman was on the loose, harassing her wife.

"So, volunteering," Emily said. "It sounds like a good idea to me. What do you think?"

Olivia blinked. "Um, well…" It was hard to switch from one difficult topic to another.

"I mean, I know you think you're not great with kids, but you actually are. You communicate with them well, and Henry has gone from hating math to processing numbers better than I do in a few short months. If you can do that with other kids, then that would be great, don't you think?"

Olivia sat on the arm of the sofa opposite Emily and considered the question for a moment. It had been a long and emotional night. From the embarrassment with Natalie to Emily's surprise return to the news that a stalker was in their midst. The idea of teaching a child how a mortgage worked seemed exhausting.

"I'm not sure," she said. "Natalie suggested it. And, to be honest, I'm not sure if I'm ready to see Natalie again. Ever."

Emily snickered. "Oh, come on, it was a misunderstanding. It will be fine."

"Will it?" Olivia asked seriously.

"Yes, it will," Emily promised. "You make a point to see her soon and then you laugh it off and get back to business. If you hide from it, then it will become an issue. She's Henry's teacher, so you can't exactly hide from her forever."

Olivia could feel her cheeks heating up.

"Henry could change schools," she half-joked.

"Putting tonight's events behind you, what do you really think about volunteering? You must have been interested to have asked her over to find out more."

Olivia sighed and got to her feet. She walked over to Emily and sat down next to her.

"I suppose I thought it was a good idea. I am bored at home all day. I simply don't know how to fill my time. I'm not interested in most hobbies, I don't have a huge number of friends to socialise with. I like to feel...useful. Volunteering would fit that brief. And it would only be for the hours that Henry is at school, which means I'd be available to look after him outside of school hours. It would also fit in with a baby, if I were pregnant."

Emily looked at her quietly for a moment. "Do you want to have a baby?"

Olivia softly nodded.

"Are you sure? You have been a little back and forth on this," Emily said.

"I have," Olivia said. "But it came from a place of fear, fear that I would have a child that may be on the spectrum. Like myself."

Emily's eyes widened slightly at the admission.

It was the first time that Olivia had made a reference to herself potentially being on the spectrum. She'd danced around the topic as much as possible, not wanting to commit to a label.

"But," Olivia said before that became the topic of discussion, "I realise that it wouldn't be the end of the world. Well, you made me realise that. And, while adoption is something I think is a great idea, I do understand your point that it isn't a great fit for us at the moment. Maybe we will revisit that in the future, maybe we won't. Either way, I understand your concerns about adoption and I do share them."

"I'm glad to hear that," Emily said. She leaned forward and placed her cup and saucer on the coffee table. She turned to face Olivia and took her hand in hers. "I know you struggle with labels, but if Henry turned out to be on the spectrum, or we had a baby that was, it would have nothing to do with you. And it would not change the way we feel about them one bit."

"Of course not," Olivia said. "We'd love them no matter what."

"Exactly."

"Unless they become very unsavoury as adults," Olivia said. "I saw this documentary about a man—"

"Nope." Emily pulled her hands back. "We're not having that conversation, whatever it is."

"But…" Olivia drifted off at the forceful glare Emily gave her.

"Nope," Emily repeated.

"Fine, fine," Olivia mumbled.

"Do you watch much of the crime channel when I'm away from home?" Emily asked.

Olivia frowned. "No, why?"

"No reason."

"How do you feel about a baby?" Olivia suddenly asked. She was keen to have the conversation that had been playing on her mind recently. She'd concluded that Emily was right about adoption. Now she wanted to gauge her opinion on more conventional methods and possible timescales.

"About you carrying a baby?" Emily asked.

"Yes."

Emily smiled. "I love the idea. I think you'd be a great mother, no, I *know* you'd be a great mother. Henry would have a little sister or brother, which is also good. I don't feel like we need another child to complete our family, but I definitely like the idea of having one. What do *you* think about it?"

"I was worried for a while. But I've had time to think about it and I think it's the right thing to do. I want to have a child. I've never really felt that way before, but I do now, strongly so."

"Then I think it's something we should investigate," Emily said.

"How do you feel about investigating it soon?" Olivia asked.

"How soon?"

"You're home now," Olivia said. She was already working out the logistics of dropping Henry off with Lucy while bribing her doctor for an emergency appointment.

Emily chuckled. "You want to go tomorrow, don't you?"

Olivia shrugged her shoulder slightly. "Maybe."

"Well, this is very you. Very us," Emily said. "We moved in together quickly. Got engaged quickly. This does seem like a logical next step."

"It does," Olivia said. "And you're not often home during the week. This would be a great opportunity to get the ball rolling."

"It could," Emily said. She remained silent for a moment, seemingly deep in thought. She nodded. "Okay, yes. Let's get the ball rolling. Then we'll have more information and we can go from there."

"You're sure?" Olivia felt herself smiling widely.

"Positive," Emily said. "I'm all in. And I know you don't suggest something unless you're all in as well."

"I'll call first thing in the morning," Olivia promised. She picked up her phone from the coffee table to set a diary reminder for herself.

Before she could save the reminder, Emily screamed.

She turned with a start, to see her jumping up from the sofa and racing to the other side of the room.

Somehow the kitten had escaped from the utility room and jumped up onto the sofa to sit between them.

"Oh my God," Emily said between deep breaths. "So…that's Captain McWhatsIt then?"

"McFluffypants the Seventh," Olivia said. "Yes. He should be locked in the utility room, but he has clearly found a way to escape."

Emily tentatively walked over with her hand stretched out. "Hello, kitty," she whispered.

The kitten jumped at her hand, claws at the ready. Emily jumped back.

"He's a demon," she said.

"He's active," Olivia said. She reached forward and picked up the tiny creature. "I'll put him back in the utility room, though goodness knows how he managed to escape. We may find him staring at us in the middle of the night."

Emily took a step back and regarded the kitten suspiciously.

Olivia took in her body language and made an assumption. "You don't like cats, do you?"

"Hate them," Emily confirmed.

"Then why on earth did we get a kitten for Henry?" Olivia moved the struggling kitten from one hand to the other as she waited for Emily to explain.

Emily sighed. "Henry really wanted one, and I didn't want to tell him that I didn't like cats. Who doesn't like cats?"

"People who fear them," Olivia said.

Emily rolled her eyes. "I'm not scared."

Olivia held it out towards Emily. She smiled as Emily jumped backwards. "Oh, yes, not scared in the slightest."

"I'm going to go unpack," Emily said, walking to the hallway. "You lock up that devil creature and I'll see you upstairs."

Olivia chuckled as she took the kitten back to the utility room. She checked his food, water, and cat litter before sneaking out the door. She wondered if the door had been slightly open or if the fluff ball had figured out how to open it himself. She hoped for the former but doubted she'd be that lucky.

She moved around the kitchen, cleaning up as she went. Her mind was spinning with all the things that had been discussed that night. The embarrassment with Natalie, the concern over the stalker, and her relief at their decision regarding the baby.

She held onto the work surface and let out a long breath. Her life had always been ordered, scheduled, and predictable. It certainly wasn't that way anymore. She'd made the decision to make a change, to break out of her protective bubble, and actually live her life. Being with Emily and Henry had thrown her headfirst into that choice. She'd expected to be terrified with the change and the pace, but if anything, she was eager to start the next chapter.

Too long her life had been static, with wasted time and potential. She wasn't getting any younger, and she was desperate to move on. Having a baby was terrifying, and yet she knew it would be so rewarding.

Of course, she knew to temper her excitement. There was a long way to go and she didn't even know if she could have a baby yet. But the journey was one she was looking forward to.

She filled the dishwasher, images of baby clothes and toys in her mind as she did. Soon she started to think about morning sickness and swollen ankles, and she grimaced to herself. So maybe the whole journey wasn't glamorous.

She heard a sound and looked around to figure out what it was.

She heard a thud and a slide. And then another thud and a slide.

Then she heard a thud and a click. She looked as the utility room door slowly opened and a furry head appeared.

"You're going to be trouble," she told him.

He meowed back at her in response.

CHAPTER TWENTY-FIVE

Olivia's ability to get things done never ceased to amaze Emily. Just a few short hours ago, they were discussing having a baby. Now, they were at an expensive clinic waiting to be seen by a specialist.

They'd stayed awake for a few hours, discussing the pros and cons of having a baby. Emily wanted to be absolutely certain that Olivia knew what she was taking on. But, as with most things, Olivia had already thought of every angle.

Emily knew that she felt ready for another baby, and she was certain that Olivia felt the same. Now came the poking and prodding, the questions, and the money. She bristled again at the idea of how easy it was for most heterosexual couples to have a baby and how much work and expensive it would be for them.

Olivia raised her wrist and looked at her watch. She tutted.

Emily put a calming hand on her arm.

"Olivia, considering you bought and bullied your way to an appointment with ninety minutes' notice, you can't complain about them being a minute late."

"Bought and bullied?" Olivia asked haughtily.

Emily fixed her with a glare.

Olivia backed down. "I'll give them another five minutes, but then I'll be asking questions."

"Fair enough." Emily closed her eyes and leaned her head back against the chair's headrest. She was exhausted. The journey home and the several long discussions were starting to take their toll. And in the back of her mind, she was already thinking about work the following week. Opening night was fast approaching, and, while she was happy about that, she was also worried about the situation with her stalker.

She had a phone call scheduled with Nicole before she flew back on Sunday, in order to get an update on what was happening. As much as she tried to push it to the back of her mind, she couldn't. The note at the hotel had scared her more than she was willing to admit.

Why someone had taken such an interest in her was a mystery. She was average, nothing special. And yet, someone was obviously fascinated by her.

She shuddered at the thought.

"Are you okay?" Olivia asked softly.

"Yes, just a chill," Emily lied flawlessly. "Probably tired."

Olivia regarded her for a moment more before nodding and looking away.

Emily hated lying to Olivia, but she knew that Olivia was probably in more of a panic than she was. Her best hope at offering Olivia comfort now was to appear unaffected.

A part of her also felt guilty for taking the focus away from what should be a happy moment. They were preparing to create new life. Olivia would, hopefully, soon be carrying a miniature version of herself, and Emily couldn't help but smile at that thought.

She'd missed a lot of Henry's childhood, and she wasn't about to let that happen again. She knew that she needed to make her name as a writer, and then she'd be able to do the job she loved from home, or at least in New York. Things were coming together; her life was getting better and better. So long as she ignored the stalker lurking in the background.

Maybe the stalker was the counterbalance in her life. Things were going well, so there needed to be some kind of spectre to keep her in line. But she'd be damned if she was going to not appreciate the good times just because of one man.

She took Olivia's hand and gave it a squeeze.

"I love you," she whispered.

Olivia looked at her curiously but smiled. "I love you, too."

CHAPTER TWENTY-SIX

Olivia pulled the car into the parking lot and looked at the building in front of her. Part of her wanted to turn around and go back home again. Another part of her knew that Emily was right—she needed to speak with Natalie again and smooth out what had happened.

She turned the engine off and took a couple of deep, calming breaths. Once she felt she was ready, she exited the car and walked into the school.

The weekend had raced by. It felt like a few short hours ago since her disastrous dinner with Natalie, but that had been four days ago. Four days where she hadn't given the matter a second thought because she had been so preoccupied.

Friday had been dedicated to the fertility clinic, where tests had been performed, decisions had been made, and a timetable of events had been put in place. Now everything was real and Olivia felt like a weight had been lifted from her shoulders. She knew that having a baby wouldn't be easy, but she also knew it was something she wanted to do. The fear of such a big decision had startled her into inaction, but now she felt positive again. Like they were moving forward. And they were moving forward quickly, just as Olivia liked. She was expecting results from her first tests the next day and had already booked her next appointment with her specialist.

Saturday had been dedicated to Henry. They'd gone to the park, seen a movie, played computer games, and eaten dinner at his favourite Italian restaurant. Olivia had deliberately kept up a fast pace, knowing that Emily was feeling nervous about her return to work the next day. Emily may have felt that she was an expert at cloaking her emotions, but Olivia was getting better and better at reading them.

But it didn't matter how action-packed Saturday was. Sunday still came around, and it was with a heavy heart that Olivia helped Emily pack her suitcase.

Despite Olivia's suggestion that she stay home, Emily was determined to return. She wasn't about to let her career be dictated by a man with an unhealthy obsession. Olivia had to admit that she was proud of Emily's resolve. Even if she was also scared of the situation in general.

Once Emily had headed off to the airport, Olivia was on the phone, informing Nicole that every precaution was to be taken. Luckily, it seemed that Nicole was five steps ahead of her and had already made provisions for Emily's security.

And now it was Monday. The first day in a long series of days until Emily would be back. It was also the day that Olivia promised she would see Natalie, apologise for the mix-up, and attempt to move on from the embarrassment of the previous Thursday.

"Olivia?"

She looked up to see Natalie walking towards her.

She sucked in a breath, not expecting to bump into the woman yet. It was just her bad luck that Natalie would be meandering around the school rather than in the classroom where Olivia expected to find her.

"Hello," Olivia said. She stood still and held her handbag in front of her, hands clasped around the hooped strap. "I wanted to apologise for the mix-up last week."

"I should be the one apologising," Natalie said. "Really, I was mortified...I've explained everything to the faculty, and everyone is now aware of the situation. I'm just so sorry that this happened."

"I hoped that we could put this behind us and move on?" Olivia asked. "I'd like to take you up on your offer of volunteering, if it's still open."

Natalie smiled. "Absolutely. Do you want to follow me? We can go to the main office, and I can give you the forms that you'll need to fill out."

Olivia nodded and fell into step behind Natalie. "If it's quite all right with you, I'd rather not discuss…any of it…"

The last thing Olivia wanted was to dissect the evening. She was already very invested in pretending it had never even happened.

"No arguments here," Natalie said quickly. "The less said, the better."

"Agreed." Olivia felt her frame soften in relief. She had been concerned that Natalie would wish to discuss the matter, or explain herself, or worse, have Olivia explain herself. Ignoring the whole matter and starting over was much better.

"Are you all right?" Natalie asked, indicating to Olivia that she had been silent too long to be considered politely acceptable.

"Emily has a stalker." Olivia decided to break the silence with a new topic.

Natalie stopped, and Olivia had to do the same so as not to run into her.

"Oh my God, is she okay?"

"She's back in London," Olivia said. "Which is where the stalker is."

"You must be beside yourself," Natalie said.

"I am. I wanted her to stay home, but she refused." Olivia sniffed and shook her head. While she appreciated Emily's independence, it was sometimes very irritating.

"She can't change her life because of some nut job," Natalie said. "Good for her for carrying on. I'd probably be terrified to go out."

"She is stubborn," Olivia said.

"Does she have friends in London?"

Olivia thought of Simon and Nicole. She knew that her friends would do anything to ensure Emily's safety.

"She does, good friends."

Natalie smiled. "That's good. They'll look after her."

"They will. It's her opening night next week. She writes plays."

"Wow," Natalie said in awe. "That's incredible. Would I have seen anything by her?"

"No, she's still pretty new to the business."

"You'll have to let me know when something is showing on this side of the pond. I'd love to go and see it."

Olivia nodded. "I'll do that."

Natalie turned around, and they continued the walk to the office.

Olivia smiled to herself. Despite the ridiculous misunderstanding, things seemed to be working out. She was actually talking to someone, making conversation with a new friend.

It was a nice sensation.

Maybe Monday was going to be a good day after all.

Chapter Twenty-seven

M onday was turning out to be horrible.
Emily was staying with Nicole in her penthouse
apartment that overlooked the Thames. Nicole was an excellent
host, and her home was nothing short of beautiful. But that didn't
stop Emily from feeling like she was intruding.

After she unpacked on Sunday night and spent at least an hour
apologising, they had sat on the balcony with blankets and a bottle
of wine. Nicole had explained that the police investigation had,
sadly, uncovered nothing.

Extra security was put in place at the theatre as an extra
precautionary measure. But, rather than making Emily feel safe, it
made her feel guilty for causing such expense and trouble.

And now Monday had arrived, and the thing that Emily was
dreading most was about to happen.

A team meeting for all theatre staff had been called for nine
o'clock. Everyone was in attendance and wondering what the big
announcement would be. They all gathered in the first few rows
of the old-fashioned theatre, some standing and some sitting, all
looking perplexed about the unexpected meeting.

Emily stood to the side, under the royal box. She looked at her
fellow employees, trying to remember names and positions and dig
into her brain for anything untoward or out of the ordinary.

From stagehands to set designers to box office staff to lighting
technicians, everyone seemed so normal. She'd met most of them

by now, easily able to put a name to at least three-quarters of the people assembled. The rest were part-time staff or people she'd yet to come across. She assumed she could eliminate them from her enquiries straight away.

"Hi."

Emily jumped and turned to see Carl standing beside her. She hadn't noticed him arrive and wondered just how long he had been there.

"Hi," she said.

"Nicole said you had a family emergency and had to go home early last week?" Carl fished.

"Yes. Everything is fine now," Emily said without expanding.

"Oh, good. Look, if you ever need anything, even just to talk, I'm here for you." He placed his hand on her shoulder.

Emily tensed up. "Thanks, Carl."

He smiled and nodded as he removed his hand. She let out a sigh of relief. His very presence set her on edge. While she still didn't have any hard evidence, deep down she was sure that Carl was her main suspect. She hoped that the very public announcement that was about to happen would be enough to make him back off.

"I'd like to think that we're not just co-writers, we're friends," he continued, clearly unable to take a hint.

"Sure." Emily smiled tightly and turned her attention back to the stage, willing Nicole to hurry up and begin.

Thankfully, Nicole appeared on stage at that moment and cleared her throat to get the room's attention.

Silence fell over the gathering, and everyone looked up in anticipation.

Nicole stood in the middle of the proscenium. Beside her were two male police officers in uniform. Gathered near the wings were the senior management of the company and some financial backers that Emily recognised from their headshots on the company website.

"Thank you for all coming here so promptly. I won't keep you long," Nicole began. "It's come to our attention that a member of the company is actively harassing a member of staff. Now, I'm not going to go into details because this matter has now been handed over to the police, and I'm unable to comment on an active investigation. However, I'd like to make it abundantly clear that this company will not tolerate any form of harassment."

Emily casually turned to look at Carl, hoping to see a reaction on his face that would confirm her suspicions. But there was nothing. He looked up at Nicole with a neutral, though maybe concerned, face.

Emily skimmed through the other members of staff, straining to see in the dim lights if anyone was having a nervous reaction. Or if anyone was looking at her. Still, there was nothing.

"So, I would highly recommend that the person responsible for this harassment ceases immediately," Nicole continued. "Because I warn you that this isn't going to go away. Continuing your current course will only serve to make things much, much worse."

Emily looked around the audience seats again, hoping for a clue.

"This matter won't interfere with our opening night next Wednesday. As we always say, on with the show. But there will be increased police and private security presence over the next few days. You will notice that security will be tightened, and you will all be required to wear your badges and passes at all times. I want to underline how seriously we are taking this matter and to advise you all that we are keeping a very close eye on proceedings. If anyone wants to discuss this matter with me, my door is always open. And now I'll let you get back to work."

There were a few moments of silence while people processed what had been said. A collective murmur bubbled up as people found their team members and left the auditorium.

"This is so scary," Hannah said as she made her way through a few people to stand by Emily's side.

"It is," Emily said.

Hannah leaned around Emily and looked at Carl. "Carl, could you leave us alone? Girl talk, you know."

Carl looked at them curiously for a moment before turning around and stalking away.

Hannah shuddered. "He's so odd. He doesn't even walk properly." She turned to face Emily. "Do you know what's going on? It's all freaking me out. I hope everything will be okay." She shuddered again and rubbed her arms. "It gives me the creeps. Will you buddy up with me when we go for lunch? Strength in numbers and all of that?"

Emily nodded. "Yeah, that sounds like a good idea."

She'd already been instructed by Nicole to not go anywhere without telling security and to certainly never go anywhere alone. She looked up and watched as people streamed towards the exits at the back of the auditorium.

Somewhere in the room was her stalker. She just hoped whoever it was would heed Nicole's warning and back off. She caught Carl's eye, and he offered her a tight smile. She swallowed before turning away and making her way backstage to talk to Nicole.

CHAPTER TWENTY-EIGHT

Olivia sat at her desk with her phone in her hand. She turned the device over and over in her palm, deep in thought.

She looked at her laptop screen. The booking page of a flight to London looked back at her. Being alone in the house for a couple of hours had sent her spiralling into a panic. She'd pictured some Gothic, shadowy figure in the wings of the theatre, watching Emily. She cursed Nicole for ever taking her to see *Phantom of the Opera*.

Now she was in a deadlock between her terror of flying again and her dread of something terrible happening to Emily.

She unlocked her phone, scrolled through her recent contacts, and quickly made a call. Holding the phone to her ear, she waited.

"Hi, boss," Simon answered.

Olivia smiled. No matter how many times she asked him to no longer refer to her as boss, he persisted. For once, though, she was going to give him an order, so boss seemed appropriate.

"I need you to keep an eye on Emily," she said without preamble.

"She already has a stalker problem," he replied.

Emily had told Olivia that she had sworn Simon and Sophie to secrecy on pain of death. So Olivia had called him over the weekend to advise him that she knew of the situation and to offer her eternal gratitude to him for caring for her.

She stood and started to pace. "You know what I mean. You're not a stalker, you're a friendly face. Someone I trust."

"You trust Nicole. And the extra security. And the police. I'm not sure what good I'd be…Ah. I see." Simon chuckled. "You're banned from calling them anymore, aren't you?"

Olivia bristled at how quickly Simon had come to the correct conclusion.

"No," she lied. "I've…decided to limit my contact."

"Uh-huh."

"And I'd feel much better if you were there." Olivia aimed for sweet talking.

"Well, I have a business to run, remember? And I'm not in the same part of town. It's not like she's five minutes away."

Olivia paused in her pacing and pinched the bridge of her nose. She'd known that ordering Simon to the theatre wasn't going to be viable, but something had pushed her to try.

"I can't stop worrying," she said.

"I know," he said. "I'm concerned, too. But I remind myself that she is surrounded by people. She's smart, she won't do anything stupid, and she has Nicole watching out for her."

"But, this person—"

"Olivia," Simon stopped her from continuing. "Listen. I know you're worried, I get that. I'd be the same if it were Sophie. But the truth is that there is nothing you can do. You need to let the security officers and the police do their job. And you need to let Emily make her own decisions. This guy is causing a huge disruption for Emily and that must be making her feel awful. You need to make her feel better. That's your job. Keeping her safe, that's the security officer's job."

Olivia leaned against the window frame and looked out at the garden. She hadn't considered that before. As a wife, she had responsibilities.

Just like at work. She had tasks she had to complete, some of those were obvious and some of them were not quite so.

She remembered the dreaded annual staff evaluations. The computerised system produced several charts showing if people had met their objectives and asked Olivia to rank them on many criteria that she felt ill-equipped to distinguish. Working well with others, problem-solving skills, social skills, communicating with senior staff. It all seemed like such a mess of questions, and she often ended up leaving Simon to fill in most of the details.

Now the whole thing was starting to make a little more sense. The ability to produce a flawless set of tax returns wasn't the only task that she expected her taxation manager to be able to complete. There was a complicated web of interpersonal skills and tasks that went hand in hand with the job.

She wondered how she had missed out on such an obvious thing during her years of management. It was only now hitting her in the face as a wife and mother. She needed to view the things she did as tasks and objectives and evaluate herself. If she was failing in an area, she needed to figure out a way to improve.

"Olivia?" Simon asked at the long silence.

"You're right," she said. "It is my job to make her feel better. And I've probably been making her feel worse. She not only has the worry of the situation, but she has to worry about my own fear."

"Exactly. Honesty is really important, but sometimes it's important to be strong for your partner, even if you don't feel it."

"You're right," she repeated.

"When is she home this week?"

"Friday evening."

"That's not long, it's Wednesday already."

"I just don't like her not being here," Olivia said. "I know it's necessary. But I don't like it."

"Mm," Simon said noncommittally.

"What?" Olivia asked.

"Nothing. You'll figure it out."

Olivia frowned. She wasn't sure if he meant that she'd figure out a solution, or if she'd figure out what he was discreetly referring to.

"I have to go," he said. "I have a telephone conference to prepare for."

She decided she would have to figure it out, whatever it was.

"Okay, thank you for the pep talk," she said. "It feels like old times."

"It does," he said. "I miss them."

"So do I," she said.

They said goodbye.

Olivia walked over to her desk and put her phone in the giraffe-shaped holder that Henry had got her for her birthday. At least, Emily said that it was Henry's idea. Olivia was fairly sure that it was Emily's idea of a joke, but the joke was on her. The giraffe's arms held the device perfectly.

Chapter Twenty-nine

So, this is where you and Olivia used to have lunch?" Emily asked Nicole as two waiters pulled out their chairs and invited them to sit down.

"Yes, more Olivia's style than mine, I do admit." Nicole sat down. "But it is delightfully out of the way of the theatre. We can talk freely here."

Emily looked at the array of cutlery and glassware on the thick cloth-covered table in front of them. It was very Olivia, all the luxuries that she assumed she wanted but didn't actually enjoy.

"I take it that there haven't been any further incidents?" Nicole asked as she picked up the linen napkin and placed it on her lap.

Emily repeated the move and shook her head. "No, nothing. Part of me is relieved, but part of me is waiting for the other shoe to drop."

"I don't blame you. It would be nice to think that it's all over with, but until we can identify who it was and speak directly to them, I won't feel comfortable."

"Neither will I," Emily said. "Just because nothing has happened this week doesn't make me feel any safer. And I feel so bad about putting you out."

Nicole waved away her concerns. "You're not putting anyone out."

"I'm staying in your apartment," Emily said.

"I love company."

"You hate company," Emily countered. "Remember that your best friend is my wife."

"Well, that's true. But I like having you staying over. You haven't mocked my Netflix list, you like cooking shows, and you clean before the cleaning lady comes…which is adorable, by the way."

"I spilled toothpaste on the sink," Emily said for the third time.

"Adorable," Nicole repeated with a grin. "But seriously, I like having you stay with me. I'm not doing it because I feel I must, or because Olivia will garrotte me if I don't. I'm doing it because I am responsible for you, and you don't seem to be safe at the two hotels we've picked so far. If I really didn't want you to stay with me, then I would have shipped you off to a private apartment with a chap from security to watch over you."

Emily looked at her and could see the truth in her eyes. It didn't stop her feeling guilty about putting Nicole out and the extra cost to the theatre company.

"Good afternoon," the tuxedoed waiter approached their table and addressed them. "Would you like to see the wine menu?"

"Yes, please," Nicole said.

"Just water for me," Emily replied.

Nicole looked at her. "Actually, you'll want a glass of wine with lunch." She turned to the waiter. "We'll have the Château Pesquié, please."

He nodded, took the menu back, and turned away to fetch the bottle. Emily furrowed her brow and looked at Nicole with concern.

"Why am I day drinking?" she asked. She'd had to cancel lunch with Hannah once Nicole had asked to speak to her. Hannah's disappointed reaction had made her feel guilty and now she was certain that she was about to feel much worse.

"It's nothing terrible," Nicole said. "But it is something I need to make you aware of, something we need to discuss."

"You're not reassuring me."

"When we first talked about you coming to work for us, we agreed to employ you as a writer to help you see how things work, so you have more experience of the industry."

Emily could feel the room heating up and started to panic. "Am I fired?"

Nicole blinked in surprise. "I literally just said it's nothing terrible."

"Yes, but am I?"

"No," Nicole said quickly. "No. Your work is exceptional. People are very happy with what you're doing. This isn't about that, it's about the future."

Emily felt just as confused.

The waiter returned and presented the bottle. After uncorking and pouring a tasting glass for Nicole's approval, he poured two full glasses, then placed the bottle into an ice bucket beside the table.

"We'll need a few minutes before we order, but some bread would be wonderful," Nicole said.

The waiter nodded politely and left the table again.

"Next week, we have opening night. By the next week, we won't require two members of writing staff on this project," Nicole explained. "And I know that we have discussed getting you work in New York, but that is seeming to be a very difficult task at the moment. There just aren't any jobs around that would suit you. As you know, it's a hugely competitive market."

Emily took a sip of wine. She had expected this conversation. Becoming a scriptwriter had been her dream, having it become a reality was incredible. Of course, logistics would make it impossible. No one was lucky enough to have everything fall into their lap so easily.

"I've spoken with some companies in London, and there are a few opportunities for you here. However, we've been supporting you with air travel costs because you have a rights interest in this play. Once you move on from this project, that will cease."

"So, there are no jobs in New York for me," Emily said. "There are jobs for me in London, but they won't cover the cost of my travel from New York."

"Exactly."

Emily took another sip. When Nicole had first come to her with the proposition of taking a royalty cut on the rights to her play in order to get free travel back and forth from New York to London, it had been like a fairy godmother had waved a magic wand.

Her play was going to be in a West End theatre, she was going to commute back and forth and be involved in its production, and she was going to have the opportunity to learn the ropes with professionals.

Of course, it couldn't last.

"So, a decision needs to be made," Nicole continued. "And I know it's not an easy one. Really I do."

"I could continue to write from home?" Emily said. "And then sell those completed scripts."

"You could," Nicole said. "But we can't guarantee that they would sell. We were lucky that your previous scripts were snapped up. That could happen again. But it might not. Theatres are making less and less profit, and therefore they are less willing to take risks. We don't even know if what we're working on now will turn a profit. Advanced sales are okay, but nothing sensational."

Emily sipped more wine, glad that Nicole had taken the decision to order a bottle. It seemed like she'd need it.

"It's not all doom and gloom," Nicole said. "You do have options, and I think it would be a terrible shame to throw away these opportunities."

"But I can't afford to commute, not on a writer's salary," Emily said. "And I can't move. I'd be taking Henry away from all his friends. And Olivia won't board a plane."

"I know this seems bleak," Nicole said softly. "But you are a great writer and you're an asset to the business. If we have a production that we could put you in, we would. But there's nothing at the moment, and I can't guarantee when the next project will be. And, even if I could, the travel would be an issue."

The waiter placed a bread basket on the table. Emily quickly reached for a wholemeal roll and broke it apart.

She felt crushed. Even though she always knew that the opportunity was a temporary one, she had expected to be able to move on to other things.

She was learning so much, and she'd barely had time to scratch the surface. She literally had the much-talked-about theatre bug. She couldn't imagine not seeing the words she'd written at three a.m., at her desk, on the subway, acted out in front of a crowd. Watching the actors and then delivering slight tweaks to dialogue that she knew would improve the performance.

"I know that Olivia would happily use her nest egg to fund your travel," Nicole suggested tentatively.

Emily snapped her head up to make eye contact with her.

Nicole held up a hand. "I know you want to be independent. I know you don't want to rely on Olivia's money."

"I want to pay her back for what she has already spent," Emily said. "I don't want to add to the debt."

Nicole picked up a breadstick and snapped a piece off the end. "It's just a suggestion. I know you don't want to feel beholden to Olivia. But if you want to continue in the theatre, then it may be your only option."

She chewed on the piece of breadstick, and Emily looked down at the mangled roll in front of her. She dusted the breadcrumbs into the palm of her hand to return the tablecloth to its pristine condition.

"Do you think there is any chance that I could make a living writing and selling scripts?" Emily asked.

Nicole let out a sigh. "Maybe. It's a hard thing to judge. Most people can't. Some people can. Such is the creative world."

"Well..." Emily raised her wine glass. "It's been a great adventure, but I think that once this project is over, I need to go back to my family."

Nicole looked at her sadly but raised her own glass. "I will continue to look for things, I'll be your agent as long as you want me to be. I really wish things had worked out another way. It's just bad timing."

"I'd love you to continue to be my agent," Emily said. "And I'm so glad that I got to experience what I did. I've learned so much, and I'm really grateful for the opportunities I've had. It's more than I ever could have dreamed of."

They clinked glasses and sipped some wine.

Emily lowered her glass to the table and chuckled.

"What is it?" Nicole asked.

"I was just thinking, I don't need to worry about my stalker so much now," Emily said. "A few more days and I'll be back in New York. And Olivia will be ecstatic as well. Not that she'd ever admit that she didn't want me to commute, but I know she misses me. And I miss her. Maybe this will be for the best."

"No, it's not," Nicole said with a pout. "Because I'll miss you."

Emily reached a hand across the table and took Nicole's. "I'll miss you, too."

Nicole squeezed her hand and then retracted her own. She took a deep breath and picked up the menu.

"Let's eat, before I get all emotional."

Emily smiled and picked up her own menu. She stared at the words on the page, but none of them made sense. Her mind was spinning. She had no idea what she'd say when she saw Olivia the next evening. She felt like a failure. They had moved everything to give Emily the best shot at a new career, at an amazing opportunity. But now that chance had effectively disappeared.

She felt like she'd been fired from her dream job.

CHAPTER THIRTY

Emily walked up the path with her suitcase in tow. She was exhausted, and the only thing keeping her awake was the knowledge that she'd soon see her family.

She hoped that this time Olivia wouldn't be entertaining a random woman, oblivious to the fact that said woman was madly flirting with her.

She had to smile, despite the potential seriousness of the situation.

It had been a long and trying week. The meeting with the police, constantly looking over her shoulder to see if anyone was following her, and then yesterday finding out that her career was effectively over.

Of course, she'd not told Olivia any of that on the phone. She'd kept things as light as she could. But inside she was desperately in need of the comfort of her family.

Landing at the airport, she had quickly regretted her decision to get a taxi home at the end of every week. She knew it was in Olivia's and Henry's best interests, but now the delay of being in the arms of the woman she loved seemed unreasonable.

As she approached the front door she waited for it to fly open. Except...it didn't. The lights were on, so she knew they were definitely home. She reached into her handbag and dug around for her house keys that lay at the bottom, having been unused for a week. She pulled them out and unlocked the door.

"Hello?" she called out as she pulled her suitcase into the hallway.

She could hear the sound of people talking, but no one replied to her greeting. She slammed the door closed and shrugged out of her jacket. While she didn't want Olivia to make a fuss of her return by dragging Henry to the airport, a hello would be nice.

"Mommy!" Henry ran around the corner and collided with her legs.

At least someone noticed, she thought to herself.

"Aidan is here," Henry said and started to pull her hand.

She reached out to put her jacket on the hook. "Aidan?"

Henry dragged her across the living area and into the dining room. When she looked in the room, her heart melted.

At the table sat an adorable blond-haired boy with thick spectacles. Next to him was Olivia. They were both focused on a sheet of paper on the table.

"So, if I gave you another two lollipops, how many lollipops would you have?" Olivia asked softly.

Aidan shrugged and looked up at Olivia helplessly.

"Let's count them together, okay?"

Emily gently pulled Henry out of the dining room and walked him into the kitchen. For some reason, Olivia was in the middle of a math lesson with an unidentified child. It was certainly a step up from the last time she came home, but still a confusing scene to walk into.

"Was that Aidan?" Emily asked as she pulled a tray down from atop the kitchen cabinets.

"Yep. He's my best friend," Henry replied. He looked at Emily with confusion. "Are we having hot chocolate?"

"Absolutely," Emily said. "And wow, Aidan is your best friend?"

Henry hadn't mentioned Aidan once, and just last week he had told her that a girl called Alice was his best friend. Clearly things moved fast in the hurly-burly world of first grade.

"Yep. And I'm his best friend," Henry explained.

Emily pulled some cups out of the cupboard. She was happy that Henry was making friends, even if she'd never heard of Aidan before.

"And what are Olivia and Aidan doing?"

"Playing math," Henry said with distaste.

Olivia had often tried to convince Henry that mathematics was a game, not realising that adding the word "playing" to the word "math" wouldn't be enough to make it a fun game.

Henry was happy to have lessons and learn about math for short periods at a time that ended with a suitable prize. But he wasn't convinced that math was something that could be played.

Clearly, Aidan hadn't caught on to Olivia's scheme yet.

"Aidan hates math. He's really, really bad at it. He cried when we had math class today."

"Did Aidan come over for dinner?" Emily asked, keen to clarify that Olivia had permission to have the bespectacled cutie in their house.

"Yes. We played in the yard, and we did some painting."

"And Aidan asked his mommy, right?" Emily said.

"Yep. His daddy is coming to get him soon."

Emily let out a sigh of relief. While she didn't really expect Olivia to have kidnapped the boy, she'd not wager money on it.

"Captain McFluffypants the Seventh peed in the sink," Henry said with some pride.

"Which sink?" Emily asked. She eyed the kitchen sink and shuddered.

"Today?" Henry asked.

Emily shuddered again and decided that the next day she'd give the house a deep clean.

Emily walked into the dining room with mugs filled with hot chocolate on a tray. As she lowered it to the table, Olivia looked up in surprise.

She watched in amusement as Olivia looked from her to the clock on the wall to the hot chocolate and back to Emily again with confusion.

"You're home." Olivia walked around the table to embrace Emily.

"I am," she replied. "You were caught up in your lesson with *Aidan*." She emphasised the boy's name, hoping that Olivia would elaborate on the boy's presence.

"I told you I had two mommies," Henry said proudly.

Olivia took a step back. "Aidan, this is my wife, Emily."

"Hi, Mrs. White," he replied, complete with lisp.

"Hi, Aidan." Emily smiled. Aidan was adorable. She turned to Olivia. "Does Aidan have any allergies…or parents?" she muttered under her breath.

Olivia picked up a piece of paper from the table and handed it to Emily. She looked at it and bit her lip to hold back a chuckle. Olivia's neat script detailed what appeared to be Aidan's full medical history, a set of emergency phone numbers, names and addresses, and his doctor's details.

"The rest is on the back," Olivia said.

Emily felt her eyes bulge and quickly glanced at the back of the piece of paper to see another full sheet of information. At this point, Olivia probably knew more about Aidan than Aidan did. She quickly checked the allergies.

"Aidan, would you like some hot chocolate?"

He swiftly nodded.

"My mommy makes the best hot chocolate in the world," Henry said.

Emily handed each of them a small mug.

"Thank you, Mrs. White," Aidan said. He held the mug with both hands, and Emily realised how small the boy was. Clearly, he hadn't had a growth spurt yet.

Olivia reached for a mug of hot chocolate, but Emily quickly grabbed her hand and tugged at her.

"Boys, we just need to clean up the kitchen. We'll be back in a moment."

Emily kept hold of Olivia's hand and pulled her towards the kitchen.

As soon as they got into the room, Olivia started to look around in confusion.

"The kitchen looks clean to m—"

Emily pressed Olivia back against the wall and kissed her deeply. Her temple rubbed against Olivia's glasses, the ones she had started to wear more upon realising how it drove Emily wild with desire.

"I thought you'd forgotten about me," Emily teased her. "But then you were there helping the most adorable boy—don't tell Henry I said that—and it made my heart melt."

"I didn't hear you come in," Olivia said apologetically. "Aidan seems to be scared of numbers. He shuts down, so I tried to make it more enjoyable for him, to show him that he could do it. We had just—"

Emily put her finger on Olivia's lips to silence her. "Later."

She removed her finger and replaced it with her lips. Olivia got the message and returned the kiss. A few moments passed, and Olivia ratcheted up the intensity.

"I've missed you," she breathed as she started to plant kisses down Emily's neck.

The kitchen door flew open, and they sprang apart.

"But Ironman is the best," Henry explained to Aidan as they entered the kitchen. "Superman is okay, but his outfit is silly."

"Superman can melt stuff with his eyeballs," Aidan argued.

Both boys placed their mugs on the counter, ignoring Emily and Olivia as they continued their debate about favourite superheroes.

The doorbell sounded, and Olivia quickly excused herself from the potentially awkward situation.

"I'll get it," Olivia said, already half out of the door.

"That's probably my daddy," Aidan said sadly.

"You can come back another day," Henry said.

"As long as it's okay with Aidan's parents," Emily added. She mentally filed away a note to talk to Henry about asking for permission before making promises. "Aidan, did you bring anything with you?"

"My bag," Aidan said.

"It's in my room," Henry said.

She hurried the two boys out of the kitchen and watched them climb the stairs. She could hear Olivia having a conversation with a man.

"He's been no trouble at all," Olivia said.

"Great, maybe you and your husband could come over at some point?"

"Oh, I don't have a husband," Olivia said.

"Well, then maybe you can come over at some point?"

Emily frowned. She didn't like the change in the man's tone. She knew that Olivia wouldn't pick up on it, and before long, would be committed to visiting Aidan's parents and presumably being ogled at by his father. She quickly walked into the hallway.

"Aidan's getting his bag," she said. "I'm Henry's other mother, Emily."

She held out her hand and smirked as he stumbled to quickly shake it.

"Oh, right, um…M-mike."

"Nice to meet you, Mike." Emily held onto his hand a moment longer than necessary, gripping it tightly.

Aidan rushed into the hallway. "Can I come again soon, Daddy?"

Mike retracted his hand and smiled at his son. "Sure, we'll talk to Henry's mommy…ies and arrange something."

"Absolutely. We'd love to have Aidan over again," Emily said while engaging in a staring contest with Mike.

After some farewells, Mike and Aidan left and Emily closed the door behind them. She wasn't happy with the way Mike continued to look at Olivia. While she would agree that Olivia was stunning, that was no way to behave. Especially not in front of her wife and two impressionable young boys.

"He seemed nice," Olivia said before turning away.

Emily felt herself seethe. She took a deep breath to calm down, reminding herself that Olivia wasn't the best at picking up on signals.

"Henry, could you make sure your room is tidy before bed?" Emily asked.

Henry, unlike Olivia, could detect the change in atmosphere and hurried off to clean his room.

Emily followed Olivia into the kitchen.

"Wine?" Olivia asked.

"Please."

Olivia pulled out a bottle of white from the fridge and picked up two glasses from the shelf.

"Mike was staring at you," Emily said as she sat on the stool at the breakfast bar.

Olivia reached for her hair to search out a stray lock that she thought was out of place, clearly the reason for any staring.

"Because he thought you were hot," Emily clarified.

Olivia blushed and lowered her hand. "You're being silly."

"I'm not. I just want you to know because he continued staring at you in front of the boys, even after I gave him the stink eye. Just…file it away in your brain for now."

Olivia poured wine into both glasses silently, considering the information she had been given.

"I'll be distant with him," she said as she handed Emily a glass.

Emily nodded gratefully and took a sip of the cold liquid. "So, if you had three lollipops and I gave you another three lollipops, how many lollipops would you have?"

"Six." Olivia frowned. "Obviously."

Emily chuckled. "I'm joking, Olivia. It was cute, seeing you teaching Aidan. For someone who used to be so scared of children, you're doing pretty well."

"Aidan is a sweet boy. Henry told me he cried when he realised he had a math lesson, I wanted to help him."

Olivia leaned backwards onto the work surface and swirled her wine glass in front of her as she thought.

"I enjoyed it," she admitted. "I still find children frightening, though."

"Everyone does," Emily said. "You get used to them."

"I think I will," Olivia said. "It had me looking forward to volunteering. If I can spend time with groups of children, then maybe I can make a difference? Maybe in twenty years I won't have to correct people when they hand me change in a shop."

"I don't think you're going to singlehandedly reverse this country's math literacy issues, but it's a start," Emily said.

She took a deep breath and looked at Olivia. It was time. She had to tell her, no matter how much she wanted to bottle it up and pretend it wasn't happening.

"Maybe you could help me with a math problem," Emily suggested.

"Of course," Olivia replied with a frown.

"If I had three lollipops and then I had no lollipops, how many lollipops would I have?" Emily knew it was a cop-out, but she didn't know what else to say.

"None," Olivia said. "Who is taking your lollipops?"

"Nicole. Well, not exactly, but she told me that my lollipops are going away."

"Going away? Nicole?" Olivia put the wine glass on the countertop. "I don't understand what you're saying."

"There's no more work for me," Emily said sadly.

Olivia continued to look confused.

"Lollipop was code for work. I'm sorry, I should have just said it outright, but it's really hard." She took a deep breath and sat a little higher on the kitchen stool. "I had lunch with Nicole yesterday, and she told me that there are no projects at her company. And she's asked around and there is nothing in New York. So, that's that."

Olivia blinked. "But…you…you love your job."

"I do. I did. It's just…it's not working out. Theatre isn't making as much as it used to, and people are being more conservative with money. Fewer productions means fewer people, more competition. And I'm the new kid on the block."

She picked up the wine glass and took a gulp.

"Really, I'm lucky," Emily said. "I had the chance to work in my dream profession. I saw behind the curtain, literally. I've learned a lot. But it couldn't go on forever."

Olivia continued to stare at her, clearly unsure what to say.

"It's okay, you can be happy. I'm sure you're happy." Emily chuckled. "Not spending so much time away from you and Henry will be really nice."

"But you'll miss it," Olivia said. "Of course, I'm ecstatic for you to be home. But I want you to be happy, and if that means only seeing you for a few hours every weekend, then that's fine."

"Well, it's all irrelevant now." Emily threw back the last gulp of wine. "It's done. I can officially say that I worked on a theatre production and that a version of one of my plays showed in the West End of London. Who else can say that?"

"Not many people," Olivia admitted. She still looked at Emily with something akin to pity.

"Smile, Olivia," Emily said. "I'll be home. I don't know what I'll be doing, but I'll be home."

Olivia tried to smile but failed. "I'm sorry, it's a little bit of a shock."

"Same," Emily said. "I always knew that this was temporary, but I just assumed that I'd work on more projects with Nicole. I assumed I'd be doing this for a few months, not a few weeks. But, that's one of the many things I learned. The theatre moves fast."

"And there are no jobs in New York? Or in other London theatres?" Olivia asked.

Emily shook her head. "I had a long chat with Nicole. She gave me a list of everyone she spoke to and told me about some potential people to approach, but she didn't seem very hopeful. The chance of a paid position is pretty much non-existent."

"Then volunteer, like me," Olivia suggested.

Emily bit the inside of her cheek hard. She was emotional, and she didn't want to lash out at Olivia. Technically, it was a very generous offer and one that came from a place of love. But Emily needed to make her own way and she needed Olivia to understand that.

"I need to earn money," Emily said softly.

Olivia looked like she wanted to argue but wisely stopped herself.

"It's for the best," Emily said. "I won't have to travel. Henry won't grow an inch every time I see him."

"Mommy, look," Henry called out as he barged into the kitchen like a streak of lightning.

He had a piece of paper in his hand and slapped it into Emily's stomach.

"For you," he said.

Emily looked at the drawing. "Wow, you're getting so good. Do you want to talk me through this?"

"Yep," Henry said readily.

Emily angled the drawing so he could reach to point.

"You, me, Olivia, Captain McFluffypants the Seventh, Tiny, and Miss Costa."

Emily smirked and looked up at Olivia. "It looks like Miss Costa lives with us in this big house you've drawn?"

"She does," Henry said.

Olivia looked panicked and opened her mouth to defend herself.

"But, Miss Costa doesn't live here," Emily told Henry. "She just came over for dinner that one time, remember?"

"Yeah," Henry said. He squished up his face as he looked at the drawing.

"Maybe this building isn't a house at all. Maybe it's a school?" Emily said. "And we're taking Captain McFluffypants to see your classroom?"

"Yes, that's it!" Henry said, pleased with the solution.

"I thought so," Emily said. "Maybe you should draw a whiteboard and a playground so everyone knows that it's a school?"

"But that will have to wait until tomorrow. It's time to get ready for bed now," Olivia interrupted.

Emily looked up at the clock on the wall and sighed. Time moved so quickly, she barely felt like she had any time to see Henry. But at least that would change soon.

CHAPTER THIRTY-ONE

Emily carried the tray of drinks out to the patio table. Irene quickly stood up and helped her to place the glasses and jugs onto the table. She thanked her, and the women started to pour drinks.

Emily looked up towards Olivia and Tom who were walking around the vegetable garden, deep in conversation. She decided to leave them to it.

"And then McFluffypants wouldn't come down," Henry told Lucy.

"Wow, what did Olivia do?" Lucy asked.

Henry, who was in Lucy's lap, turned to face her. "She got a broom and she tried to push him from the top of the bookshelf. But he just jumped over the brush."

"This cat of yours sounds like a hassle," Irene told him with a smile. "Maybe you should send him back and get a goldfish instead?"

"Nah." Henry shook his head. "I'm going to go and play with him, in case he's lonely. Because he isn't allowed outside with us."

Emily watched him slide from Lucy's lap and pick up his drink.

"Make sure you keep the door closed," Emily said. "You don't want him running off."

"I will," Henry called behind him as he walked back into the house.

Emily flopped onto a chair. "That cat is the devil."

Lucy and Irene laughed.

"Surely he can't be that bad?" Lucy asked.

Emily held up her hand to show some deep scratch marks.

"What did you do?" Irene asked.

"Me? It was him!" Emily said. "I was just minding my own business when he came flying out of nowhere and launched himself at me."

"He can probably detect that you're scared," Lucy said. "Like dogs do."

"At least you only see him on weekends," Irene chuckled.

"Yeah, well…" Emily took a deep breath. "I'm not going to be working in London for much longer."

Lucy frowned, and Irene's mouth formed an O.

"Why's that?" Lucy asked.

"There are no new jobs in London, and the project I'm working on is nearly finished. It was always going to be temporary. I had hoped to move on to something else, but it's just bad timing. Still, I get to be home more with Henry, Olivia, and the devil cat."

Irene picked up her glass of juice and took a sip. Emily respected that Irene knew when silence was appropriate. Irene wasn't one to sugar-coat things, remaining quiet rather than blurting out platitudes.

"It's for the best, I'm sure," Lucy said.

Lucy was the opposite to Irene. Lucy would search high and low for the bright side, the silver lining in any piece of potentially disastrous news.

"You'll find something else, and, in the meantime, you can spend more time with Olivia," Lucy said. "And Olivia did mention that you're both on the path to getting her pregnant now."

Irene looked up with interest.

"We are. Olivia's been racing along. She's been cleared by the doctor, and now we're choosing a sperm donor. In fact, that's our plan for this evening. Never did I think I'd spend an evening looking at profiles of men who I think would be a good fit to impregnate my wife!"

"It's a different sort of evening in," Lucy said.

"How many do you have to choose from?" Irene asked.

"Olivia's already streamlined the list down to five."

"Has she done a pros and cons list?" Lucy chuckled.

"Oh yes, of course!" Emily laughed.

"She'll be pregnant before you know it, and then you'll forget all about working for a while. You'll be too busy looking after Olivia and then a new baby." Lucy clapped her hands together. "Oh, it's so exciting! And if you ever need a babysitter, you know where I am."

"Yes, you're right in line behind the grandmother," Irene said with a grin.

"No arguing over who gets to babysit." Emily laughed. "At least not until we know we're having a baby."

"Everything will work out; things have a way of doing that," Irene said. "The work thing will seem like a blessing in disguise soon, I'm sure."

"I just can't get my carrots to grow properly. They're skinny and weird looking," Tom complained.

"Carrots are challenging," Olivia said. "People think because they are so common that they must be easy to grow, but they are very fussy. Try the soil I told you about, it might help. And I'm serious about knowing the temperature of the soil."

"I'll get the thermometer," he said.

Olivia walked over to the tomato plants and picked a couple of weeds out that had sprouted near them.

"It's a shame about Emily," Tom said conversationally.

"It is," Olivia said. She wasn't sure what was a shame, but she knew that Tom would elaborate soon enough.

"She loves writing. And working in the theatre, it must have been a dream come true."

"It was."

Tom leaned on the shovel that was wedged into the ground beside the celery.

"Can you imagine having a dream job and then having it taken away? That would be hard."

Olivia could imagine. She loved her job until Marcus took it away.

"It's like if someone told me I couldn't fly anymore. Not being able to pilot a plane would be crushing." Tom tutted and shook his head. "Still, bad timing, I suppose. I know Em. She'll put a brave face on this, but it's probably destroying her on the inside."

Olivia didn't understand Tom's need for dramatics. He always seemed to overreach a point. It was a trait she also saw in Lucy, so suspected that was the cause. The two played off one another.

"I don't know about destroying her," Olivia said.

"Brave face," Tom said.

Olivia looked over to the patio table where Emily, Lucy, and Irene were all laughing about something.

"Very brave," Olivia mused. "She's probably relieved to be honest."

"Why relieved?"

"While no longer working in the theatre has definitely been a blow, at least she no longer has to worry about the stalker."

Tom frowned in confusion. "How so?"

"She won't be in London, so…no stalker," Olivia said.

"Maybe so, but that won't suddenly go away," Tom said. "In fact, if it's not properly resolved…will it ever go away?"

Olivia looked down at the tomato plants, lost in thought. Tom was right. Emily may put a brave face on things, but Olivia knew that the whole stalker business terrified her. Even when she was at home, she was different. Every noise, every curtain twitch had Emily grabbing Olivia's arm in panic. She tried to claim that it was just nerves, but Olivia had noticed a change. Would that change go away if the identity of the stalker was never revealed?

"And the stalker won't be happy to hear that Emily's leaving," Tom added.

Olivia snapped her head up to stare at him. "What do you mean?"

"N-nothing," Tom stammered.

Olivia knew exactly what he meant. Worse, she agreed with him. It hadn't occurred to her before now. How would Emily ever get over the fear of being stalked without finding out who the stalker was? It was all well and good saying that it was over, but was it?

She angrily ripped another weed out of the ground.

CHAPTER THIRTY-TWO

Emily heard Olivia arriving in the living room before she saw her. Which was strange, as Olivia was usually very graceful and calm. But as Emily looked up to see Olivia's face, she realised she was anything but calm.

"What's wrong?"

"The cat's a murderer," Olivia said.

Emily put down her book and edged backwards. "It's not a mouse, is it?"

"Worse." Olivia looked around to ensure they were alone before producing Tiny from behind her back.

Well, it had been Tiny at one point. Now, the weathered giraffe cuddly toy was ripped to shreds, his eye hanging loosely on a piece of stuffing that hung from his gouged socket.

"Captain McFluffypants has killed Tiny the Giraffe," Olivia said seriously. She took a breath as she realised what she had said. "And my life has become a farce."

Emily walked over to the bottom of the stairs and looked at Tiny's lifeless form.

"It's beyond repair," Olivia said. "That cat is a menace."

"He is," Emily said. "But Henry loves him."

"Henry also loves Tiny. What's he going to say when we tell him that one of his great loves has disembowelled his other great love?"

"He'll ask what 'disembowelled' means, and you won't be explaining that one," Emily said.

An unfortunately timed news article had caused Henry to ask Olivia what waterboarding was. Just an hour later and one of Emily's old Barbie dolls was taped to a ruler and being introduced to the toilet headfirst.

"He showed an interest in the news," Olivia argued.

Emily let out a sigh. "Can we just agree to not discuss methods of torture with our son until he is at least ten? And then both of us will be present?"

"Fine. What do we do about Tiny? How do we tell Henry?" Olivia asked.

Emily bit her lip and took a step back. She'd hoped that she wouldn't have to do this. Yes, Olivia was an adult, but she was also woefully bad at keeping secrets. And now Emily was in a situation where she was going to have to trust Olivia by showing her the inner workings of the most well-guarded magic trick in existence.

"Where's Henry?" Emily asked.

"Colouring in his room. I managed to take Tiny before he noticed."

Emily took hold of the stuffed animal's broken form. She looked Olivia in the eye.

"I'm going to tell Henry that I've taken Tiny to be washed. It happens every now and then, so he won't be suspicious. Don't say anything. I'll meet you in the bedroom after Henry's gone to bed."

Olivia nodded. "But—"

"No buts," Emily said. "Operation Save Tiny is a go."

Olivia closed Henry's bedroom door and let out a relieved breath. He hadn't asked once about Tiny, satisfied with Emily's explanation that Tiny was in the washing machine and, yes, had been provided with the customary scuba gear.

She had no idea how they were going to break the news to him the next day. Olivia surmised that some kind of washing machine accident would be held responsible for the mangled toy. Henry would be heartbroken, so Olivia had been planning a week of activities that would help to cheer him up.

"Psst."

She turned around. Emily stood in the doorway to their bedroom, gesturing for Olivia to follow her.

"Is he asleep?" Emily whispered.

"He is. What are you doing?"

"What are *we* doing," Emily said.

She pulled Olivia into the bedroom and closed and locked the door behind them. All the lights were on, and in the centre of the bed, like the star of a horror movie, was Tiny. Olivia cursed herself for finding the only murderous kitten in New York. She'd seen videos online of kittens doing all kinds of adorable things. And yet, she had managed to pick out a monster who was content to rip things up and shit in inappropriate places. She'd still not told Emily about the faeces in the bathtub.

"Don't just stand there, help me," Emily said.

Olivia turned around. Emily was on top of the small set of steps, reaching into the back of the wardrobe's top shelf. She heaved a box from the very back and lowered it down towards Olivia's outstretched arms.

In a flash, Emily was down the ladder and had taken the box from Olivia's hands. She placed it on a chair and picked up a decorator's dust sheet and placed it on the floor in front of the bed.

Tiny was moved from his bed shrine and placed on the sheet. The box was placed beside him.

"Come, sit." Emily patted the space beside her.

Olivia sat down, confused but fascinated with whatever was happening.

Emily lifted the lid on the cardboard box.

Olivia gasped. "You…but…" she started.

"No one knows about this," Emily said seriously. "No one."

Emily pulled a cuddly toy giraffe out of the box. It was Tiny, but new and wrapped in cellophane.

Olivia sat up and looked into the box. It was stuffed full of new Tiny toys.

"We just saw the demise of Tiny Mark Seventeen," Emily said. "This one has lasted the longest. The first Tiny you ever saw was Mark Fifteen. You don't even want to know what happened to him."

Olivia gasped. "Y-you've replaced Tiny since we've been together?"

"Twice," Emily confirmed. She continued to unwrap the toy.

"And you never told me?"

"I didn't know if you could be trusted."

"We're married!" Olivia cried.

"Less talking, more fluffing," Emily thrust Tiny into Olivia's hands. "He needs to feel soft, pliable. Get fluffing."

"Fluffing?" Olivia held the new toy in shock.

"Fluffing. Bend him, punch him if you have to." Emily sealed the box and climbed back up the ladder to replace it.

"What happened to Sixteen?" Olivia asked as she squished the giraffe.

"Left in Lucy's garden and run over by a lawnmower. There wasn't much to work with that time, so I had to do most of it from memory."

Olivia winced at the mental image of Tiny being ripped through the blades.

"No, no, no," Emily said as she returned with another box. "You need to really go for it, this is a toy that has been around for years! He's soft. If you keep on like that you'll be at it all night."

"But he hasn't been around for years," Olivia said as Emily snatched the imposter away.

"But Henry needs to believe he has been." Emily put the new toy on the ground and started to walk on him. "Open the box."

Olivia tore her eyes away from her sweet, mature wife trampling a toy giraffe. She opened the new box that Emily had placed on the protective sheet and looked inside.

"What's all this?"

"Mud, grease, grass clippings, paint, scissors…"

A light-bulb moment occurred. "We're going to…"

"Re-create Tiny, yes." Emily picked the new toy up and walked over to the en suite. She placed the toy on the edge of the doorframe and then looked towards Olivia with a grimace. "You might want to look away."

Olivia turned away and heard the sound of cotton stuffing being smashed between the door and the frame. She shuddered.

"As you know," Emily said, "Tiny is a bit floppy in the neck."

"You disturb me," Olivia said.

Emily dropped the toy onto the sheet and sat next to Olivia.

"Yeah, yeah," Emily muttered. "Now, get the jar marked fake blood. Henry cut himself and there's a tiny drop of dried blood on Tiny's left ear."

Olivia dug out the jar and handed it over. She watched as Emily picked up a small paintbrush and started to drab the tiniest amount of fake blood onto the ear.

"Wouldn't all of this dirt have been washed away in the machine?" Olivia asked.

"Some of it, some of it is so ground-in that it stays. That's the real challenge, making it look like clean dirt and not just dirt. There's a science to this. I'll teach you."

She'd never much rated Emily's artistic skills, but, clearly, they were of an extraordinary level if they were on Tiny Mark Eighteen. She couldn't believe that Tiny had been replaced twice and she hadn't noticed.

"Does this mean I'm here to stay?" Olivia asked with a grin.

"Yep." Emily popped the word. "Or I'd have to kill you to protect my secret."

Olivia chuckled.

She picked up the battered Tiny and started to examine him.

"He's a little bald on his backside," Olivia said.

"There's a disposable razor in the box," Emily said.

Olivia searched through the questionable arts and crafts supplies and found the razor.

She watched Emily work with such care and precision. The entire production was born out of an incredible love and need to protect her son as much as she could. Olivia didn't think it was possible to love Emily any more. But here she sat, cross-legged on the floor of their bedroom, preparing to shave the butt of a toy giraffe.

CHAPTER THIRTY-THREE

Henry walked into Olivia's office with Tiny clutched under his arm. Emily had been gone for an hour, and Henry had already claimed his eternal boredom several times. Luckily, he was none the wiser about the imposter Tiny, or so it seemed. Olivia was on edge, waiting for him to quiz her about the toy.

"Bored," he said.

Olivia looked up from the bank statement she was checking. Henry was lying spread-eagled on the ground and staring up at the ceiling.

"I wish I was in London with Mommy," he sighed.

She glanced at her watch. "Mommy isn't in London yet. She's probably barely at the airport."

"I wish I was at the airport with Mommy," he said.

"Yes, well, you have school tomorrow." Olivia picked up her pen and returned her attention to the bank statement in front of her.

"Mommy is going on a plane."

"She is."

"Will I ever go on a plane again?"

Olivia kept her head down but glanced up at Henry. She'd tried to avoid this conversation, but Henry didn't look like he was going to be distracted.

"I'm sure you will," she said without making promises.

"You don't like planes anymore, do you?" Henry turned onto his front and rested his chin on his hands as he looked up at her.

She'd promised Emily that she wouldn't tell Henry the gruesome details of the plane crash. They didn't want him to be afraid of flying. But she couldn't lie to him. It wasn't in her nature.

"I don't," she said.

"Are you still scared?"

Olivia bit the inside of her cheek as she wondered about all of the ways the conversation could potentially backfire.

"Because I used to be scared of spiders," Henry continued. "But you taught me that they aren't scary."

Olivia lowered her pen and removed her glasses. She smiled at him as she remembered the day they had spent in the garden seeking out spiders.

"So, maybe I can help you not be scared of planes?" he suggested.

"Maybe," she said. "How do you think we could do that?"

Henry thought about it for a second. "We play airplane!" He jumped to his feet and ran around the desk to grab Olivia's hand. He pulled her to her feet and dragged her towards the dining room.

He let go of Olivia's hand and started to pull the dining chairs into the space beside the table. She helped him to straighten the chairs into four rows of two, similar to airline seats, as they had done the last time they played the game.

"Sit," Henry commanded, pointing to one of the chairs.

She considered reminding him of manners but decided to let him get away with it just this once.

She sat down and felt a familiar constricted feeling in her chest. It was the same jet of panic that rushed her whenever she thought about boarding a plane.

"You need to sit by the window," Henry said. He pointed to the chair next to the one she was on.

She shuffled over.

"Look out the window," he said.

She smiled to herself and turned to look out of the make-believe window. She noticed the carpet needed to be vacuumed.

"What do you see? And put your seat belt on."

She buckled the imaginary belt and peered out the non-existent window.

"Clouds."

Henry sighed. "We haven't taken off yet."

"It's a cloudy day," she amended.

Henry walked up to the front of the chairs and placed Tiny on the floor. He walked back down the rows and sat on the chair next to her and fastened his seat belt.

"Is Tiny the captain again?"

Henry nodded.

"Don't you want to be the captain?"

He took her hand. "No, silly. I need to hold your hand because you're frightened."

She looked at their joined hands and swallowed awkwardly.

Just like the last time they had played, she was taken back to the first time she saw Henry. He looked so small in the first-class seat across the aisle, clutching onto the giant armrests and looking fearful. And he had a lot to be fearful of, his first time on a plane, flying to another country for surgery.

Olivia had instantly wanted to soothe him, and Emily, too. Inviting the small boy over to sit with her, have dinner with her, was the first step in what had become her future.

Things had changed. Now she was the one frightened and Henry was here for her, holding her hand and animatedly chatting about everything and nothing to keep her composed.

She turned to look out the imaginary window. Henry kept chattering next to her, talking about a future business plan of his that involved crash helmets for bees. She tuned him out and imagined being in the air, clouds floating by and the sound of the engines whirring away in the background.

Flying had always been a pleasure. Especially flying first-class. While she wasn't an aviation buff, she had a fascination and a respect for the dynamics of flight. The crash had been horrific, but she was aware of the statistics enough to know that it was a rarity.

"Olivia?"

She turned to look at him.

"If we ever went back to London, I think I'd like to go to the zoo again."

Olivia licked her lips nervously. Sitting on some chairs in the dining room was very different from actually flying.

"We'll see," she said diplomatically.

CHAPTER THIRTY-FOUR

Emily walked up the spiral staircase to the top of the theatre. The auditorium was becoming too loud and hectic to work in. As fascinating as it was to see the inner workings of the theatre, she didn't need to hear the director screaming at the actors for hours at a time.

Hannah had told her about the old admin rooms at the top of the building. Behind a door marked "private" and up a few flights of concrete stairs, and, suddenly, it was like she was in another world. The rooms were painted white and had windows that overlooked the city. It was like being on a movie set, seeing all of London laid out before her.

Seamstresses busied themselves in a couple of the rooms, needing the natural light to see what they were doing. Another room contained an old piano, which had Emily wondering how on earth anyone had gotten it in there. At the end of the corridor were two rooms, one being used by a poor marketing intern who was stuffing envelopes, and the other for Emily's use.

At this late stage, the changes were few but frantic in their pace. The actors would run through one scene at a time while the production management team mulled over each sentence they spoke. If they required changes, Emily had only a couple of hours to make them.

Luckily, she was good at thinking on the spot and didn't buckle under pressure. She understood what people meant when they said there was a buzz to working in the theatre. The atmosphere was electric. Armies of people rushing around to bring together what seemed impossible. And yet there was an air of certainty that everything would be all right on opening night, even if it was held together by string behind the scenes. The illusion of the show was everything, the need for perfection in the eyes of the audience was essential.

She opened the door to her makeshift office and dropped her notepad and papers onto the small desk. She walked over to the window and looked out at the amazing view of London's West End.

"Hi, Emily."

She spun around and saw that Carl had entered the room. He must have been right behind her coming up the stairs. She wondered if he had followed her or if he had already been on his way to the room.

"Hey," she tried to sound casual.

"I have an extra ticket for the preview on Wednesday, I wondered if you wanted it?" Carl asked.

Everyone had been allocated four tickets for the preview. It was the day before the actual opening night with paying guests and a good way to run through with a real audience without running the risk of bad reviews if anything went wrong.

Emily had already returned two of her four tickets. The only people she knew in London other than Nicole were Simon and Sophie. Any unused tickets were to be given back to the box office to be handed out to people who had requested more. The chance to see a West End show for free was highly sought-after, and the list for extra tickets was known to be enormous.

"Thanks, but I already had to return two of mine," Emily said.

"Oh, yes." He gently smacked himself on the forehead. "Of course, you don't really have anyone, do you?"

Emily bristled. "Not in this country," she replied.

Carl winced. "Sorry, didn't mean that to sound bad."

"It's fine." Emily picked up her pen from the desk. "Thank you, but I don't need the tickets. Was there anything else? I need to get these changes done."

"Do you want some help?" Carl asked.

Carl was supposed to be working on a new production for the company. A fact that had caused Emily to breathe a huge sigh of relief. While he had helped her to learn the ropes, he was also uncomfortable to be around. More so now that Emily was convinced that he was the stalker.

"No, it's fine," Emily replied. "Just some last-minute things. Jonathan is being a diva again."

"Yeah, that's Jonathan for you. Be warned, he usually has a strop right before show time as well."

"Thanks for the warning," Emily said frostily. "I'll be fine."

"Sure? I don't mind helping." He edged forward, and the room suddenly felt a lot smaller.

Emily wondered if the marketing intern next door would hear her if she screamed. Or maybe Carl would back off if she did. Maybe if she told him that she knew it was him, told him that she'd report him to the police, he might leave.

"Ah, here you both are," Nicole said as she entered the room.

Emily felt relieved to have company

"I have a spare ticket for the preview," Carl explained. "I wanted to see if Emily wanted it, but she doesn't."

"I'll have it," Nicole said. "I was just speaking to Amy, and she needs another seat. Can you drop it into the production office?"

"Sure." Carl nodded and started to leave the room.

"Thanks, Carl, you're a darling," Nicole called after him.

Emily licked her lips. She wanted to say something, but it was clear that Nicole was fond of Carl. While she was sure that Carl was the stalker, she didn't have any evidence and she didn't want to rock the boat. Nicole was her agent, and Olivia's friend.

"Are you okay? You look like you've seen a ghost," Nicole said.

"Fine, just skipped lunch," Emily replied quickly.

Nicole didn't seem convinced, but luckily, she didn't seem to want to push the issue either. "I just wanted to check if you had received the paperwork for the dual taxation thing?"

Emily nodded. "Yep. Didn't understand a word of it," she said jokingly.

"No one does, darling. That's why accountants are filthy rich. The rest of us haven't got a clue what we're signing." Nicole smiled.

"The trick is to marry one." Emily chuckled.

"I'm trying!" Nicole bemoaned good-naturedly. "Anyway, I'll let you get on. I know you must be swamped."

"Yes, these minor rewrites are coming in thick and fast," Emily said. "You weren't kidding when you said it got hectic as we get closer to opening night."

"Preview night will be the worst," Nicole said. "That's when we have the audience in and we can see people's reactions. From preview to opening night there will be a lot of changes."

"Carl mentioned that. I've put aside some extra hours, and I'll be in early on Thursday."

"Fantastic. I'm glad Carl prepared you for the horrors! Stick close to him, he knows everything there is to know about the writing side of the business. And if you need any assistance we can always pull him off his current project. This is more important."

Emily tried to fix a smile on her face. "I'm sure I'll be fine."

"Lovely, just keep it in mind. I don't want to work you into the ground in your last couple of weeks." Nicole's phone beeped, and she looked at the device that she'd been holding. "Better get back to it, I'll catch up with you later."

Emily said goodbye and let out a sigh. She'd be gone in less than two weeks, so there really wasn't much point in saying anything to Nicole about Carl. Presumably this situation had never occurred before or Nicole would have mentioned something. And while Carl was creepy, he was never pushy when they were in the same room. Almost as if he was frightened of her. Emily assumed he was one of those men who was full of bravado and swagger up until he was in front of the woman he was trying to impress. And then he crumbled.

If she felt that Carl was a bigger issue, a predator who may bother other women, she'd take more action. But, as it was, he just made her feel uncomfortable. Knowing that she'd be leaving in a couple of weeks was a relief. Even though she'd rather not spend another minute with Carl.

Chapter Thirty-five

Olivia pressed the button on the steering wheel to connect her call. After days of wondering what she'd do to fill her time, everything was happening at once. It was her first day volunteering at Henry's school and Emily's opening night preview was the next day. Although Olivia wasn't going, she wanted to make sure that Emily knew she was thinking about her.

"Hello, darling," Nicole said.

"Hi, could you send me the best address to have flowers delivered to Emily tomorrow? I'm not sure if I should send them to the theatre or to the offices."

"You never send me flowers," Nicole groused.

Olivia smiled at Nicole's joke. "Well, you never agreed to sleep with me," she joked back.

"That's true," Nicole said. "Very well, I'll email you the address. But don't send anything too massive. They'll end up at my apartment anyway."

Olivia considered that. "Maybe I should send them to your apartment in the morning?"

"That sounds like a good idea. It would mean that she wouldn't have to travel on public transport with the no doubt enormous bouquet you intend to send."

"It's not enormous," Olivia argued.

"I'll believe it when I see it. I'm sure it will block the sun. And then Emily will run off back to New York, and I'll be left in the shade of the enormous bouquet you sent."

"Such a drama queen," Olivia sighed with a chuckle.

"I'll miss Emily. My cleaner will miss Emily, too."

"She'll miss you, and the work. I'm not sure about the cleaner, but, knowing Emily, she'll probably miss her, too."

"She wasn't too devastated, was she?" Nicole asked.

Olivia mulled over the question for a moment. Devastated seemed an overstatement. But then Emily was clearly upset by the developments. Olivia didn't want Nicole to feel guilty, so she decided to err on the side of caution.

"She's disappointed, but she understands that there is a lack of jobs for her now."

"Yes, it's just a shame that she couldn't make the commute work. If she were based in London then it wouldn't be an issue."

"What do you mean?"

"Just that it's a shame she has to give up so early on. Obviously, I don't expect you to finance her commute to London, and I know Emily would absolutely hate to be further indebted to you."

"But I thought there were no spots open?" Olivia asked. Suddenly, everything was becoming quite confusing, and she had no idea what Nicole was talking about.

"In New York," Nicole said. "Oh."

"Oh?"

"I think I've put my foot in it," Nicole said softly. "She didn't tell you, did she?"

"I don't know, but I'm very confused. Maybe you'd care to enlighten me?"

Olivia heard Nicole blow out a breath. She could mentally see her weighing up her options.

"When I spoke to Emily," Nicole said, "I told her that there were no jobs in New York. But there are companies I could get her into here in London. I'm based in London, so I obviously have more sway here. There are a couple of companies who would be really keen to help her grow her career."

Olivia reached for the turn signal and pulled off the main road onto a side street. She wanted to listen to what Nicole was telling her without having to focus on driving.

"So, there *are* jobs?" Olivia asked.

"Yes, but those jobs obviously wouldn't be willing to fund her commute. And the salary they pay wouldn't cover the commute either. Flights to and from New York don't come cheap."

"She didn't tell me," Olivia murmured. "She only said that there were no jobs."

"The commute was getting her down," Nicole stated. "She hated being away from you and Henry. Maybe she didn't mention it because she doesn't want to travel?"

Olivia recalled Emily despondently walking around the house at the weekend when she thought no one was looking. She'd been lost in her own world, quickly claiming that she was fine. But Olivia knew the look of someone who was no longer doing a job they loved. She'd seen it in the mirror.

"But why not even mention that there were jobs in London?" Olivia asked.

"That's something you'd have to ask her."

"Being in a relationship is extremely complicated sometimes," Olivia said.

Nicole chuckled. "It is, it really is. I am sorry I put my foot in it. I shouldn't have said anything. It was for Emily to tell you or not, not me."

"I'm glad you did. I'll approach it with care," Olivia said.

Nicole laughed again. "Oh, please don't. You're like a bull in a china shop when you want to subtly let someone know that you know something."

"I am not," Olivia said.

"Darling, I love you with the power of a thousand suns, but you are not subtle."

Olivia opened her mouth to deny the accusation, but realised that Nicole was absolutely right. She steamed into situations without much thought. She felt a need to speedily deal with anything that fell into her path, and sometimes that meant losing the soft touch.

"By the way," Nicole said. "While I'm putting my foot in it, have you spoken to Sophie lately?"

"Sophie? No, why?"

"The baby is due in a couple of weeks, and she and Simon are desperately trying to come up with a way to tell you that Simon is really not enjoying his job. I assumed that one of them would have done so by now, but they are running out of time before that baby comes."

Olivia spluttered. "B-but…Simon's fine. He told me he was happy."

"When?"

"A few days after he took the job."

"That was months ago. He's settled in. Now the charm has worn off, and it's all late nights and stress. He's very good at his job, but it's just not him."

Olivia took in a deep breath and held it. She turned to look out the window at people walking their dogs. She slowly let out the breath and shook her head. She was used to missing things, the finer points in people's tones or a joke slipped into a serious discussion. But to miss such things about the people closest to her was infuriating.

"So, he's leaving?" Olivia asked.

"I don't know. He's been agonising mentioning it to you for a while. He knows all of the hassle you went through to set the deal up and he doesn't want to let you, or the other Applewoods staff, down."

"He wouldn't be letting anyone down. I want him to be happy," Olivia said.

"I know that, you know that, somewhere deep down Simon knows that. He just doesn't want to disappoint you. And I know you won't be disappointed in him, which is why I'm mentioning this."

"Thank you. I appreciate you being honest with me."

"I always will be," Nicole said.

Early in their years-long friendship, Olivia had made the request that Nicole was always to be honest with her. Nicole had quickly agreed, commenting that there would be times when Olivia wouldn't want the level of honesty Nicole was willing to deliver. It had happened on occasion, but, on the whole, Olivia knew that their relationship worked because of the level of trust and honesty they shared.

She looked at the clock on the dashboard. "I have to go," she said. "I'm about to teach at the school. Any advice?"

"Tell them all to invest in the arts," Nicole said.

"I dread to think how I'd explain investments to them. We're starting off small and looking at easy ways to add and subtract."

"I could do with that course. Are you going to stream it live?" Nicole joked.

"No, you'll have to wait for the DVD."

"Fine, go, teach children how to be financial masterminds. I'll speak with you later."

Olivia chuckled and hung up the call.

She considered the conversation. There were some things that she needed to clear up. But first she needed to get to the school.

"Does anyone know the answer?" Olivia asked.

Henry put his hand up high and started squirming in his seat.

"Someone other than Henry?" she said. She offered him a warm smile, but she wasn't about to let him take credit for knowing the answer to her question.

A young girl at the back of the class carefully raised her hand.

"I think Lauren may have an answer for you," Natalie said.

"What do you think the answer is, Lauren?" Olivia asked.

Lauren put her hand down and stretched up her body to see the white board. Her eyebrows knitted together, and she counted under her breath. Olivia was intrigued by the way Lauren was starting to come out of her shell as the lesson was coming to an end.

"Is it…thirteen?" Lauren eventually asked, her voice barely above a whisper.

"It is," Olivia confirmed. "Well done, Lauren. That's marvellous."

The girl beamed with the praise and flopped back into her seat, seemingly exhausted with the strain of being the centre of attention.

"I think you just earned a star for participation," Natalie told Lauren.

"Thank you, Miss Costa," Lauren said softly.

A bell rang, and the children started to excitedly gather their things and stand up from their desks. Olivia barely had time to step back before they were all running for the exit. As Henry raced past her, he smiled brightly and waved goodbye.

A few short seconds later, and the classroom was empty save for Olivia and Natalie.

"Is it always like that?" Olivia asked.

"Like what?" Natalie asked as she picked up a stray pencil from the floor.

"Mayhem."

Natalie chuckled. "Yep. It's always like that. But the exit aside, what did you think?"

"I enjoyed it," Olivia said. "They had a lot of questions."

"They did, they enjoyed it. When I told them this morning that you were coming in, they weren't too sure. But you made it interesting for them and got them involved."

"It didn't start off too well," Olivia said.

She shuddered at the memory of having twenty-five sets of eyes staring at her. At first, no one wanted to speak. Olivia had been effectively talking to the back wall for the first few minutes. That was until she got Henry to come up to the front of the class and help her demonstrate a magic trick that she remembered seeing online.

She wrote the number fifteen on a piece of paper and gave it to Natalie to hold up high but backwards so the class couldn't see the number.

She asked Henry to choose any number at all and write it on the whiteboard. She'd given him a calculator and asked him to multiply the number by three, and then add forty-five. Once he'd done that she instructed him to double the number he had, divide the answer by six, and then remove the original number he'd written on the board.

It came to fifteen and she asked Natalie to show the class the piece of paper she'd written before Henry had chosen his first number. The children's eyes had widened, and when she had asked who wanted to be next, at least two-thirds of them shot their hands into the air.

Even Natalie had looked confused and impressed.

"How did you guess the number?" Natalie asked.

"It will always be fifteen," Olivia said.

Natalie opened her mouth but then closed it again and shook her head. "I was going to ask you to explain that to me, but I bet that you would and then my head might explode."

Olivia decided against explaining. She'd almost gotten into an argument with Emily over the numerical anomaly.

"It's magic," she said finally.

"Sounds good to me," Natalie said. "So, it wasn't too horrible? You think you'll come back?"

"I'd like that," Olivia said. "Although, things might be changing at home, so I will need to speak with Emily."

Natalie leaned on one of the children's desks. "Oh?"

Olivia licked her lips nervously. She didn't know if this was something up for discussion. But she also knew that she needed to discuss what she had recently learned.

"Emily's project in London is coming to an end," Olivia said.

"So, she'll be back home? That will be great. I know Henry misses her a lot."

"Yes." Olivia stood still and thought about how to bring up the rest of the subject.

"Is there more?" Natalie asked.

"Yes."

Natalie chuckled. "Is it top secret?"

"Emily told me that her agent said there are no available jobs for her at the moment. But I've discovered from her agent that there are jobs, but they are in London."

"But she didn't tell you about them?" Natalie asked.

Olivia shook her head. "She implied that there were no jobs whatsoever."

"Maybe she doesn't want them? Maybe she wants to do something else?"

Olivia shook her head again. "She loves her job. She was very upset when she found out that there were no new projects for her."

"Maybe she doesn't want to fly back and forth? That must be hard."

Olivia frowned. It did seem like the logical conclusion, and the one she had come to herself.

"And it must be expensive," Natalie continued. "I don't want to pry into your financial situation, but I can't begin to imagine the cost of flights to and from London every week."

"She knows I'd pay that." Olivia folded her arms and walked over to the window to watch the children playing.

"Maybe she doesn't want you to pay? I don't think I could accept a gift like that, even if it were from my wife."

"But everything we have is jointly owned," Olivia said.

"Maybe that's how you see it." Natalie walked towards the front of the class and sat down at her desk. "Excuse me if I'm being nosy, but would I be right in guessing that you come from a wealthy family?"

Olivia debated questioning the word "wealthy," but quickly put it to one side. She knew without a doubt that her family and her own financial situation put her into the wealthy category as far as most people were concerned.

"Yes, I suppose so," she said.

"So, you have money and you are happy to share it with Emily?"

"Of course."

"That's great and very kind, but I can kind of see how Emily wouldn't want that."

Olivia turned to look at Natalie. She was confused by how the teacher could possibly have any understanding of the workings of Emily's mind.

"How come?"

"Because money is a hot topic. It makes the world go 'round and causes more wars and arguments than anything else. People who were once deeply in love can quickly come apart when money is involved."

"But we've talked about money. Emily is comfortable that we live off my funds."

"That may be true, but you funding her expensive commute is a completely different story."

Olivia leaned against the wall and looked down at her feet. In her heart, she knew that Emily still had a different view towards money than she did. No matter how often they spoke about it and how much reassurance Olivia gave, a part of Emily was still unsure about spending their communal funds.

She wanted Emily to be comfortable, but that didn't necessarily mean that she was.

"I'm sorry," Natalie said. "I shouldn't get involved. It has nothing to do with me, I just sometimes spurt things out."

"I'm happy for you to spurt things out," Olivia said. "Sometimes I need to hear them. What should I do?"

Natalie blinked. "Um, I have no idea. That's up to you. And Emily, of course."

"Should I encourage her to take the jobs and pay for her flights? Maybe book them to ensure she does?"

Natalie looked uncertain. "I don't know Emily very well, hardly at all. But I know that I wouldn't want someone to force me into a situation like that. Booking a flight for someone without telling them doesn't sound like a great idea."

Olivia knew all too well what she meant. One of her first arguments with Emily had been because she had done just that. The following events nearly ended their relationship.

"True," Olivia said. "But then what?"

"You'll have to speak to Emily," Natalie suggested. "There must be a way for her to do the job she loves."

"I don't know how I can speak with her if she refuses to even tell me about this. As far as I'm supposed to know, there are no jobs."

"Maybe she didn't tell you so she could protect you?"

"Protect me?"

"You seem like the kind of person who wants to fix things, the kind of person who wants to ensure that everyone is happy."

Olivia chuckled. "I don't like to see people suffering from problems that can easily be fixed."

"Maybe Emily didn't tell you about the other jobs so you didn't feel obligated to fix things for her?"

"Maybe," Olivia said. "But that's beside the point because now that I know…that's exactly what I intend to do."

Natalie laughed. "Sounds like trouble to me."

Olivia nodded. "Probably, but I'm used to it."

CHAPTER THIRTY-SIX

Emily stood to the side of the stalls and watched as the audience started to take their seats. She'd been so busy organising the last-minute changes to the script that it had completely escaped her that she was about to experience her first opening night ever.

While it was just friends and families of the company, and no one had paid a penny for a ticket, Emily felt quite overwhelmed by what was happening. She'd had dreams of entertaining people with her writing for years, but they'd always been dreams.

She'd seen the play at least a hundred times in different variations, and on opening night, she had no intention of watching it again. This time she was going to watch the audience. She was going to soak up the atmosphere of a room full of people watching her words on a stage.

Everything had been so hectic that she'd almost forgotten the enormity of what was happening.

"Hello, famous scriptwriter lady."

She turned around and smiled at Simon. "Hey, so glad you could make it!" She hugged him in greeting.

"Wouldn't miss it for the world. Unless this one goes into labour, in which case we're out of here." Simon gestured to Sophie who had entered the auditorium with an armful of snacks.

"Wow, you look ready to pop," Emily said.

"I wish I would," Sophie groused. "I suddenly ballooned up. I can't go on like this much longer."

Emily gave her a hug, being careful to avoid the popcorn and the packs of sweets.

"Don't worry, it goes really fast at this point," Emily lied. The truth was it dragged more in the last couple of weeks. But Sophie didn't need to hear that. A little fib would hopefully make her feel better.

"I hope so," Sophie said. "I'm like a house. Two houses. And I'm comfort eating so I'll still be like a house when the baby comes out."

Sophie looked at the array of treats in her arms. She looked up at Simon with a sad expression, her bottom lip jutting out.

"What do you need?" Simon asked her.

"Chocolate."

Simon pulled the tickets out of his pocket and went to hand them to Sophie. He saw her full arms and then handed them to Emily instead.

"I'll be back in a minute," he said.

Emily looked at the row number and walked Sophie towards their seats.

"How is everything? No more creepy notes?" Sophie asked in a whisper.

"No, nothing," Emily replied. "I think I know who it was. Since the police have been involved, he's been very quiet."

"Was it the strange guy you mentioned?"

Emily looked around the sparsely filled auditorium to check they were alone.

"Yep. My co-writer, Carl."

Sophie's eyebrows raised. "Your co-writer? Oh, creepy!"

"Yeah," Emily said. She took the large bag of popcorn from Sophie's hands and gestured down the row.

The theatre was very old, and the seats were the original ones. While they had been reupholstered over the years, they were still very narrow and a heavily pregnant woman carrying half of a sweet shop would never pass without help.

Sophie made her way down the row and sat in her designated seat. Emily sat next to her and handed her the popcorn.

"He's still creepy," Emily explained. "Just no notes or flowers or anything like that."

At that moment, Carl walked onto the stage with Hannah and started to adjust something with the trap door.

"That's him," Emily said with a nod.

Sophie looked up with interest. "Oh yeah," she said. "He looks a bit weird."

"I don't have any proof, of course. Just a feeling."

"Well, you have to trust your instincts," Sophie said. "Sometimes you can just tell."

"Tell what?" Simon asked.

"Girl talk," Sophie said. "Did you get the chocolate?"

"I did, master." He handed her a large bar of chocolate with a grin.

Emily looked up and saw Nicole walk into the auditorium. She spied them and walked up the row in front of theirs to greet them. "Hello, all!"

"Hey," Simon said. He leaned over the row of seats and hugged her.

Nicole looked at Sophie. "Don't get up, darling. And don't give birth until the curtain goes down."

"Can't promise anything," Sophie joked.

"On second thought, if it starts to nosedive, I'll give you a signal and you can pretend your water has broken."

"Hey, it's not going to nosedive," Emily said.

"We might be without an actor if Jonathan doesn't stop going on and on about his closing line before the intermission."

Emily sighed. "Is he still going on about that?"

The actor, Jonathan, wasn't even playing a major part. Emily had expected the lead actors to be divas, but it turned out they were both lovely. Jonathan, however, who was on the stage for less than five minutes in total, was a pain.

"He is," Nicole said. "Could you go and see if you can add that extra line in that you were talking about? It's the last line, so it makes no difference to anyone else, and if it gives him his moment of glory, and, more importantly, shuts him up, then great."

"Absolutely," Emily said. She turned to Simon and Sophie. "I'll catch you guys at the end of the show."

"I'm sure it will be great," Sophie enthused.

"It is great," Nicole said.

Emily edged her way down the row and walked into the corridors. She hoped it was great. When she'd written the play, she had no idea it would ever actually get to be performed on a stage. Or the enormous amount of work it took a huge number of people to get it there. Now she felt jittery. It was the acid test for her work. In a couple of hours, she'd know whether she was actually any good.

Emily didn't have time for Jonathan's dramatics. She just wanted the show to go on, whether he ended the scene with one line or three didn't bother her in the slightest. But Jonathan was adamant, and as long as he was unhappy, a darkness hung over the production. Nicole had warned her about working with actors and explained how sometimes it was easier to let them have their own way. Emily couldn't agree more.

She stood in Jonathan's dressing room. Not his original dressing room, the one that he claimed was too near the stage door and therefore had a draft. The dressing room he forcibly switched with another member of the company.

That should have been their first indication that he was trouble.

"Of course, I'm not sure why it was changed to begin with," Jonathan said. He peered into the mirror at his reflection. He held a comb in his hand and occasionally swept aside a stray strand of hair.

"Well, we'll change it back for now and see how it goes," Emily said. "But it may revert to the new script for the opening night. We can compare how it is received."

"I think I know which will be preferred," Jonathan replied haughtily.

Emily resisted the urge to roll her eyes. She knew she needed to play this one more carefully.

"Yes, I think they'll prefer the shorter version," Emily said. "Of course, if it were a less accomplished actor, then I wouldn't even consider it. As you know, it takes someone with experience and ability to pull off a less-is-more performance. I think it's very brave of you to try both versions to see which one is better received. I think we both know that the audience needs to be left wanting more. And the way to do that is with an understated performance, like we know you can give. But we'll try both...just to be absolutely certain."

Jonathan paled.

Emily subtly looked up from her paperwork to regard his reaction in the mirror.

"W-well, yes, of course," he gulped. "You know what, maybe we should keep it as the shorter version. For now. Maybe try out the longer version later? I wouldn't want to confuse lighting. You know how they are when there's a last-minute change at the end of the act."

Emily pretended to consider the idea for the first time. "If you're sure?" she asked.

"Absolutely." Jonathan placed the comb back on his dressing table and stood up. "I better get going. I need to speak with costume before we go on."

Emily watched him leave and smothered a smirk behind her hand. She knew he was off to terrorise his next victim, but she couldn't bring herself to care. She'd gotten him off her plate, and that was all that mattered.

Hannah appeared in the doorway.

"Oh, here you are." She stepped inside the dressing room and closed the door behind her. "It's manic out there."

"It is! Is it always like this on opening night?" Emily asked.

"Yes, I try to keep my head down. Or Jonathan will have me repainting every piece of backdrop behind him so it perfectly matches his eyes."

Emily chuckled. "He is a bit high-maintenance."

"A bit?" Hannah joked. "He's the worse. For a third-rate, bit part actor, he has a list of demands longer than I've ever seen. Anyway, enough about him. How are you feeling? Nervous?"

"Yes, very," Emily admitted.

"Okay, you need to do some theatre breathing. It sounds weird, but it fixes everything."

Hannah stepped forward, took all the paperwork from Emily's hands, and laid it on the dressing table. She guided Emily to stand in front of the tall dressing mirror, then she stood behind her and looked over Emily's shoulder at their reflection in the mirror. Without a second thought, she placed her hands over Emily's stomach.

"Breathe in slowly," Hannah instructed.

Emily did as she was told.

"You can close your eyes, if you like," Hannah said.

Emily's eyes fluttered closed. She could feel Hannah's breath by her ear.

"Breathe out," Hannah whispered. "Nice and slow."

Emily released the breath.

"You feel so tense. Try again."

Emily took another long, slow breath in.

"That's it," Hannah said. "And out again."

Emily started to slowly breathe out. She had to admit that the calm breathing was helping. She knew she was stressed, and she couldn't remember the last time that she had taken a few moments out to relax.

Suddenly Hannah's lips were on her neck.

Eyes springing open, Emily jumped to the side and stared at Hannah in surprise.

Hannah grinned. "Sorry, I had to."

Emily continued to stare. She hadn't expected to be in this situation, and now she had no idea what to do or say. Her feet were glued to the floor, and her arms felt like they were made of lead.

Hannah took a step forward, so Emily quickly retreated the same distance. She hit her back on the wall behind her. She swallowed as Hannah took another step forward.

"I'm sorry," Hannah said. The grin remained on her face. "I just…I can see that we fit together. But, don't worry, I know that you can't see that yet."

"I-I'm married," Emily spluttered.

"Yes, but I know you're having trouble. You told me, remember?"

Emily furrowed her brow. "No. I didn't say that."

"You did. She refuses to fly and see you, remember? You told me. But anyway, enough of that. I know that you're going home soon, and I want to make sure you don't make a mistake. One you'll regret."

"Hannah, look, I don't know what you think you know, but you don't get it. I'm happy. Very happy. With my wife."

"You think that, but you're not." Hannah made a sad face, pitying Emily's apparent naivety. "I realise you don't know me that well at the moment, but I know you. And I know we fit together."

The words hit her like a punch to the stomach.

"You sent the flowers," Emily guessed.

"Yes. I didn't mean to frighten you. I was trying to show you how caring I am. Prove to you that I'm the one."

Emily looked towards the closed door and knew she had to get out of there. Hannah was clearly deluded, not to mention potentially dangerous. She seemed to have some fantasy where they would be together.

She edged to the side, but Hannah quickly did the same, bringing them closer together.

"Now, now," Hannah said. "Let's talk. No need to run off."

"Hannah, I want to leave," Emily said firmly, though a quake was detectable in her voice.

"And I want to talk to you," Hannah said. "I don't want you to run off before I've had a chance to explain."

"Hann—" Emily was cut off by Hannah's hand covering her mouth.

"Shh, just let me explain everything. You'll see what I see soon, I promise."

CHAPTER THIRTY-SEVEN

Hannah was clearly unstable, and Emily had no idea what she would do next. Hannah's hand was tightly clamped against her mouth.

The door opened with such a force that it cracked against the wall behind it.

Hannah jumped back in shock, and Emily shuddered in relief. Relief quickly turned to shock as Olivia barrelled through the doorway with a murderous look on her face.

"That's her." Olivia raised her hand and pointed to Hannah.

"Come with us, please, miss," a police office said as he entered the room. Another police officer followed him, blocking the door.

"Go away!" Hannah screamed. "I'm not doing anything!"

"We know your real identity, and we want to have a word with you down at the station. Don't make this any more difficult than it needs to be."

Hannah rushed towards the police officers, but they quickly managed to contain her, each taking an arm as they quickly escorted her from the room.

Hannah screamed as they pulled her down the corridor.

Emily stared at Olivia as if she were a hallucination.

"Did she hurt you?" Olivia asked. Her eyes raced over Emily's body in search of damage.

Emily caught her breath. "What are you doing here?"

"Having the authorities arrest that crazy woman," Olivia explained.

"I mean in this country!"

"Oh. I came here to support you on your opening night. It was meant to be a surprise. So, yes. Surprise."

Emily launched herself into Olivia's arms, and Olivia tightly wrapped her in a hug.

"Did she hurt you?" Olivia repeated.

"No." Emily shook her head into the material of Olivia's woollen trench coat. She gripped at the soft fabric.

"And you're okay?" Olivia asked.

"I am now. How did you know?" Emily rested her head on Olivia's shoulder. She breathed in her familiar perfume and forced herself to relax a little.

"Sophie told Simon who you suspected, Simon told me when I arrived. We went to talk to him, and he told me that he suspected Hannah. Apparently, he was aware that she had done this kind of thing before, but he was afraid to speak out."

Emily leaned back a little and looked Olivia in the eye. "Carl suspected it was Hannah?"

"Yes."

Emily looked at the ceiling and shook her head. "I can't believe I got it so wrong."

"Why did you think it was him?" Olivia asked.

She lowered her eyes and guiltily met Olivia's. "He seemed weird."

"Weird?" Olivia frowned.

"Yes." Emily took a deep breath through her nostrils. "I clearly misjudged him."

"He seems like a nice guy," Olivia said.

Emily suddenly made the connection that maybe Carl wasn't weird. It was possible that he just processed things differently, much the same as Olivia did. She felt guilt in the pit of her stomach. She'd judged him unfairly. Worrying about the stalker had caused a knee-jerk reaction, one she wasn't proud of.

"And if I hadn't spoken to him, I-I might not have found you so soon," Olivia said. Her arms tightened around Emily's middle.

"I would have kicked her in the kneecaps eventually. I was a bit startled," Emily said.

She wasn't entirely sure whether that was true. She felt stupid for her inactivity, but Hannah had literally scared her stiff.

"Mm." Olivia sounded unconvinced.

"Emily? Is everything okay?"

Emily pulled away from Olivia's embrace to see Carl standing awkwardly in the door.

"It is now," Emily replied. "Thank you for sharing your concerns with Olivia. Why didn't you tell me?"

Carl shoved his hands into his pockets and shrugged. "I didn't know for sure. I didn't want to get her in trouble. You know what it's like when someone accuses someone, and they didn't do anything wrong."

Emily stifled a bitter laugh. "I know what you mean."

"I went to college with her. She used another name back then. She told me that the rumours weren't true, and if I told anyone, she'd get her brother to hurt me," Carl explained. "I should have said something sooner, but then I worried that you would think I was blaming someone else to put myself in the clear and—"

Emily held up her hand to calm him. "I get it," she said. "Thank you for saying something."

"Well, I didn't have much choice." Carl gestured to Olivia. "She had her hand around my neck."

Emily spun to regard Olivia.

"I thought you'd been harassing my wife," Olivia said, as if that was a perfectly reasonable excuse for throttling the man.

"I'm glad you're okay," Carl said and turned to leave.

"You throttled him?" Emily asked.

Olivia smiled. "I helped him to remember pertinent facts, quickly."

"You're a little scary sometimes," Emily said. But then her brain clicked into gear. "You're here!"

"I am," Olivia said carefully, probably thinking that Emily had lost her mind.

"You…you flew here. You said you'd never fly again."

"I had a little help," Olivia said. "Henry's here, too."

"Henry?" Emily blinked. She was torn between being embarrassed at having forgotten to even ask where Henry was and being stunned that both Olivia and Henry were in London.

"He's asleep. It was rather a busy day. I have the hotel babysitting service watching him." Olivia looked uncertain. "Should I have left him at home? With Lucy?"

Emily shook her head. "No, that's fine. I'm glad he's here. He…he helped you get on a flight?"

"Yes, we've been playing airplane."

Emily was about to ask Olivia to explain what she meant when Nicole came rushing into the dressing room.

"I just heard about Hannah. Are you okay?" She turned to look at Olivia. "What on earth are you doing here?"

"Feeling very unwelcome," Olivia replied.

"I'm fine. My knight in shining armour saved me," Emily replied.

Nicole turned away from Olivia to look at Emily. "Hannah had been using someone else's credentials to work here. It's all coming out now. I'm so sorry. Clearly, our recruitment procedure leaves a lot to be desired. I've spoken with the company solicitor, and he is going to go to the police station now."

Emily felt some panic. "I don't want to miss tonight."

"No need. The lovely, tall, and handsome sergeant tells me they have enough to hold her with the identity theft alone. They want you to call them in the morning. I have all his details."

"I bet you do," Olivia said.

Nicole turned around. "What *are* you doing here?"

"Throttling Carl," Emily mumbled.

Nicole gave her a look, but then shook her head and held her hands up. "I don't want to know. I have a play opening in less than fifteen minutes. I'll catch up with you both later."

Nicole rushed out of the room, and Emily turned to Olivia again.

"Not that I'm not glad to see you, but I have to echo Nicole's question, why are you here?"

"I had an idea," Olivia said.

Emily itched to point out that having an idea wasn't a prelude to flying halfway around the world. Before she got a chance to say anything, the corridor outside the dressing room started to thrum with people. Everyone was getting ready for curtain up. It wasn't the best place to have whatever conversation they were about to have.

Emily grabbed Olivia's hand.

"Come with me."

CHAPTER THIRTY-EIGHT

Olivia allowed Emily to drag her through the back corridors of the theatre. The behind-the-scenes world was just as chaotic as she had imagined. People were getting changed in corridors, and heavy props were being carried through narrow gaps.

She was thankful when they got out of the busy area and started to climb a set of concrete steps.

"Where are we going?" Olivia asked.

"Somewhere where we can have a conversation without being in the middle of the mayhem," Emily replied.

Soon, they were at the top of the theatre. Windows showed the London skyline at night. Olivia smiled to herself at the familiarity.

Emily opened a door and gestured for Olivia to step inside. It was small, but there was a desk and a chair.

"Do you work here?" Olivia asked.

"Sometimes."

"It's a cupboard."

"It's quiet," Emily said. She gestured to the single chair and Olivia sat down.

Emily sat on the edge of the desk and looked down at her. "I'm so happy to see you," she said.

"I'm very happy to be here."

"You said you had an idea?"

"I did," Olivia confirmed.

"An idea that caused you to board a plane, which you said you'd never do," Emily pressed gently.

"I spoke to Nicole," Olivia said.

"Okay?" Emily sounded confused, clearly not picking up on the connection.

"She told me about the jobs in London."

Emily's eyes widened. "Oh."

"I don't want you to give up your dream."

"It wouldn't be giving up my dream exactly," Emily explained, but even Olivia could tell that it was half-hearted.

"You love working here," Olivia said. She looked around the cold and barren room at the top of the theatre. "I may not understand *why*, but I can see that you love it."

"I do. But I also love you and Henry. And I miss you both so much when I'm here. That's one of the reasons I didn't mention anything. I don't want to keep commuting and seeing so little of you both. I don't want Henry's teachers to think I'm dead." She chuckled. "And the cost. As much as I love the work and the experience and opportunities, I can't justify the expense."

Olivia started to open her mouth.

"And I don't want you to pay for my travel expenses," Emily said quickly.

"I know," Olivia said.

Emily frowned, clearly having expected Olivia's grand plan to be her funding Emily's flights. But luckily, Olivia had learned.

"I know you don't want me to pay for your travel. And I know you want to pay me back for the debts I paid off. I don't quite understand why, but I know it's very important to you. The last thing you would want is to add to those…perceived debts. I understand that."

Emily smiled. "I'm so glad you understand. I know it must sound odd to you, but I like to do things on my own. If I'm going to succeed, I want to have done it myself."

"I know," Olivia said.

"So, I didn't mention the potential jobs in London because there's no way I could afford the commute."

"You don't have to commute," Olivia said. "We could all live in London."

Emily stared at her.

"We can buy a house. Here," Olivia clarified.

Emily continued to stare.

"So that you can work here. And not commute," Olivia continued.

"You'd do that?" Emily whispered.

"Of course!"

Emily slid from the desk and paced the small room.

"What about Henry and school?"

"He's learning the alphabet and basic math, which he already knows. He'd easily integrate into a new school."

Olivia watched Emily pace.

"What about the house?"

"I think we should leave it for now. If we think the move would be permanent, then we could rent it out or sell it."

"What about a visa? There are rules about working in countries," Emily said.

"There are, but you'd have a job and they'd help with the legal side of things."

Emily stopped and looked at Olivia seriously. "You mean this?"

"Of course."

"What about you?"

"What about me?" Olivia frowned.

"Do you want to live in London?"

Olivia shrugged. "I've spent more time in London than I have in New York in recent memory. And I-I'm sure I could find something to occupy myself."

Emily narrowed her eyes. "Spill it."

Olivia sighed and shook her head. She still didn't know how Emily managed to see right through her.

"I might have a business idea that would solve a few outstanding conundrums."

Emily smiled. "Go on."

"Well, volunteering at Henry's school was very enjoyable. And it reminded me how much I enjoy work. But I wouldn't want to go back to the hours I was working previously. I was thinking of establishing a charity that links businesses and schools. I have a vast network of people I could ask to go and speak in schools about finances."

"You can't ask five-year-olds to apply for mortgages," Emily said.

Olivia gave her a look. "Clearly not. That would infringe on the Financial Services and Markets Act 2000."

Emily chuckled. "So, what would these businesses say?"

"For example, someone working in an accounting firm could volunteer their time to go to a school and talk about the importance of savings. Keeping things simple so children understand. That person has then done something worthwhile, and they have something to put on their résumé."

Emily smiled. "Meanwhile, the school has a visitor to talk about something practical."

"Exactly, and the business gets some positive PR," Olivia finished. "It works well for everyone. Especially the children."

"Is this something you want to do?" Emily asked.

"It is. I've previously done charity work and been involved in outreach programs, and I find them very rewarding. And I've always thought that catching children when they are young is the key to avoiding debt issues when they are older."

Emily nodded. "If I'd been taught more about debt, then I wouldn't have been in the situation I got myself into."

"Well, selfishly, I'm glad you did," Olivia quietly admitted.

"It sounds like a big project to undertake," Emily said. "Setting up a charity, arranging all the schools and businesses to work together. Presumably there will be legal points to take care of? Training?"

"Yes, but I think I know someone who can help me."

Emily frowned.

"Simon," Olivia said. "It's come to my attention that he isn't happy at Applewoods. He's staying in the position because he feels I'd be disappointed if he didn't. I enjoy working with him, and it's a role where the first few months would be a start-up stage that we can take at our leisure."

"So, he can take time off when the baby comes," Emily said.

"Exactly. He can adjust his hours, work from home. Whatever he needs. I'm sure he'd like the idea."

"I think so, too," Emily said. She blew out a long breath, folded her arms, and stared towards the window.

Olivia looked from her to the window and back again. She knew it was a lot for Emily to take in. Maybe a normal person would have phoned, or even waited for Emily to return home, possibly given out the potential plan in small, easy-to-manage chunks, but Olivia had been consumed with the plan. It solved every issue. It was a solution, and she loved solutions.

"I guess you're already planning to look at houses?" Emily asked without making eye contact.

Olivia couldn't read her tone. "Yes, I have several appointments lined up for tomorrow. J-just as a starting point, I hadn't made any decisions. Obviously."

Emily turned away from the twinkling skyline and looked at Olivia.

"Well, it's an improvement. Last time you bought a house without telling me."

"Technically, it was a house for me that I then asked you to move into," Olivia said.

"Yes, because you really needed all those bedrooms," Emily said.

"Well, yes, okay, maybe I bought it with every intention of hoping you'd live with me."

"It would be nice to go house-hunting with you," Emily said.

Olivia felt her heart soar. "So…you agree?"

"How could I not?" Emily asked. "You've come up with the perfect solution. You're right, I do love my job. And it was painful to think I wouldn't be able to do it anymore. If I can continue to do it, and you can work on something you like, and Simon can work with you again, then that's obviously a solution that works for everyone. And, frankly, I'm still a little shell-shocked that you got on a plane and you're here."

Olivia stood up and held out her arms. Emily crashed into them.

"A new life in London, I like the sound of that," Olivia said.

"I'll miss Tom and Lucy, and Irene," Emily whispered into her hair.

"We'll visit them often," Olivia said. "I can't stay afraid of plane travel. It will be good for me to have a reason to fly now and then."

"I don't mean to interrupt…"

Olivia looked up to see Nicole standing in the doorway.

"It's just that your play that has just opened on the West End is about to start, and I thought you might like to see it?"

Emily pulled away from Olivia. "Oh my God, yes, I lost track of time!"

"We're a little delayed," Nicole explained. "But it will be starting in a moment, so come on."

Nicole turned around, and Emily quickly followed her.

Olivia exited the cramped room and closed the door behind her.

"I need to talk to you about those jobs in London…" She heard Emily say.

"I assumed as much. I have a telephone interview set up for you for tomorrow," Nicole replied.

Chapter Thirty-nine

Emily couldn't focus on a single word of the play. As she'd taken her seat and the lights had dimmed, she'd been wildly excited. But within a few moments her mind had drifted. She couldn't believe how Olivia had appeared without warning, like a knight in an expensive, woollen trench coat.

She'd never considered moving to London. The idea of uprooting Olivia and Henry for her own needs had seemed so selfish. But Olivia had offered the idea up as if it were obvious. Emily knew that Olivia was invested in her happiness. Olivia demonstrated it every day. But it was something else to offer to move to a new country.

Emily mused that this was another way that they were different. Emily saw obstacles and difficulty where Olivia saw opportunity and solutions. Olivia had lived and worked in London before. To her, it wasn't as enormous a deal as Emily felt it would be.

It was where their difference really shone and made them stronger as a unit. Where Emily wouldn't even consider something because it seemed too much to ask, Olivia was already well into the planning stages of making it happen.

Emily turned to regard her. Despite the actors arguing on the stage and the ominous music building a crescendo, Olivia had quickly fallen into a deep sleep. She couldn't be sure if it was the contents of the play or the jet lag. With Olivia, it could be either.

She subtly turned around and looked at the rows behind her. People were staring, enthralled at the show in front of them. Emily wasn't sure what she should be looking for on a preview night, but the open mouths and the occasional person hiding behind their hand seemed to be a good sign.

She turned back and watched the stage. Jonathan was a good actor. He was a drama queen, but he almost deserved the title. She shivered at the memory of being in his dressing room with Hannah. She still couldn't believe that she had been frozen into inaction. She didn't know what might have happened if Olivia hadn't shown up when she did.

Suddenly she remembered Carl. Carl whom she had blamed, who'd had Olivia's hands around his throat. She spied him a few rows in front of her, on the end seat, the same as she was. Staff were positioned on the end of rows so they could pop out of the auditorium if they needed to.

She turned to ensure that Olivia was asleep and then stood and quickly walked up the rows. She tapped Carl on the shoulder and gestured towards the door. Carl looked terrified but followed her regardless. Once they were in the corridor, they waited for the fire door to slowly close so that their conversation wouldn't bother the audience.

"I just wanted to say thank you," Emily said in a quiet voice. "And sorry. My wife is a little protective."

"You're lucky to have her," Carl whispered. "I'm sorry I didn't say anything about Hannah sooner. I'm, um, not very good with people and stuff. And she's pretty scary."

Emily nodded. "She is; she did a one-eighty with me. One minute she was fine, and the next it was like Kathy Bates in *Misery*."

Carl grinned. "Yeah, she's pretty weird. I should have said something. But then you didn't say anything to me, so I thought you wanted to ignore it. And I didn't know for sure that it was you who was being harassed. Or that it was Hannah doing the harassing. It was a bit of a mess. I'm sorry."

"It's fine, really. Don't apologise." Emily felt awful. She'd misjudged Carl in a big way.

"I'm sorry that you thought it was me," Carl said. "I-I like you, but I don't think of you like that."

"Oh, I know…I was getting paranoid," Emily said.

"Could you, um, tell your wife?" Carl asked.

"Yes, don't worry, there won't be a repeat performance of that. Again, I'm so sorry. I feel like this has really put a damper on everything. I did enjoy working with you, I probably should have been more patient with you."

"It's fine, I know I'm a bit awkward to work with," Carl said. "For what it's worth, I really liked working with you, and I think you have a lot of talent."

"Thank you, Carl, that really means a lot."

"Nicole said that you'd be going back to New York. It's a shame that you're not staying. I'm presenting a scriptwriting course at a local college, and I was going to ask if you wanted to come along and help me present."

"Me?" Emily was flabbergasted.

"Yes, you know more than you think. You have a natural storytelling ability that not everyone has. And you could learn from the bits of the presentation that I was doing. But you're not going to be here, so maybe I could film it and send—"

"Actually," Emily interrupted with a grin, "there might be a change of plans."

Chapter Forty

Ten Months Later

"I cannot believe you talked me into this," Olivia grumbled.

"Me?" Emily laughed. "You were the one who wanted a baby, you were the one who moved a million miles an hour. Doctor's appointment in a few hours, sperm donor picked within a couple of days."

"You should have held me back." Olivia licked the ice cream spoon clean. "This baby has completely changed my personality. I don't even like ice cream, and I've somehow eaten an entire tub."

"No one doesn't like ice cream." Emily took the empty cardboard container and the spoon from Olivia and placed them on the coffee table.

"What if the baby never comes out?" Olivia asked. "What if it just stays in there?"

"Then you'll be fat forever," Emily said.

Olivia whined. "You're not helping me at all."

"You're four months along," Emily said. "You're not even halfway there. You can't be moaning this much now. You'll have run out of things to complain about."

"Doubt it." Olivia held up her hand. "My ring doesn't fit. Some of my fingers are fat."

"You're retaining water, not fat," Emily said.

She stood and picked up the ice cream container, worried that Olivia would soon start to lick the inside if the tempting treat was near her any longer.

"You're gorgeous," Emily said. She leaned forward and kissed her forehead.

She walked out of the living room and into the kitchen. She placed the container in the recycling bin and put the spoon in the dishwasher. As she wiped down the work surface, she looked out the window. Henry ran around the garden, chasing and then being chased by Captain McFluffypants.

He loved his new London school. They thought he might not like the school uniform he was now required to wear daily, but he thought it made him look like Harry Potter.

Olivia walked into the kitchen. "Can I help with anything?"

"No, all done," Emily said. She turned around and opened her arms. "A big hug would be nice, though."

Olivia smiled and walked into the embrace.

Emily loved to feel Olivia's slightly protruding stomach. Olivia was already complaining about being fat, and Emily didn't have the heart to tell her that she had a lot of growing to do yet.

"I spoke to Henry's teacher," Olivia said. "He passed his last marker evaluation. They're going to schedule one in for next year."

"Okay."

Henry's tests had come back as negative, but the results showed that he was on the border of Attention Deficient Disorder. While he hadn't been diagnosed, the school was keeping an eye on him to see how he developed.

"And Simon wants to look at offices tomorrow morning."

"Okay," Emily said. "I can take Henry to school, my morning catch-up was pushed back to ten."

"Remember to leave early on Friday," Olivia said. She took a step back from the hug. "You'll need extra time to pack if we're getting the early flight on Saturday morning."

Olivia edged towards the freezer.

Emily coughed.

"Some ice for a glass of water," Olivia said.

It didn't matter. Emily had hidden the rest of the ice cream stash the moment she got home.

Henry came in from the garden, panting for breath. Emily smiled and let out a long, contented sigh. Seeing Henry fit and healthy was never going to not make her happy.

"Shoes," Olivia reminded him.

He kicked off his shoes and slammed the door behind him.

"I'm taking you to school tomorrow," Emily said. "So, make sure you're ready a little early."

"Okay."

"And I'm picking you up on Friday afternoon," Olivia told him. Probably for the eighth time that week.

"I know, Mom," Henry said with a smile. "I can't wait to go to New York and see Tom and Lucy and Grandma. I made Grandma a birthday present."

"What did you make her?" Emily asked.

"A dinosaur out of LEGOs."

Emily could just imagine Irene looking for a place to put such a gift in her immaculate house.

"When we fly, can I sit by the window?" Henry asked.

"We'll all be sitting by the window," Olivia replied.

Emily rolled her eyes. "I thought I told you not to book first-class?"

"It's the pregnancy, my hearing is going." Olivia smirked.

"Uh-huh," Emily replied, shaking her head.

"First-class is where I first met Olivia," Henry said.

Emily looked at him dumbstruck. "Do you remember that, Henry?"

He nodded. "Yeah. I don't remember much before that. But I remember flying for the first time. And meeting Olivia. It was like Christmas and my birthday all at the same time!"

Olivia bent down and pulled him into a hug. "It was the same for me."

Emily could feel tears starting to form in her eyes. She knelt beside Henry and hugged him, too.

"Ick. You guys are weird," Henry complained with a smile on his face.

"Yep, and you're stuck with us," Emily told him.

"Forever," Olivia said.

About the Author

Amanda Radley had no desire to be a writer but accidentally turned into an award-winning, best-selling author. Residing in the UK with her wife and pets, she loves to travel. She gave up her marketing career in order to make stuff up for a living instead. She claims the similarities are startling.

Books Available from Bold Strokes Books

Cold Blood by Genevieve McCluer. Maybe together, Kalila and Dorenia have a chance of taking down the vampires who have eluded them all these years. And maybe, in each other, they can find a love worth living for. (978-1-63679-195-1)

Greener Pastures by Aurora Rey. When city girl and CPA Audrey Adams finds herself tending her aunt's farm, will Rowan Marshall—the charming cider maker next door—turn out to be her saving grace or the bane of her existence? (978-1-63679-116-6)

Grounded by Amanda Radley. For a second chance, Olivia and Emily will need to accept their mistakes, learn to communicate properly, and with a little help from five-year-old Henry, fall madly in love all over again. Sequel to Flight SQA016. (978-1-63679-241-5)

Journey's End by Amanda Radley. In this heartwarming conclusion to the Flight series, Olivia and Emily must finally decide what they want, what they need, and how to follow the dreams of their hearts. (978-1-63679-233-0)

Pursued: Lillian's Story by Felice Picano. Fleeing a disastrous marriage to the Lord Exchequer of England, Lillian of Ravenglass reveals an incident-filled, often bizarre, tale of great wealth and power, perfidy, and betrayal. (978-1-63679-197-5)

Secret Agent by Michelle Larkin. CIA agent Peyton North embarks on a global chase to apprehend rogue agent Zoey Blackwood, but her commitment to the mission is tested as the sparks between them ignite and their sizzling attraction approaches a point of no return. (978-1-63555-753-4)

Something Between Us by Krystina Rivers. A decade after her heart was broken under Don't Ask, Don't Tell, Kirby runs into her first love and has to decide if what's still between them is enough to heal her broken heart. (978-1-63679-135-7)

Sugar Girl by Emma L McGeown. Having traded in traditional romance for the perks of Sugar Dating, Ciara Reilly not only enjoys the no-strings-attached arrangement, she's also a hit with her clients. That is until she meets the beautiful entrepreneur Charlie Keller who makes her want to go sugar-free. (978-1-63679-156-2)

The Business of Pleasure by Ronica Black. Editor in chief Valerie Raffield is quickly becoming smitten by Lennox, the graphic artist she's hired to work remotely. But when Lennox doesn't show for their first face-to-face meeting, Valerie's heart and her business may be in jeopardy. (978-1-63679-134-0)

The Hummingbird Sanctuary by Erin Zak. The Hummingbird Sanctuary, Colorado's hottest resort destination: Come for the mountains, stay for the charm, and enjoy the drama as Olive, Eleanor, and Harriet figure out the meaning of true friendship. (978-1-63679-163-0)

The Witch Queen's Mate by Jennifer Karter. Barra and Silvi must overcome their ingrained hatred and prejudice to use Barra's magic and save both their peoples, not just from slavery, but destruction. (978-1-63679-202-6)

With a Twist by Georgia Beers. Starting over isn't easy for Amelia Martini. When the irritatingly cheerful Kirby Dupress comes into her life will Amelia be brave enough to go after the love she really wants? (978-1-63555-987-3)

Business of the Heart by Claire Forsythe. When a hopeless romantic meets a tough-as-nails cynic, they'll need to overcome the wounds of the past to discover that their hearts are the most important business of all. (978-1-63679-167-8)

Dying for You by Jenny Frame. Can Victorija Dred keep an age-old vow and fight the need to take blood from Daisy Macdougall? (978-1-63679-073-2)

Exclusive by Melissa Brayden. Skylar Ruiz lands the TV reporting job of a lifetime, but is she willing to sacrifice it all for the love of her longtime crush, anchorwoman Carolyn McNamara? (978-1-63679-112-8)

Her Duchess to Desire by Jane Walsh. An up-and-coming interior designer seeks to create a happily ever after with an intriguing duchess, proving that love never goes out of fashion. (978-1-63679-065-7)

Murder on Monte Vista by David S. Pederson. Private Detective Mason Adler's angst at turning fifty is forgotten when his "birthday present," the handsome, young Henry Bowtrickle, turns up dead, and it's up to Mason to figure out who did it, and why. (978-1-63679-124-1)

Take Her Down by Lauren Emily Whalen. Stakes are cutthroat, scheming is creative, and loyalty is ever-changing in this queer, female-driven YA retelling of Shakespeare's Julius Caesar. (978-1-63679-089-3)

The Game by Jan Gayle. Ryan Gibbs is a talented golfer, but her guilt means she may never leave her small town, even if Katherine Reese tempts her with competition and passion. (978-1-63679-126-5)

Whereabouts Unknown by Meredith Doench. While homicide detective Theodora Madsen recovers from a potentially career-ending injury, she scrambles to solve the cases of two missing sixteen-year-old girls from Ohio. (978-1-63555-647-6)

Boy at the Window by Lauren Melissa Ellzey. Daniel Kim struggles to hold onto reality while haunted by both his very-present past and his never-present parents. Jiwon Yoon may be the only one who can break Daniel free. (978-1-63679-092-3)

Deadly Secrets by VK Powell. Corporate criminals want whistleblower Jana Elliott permanently silenced, but Rafe Silva will risk everything to keep the woman she loves safe. (978-1-63679-087-9)

Enchanted Autumn by Ursula Klein. When Elizabeth comes to Salem, Massachusetts, to study the witch trials, she never expects to find love—or an actual witch…and Hazel might just turn out to be both. (978-1-63679-104-3)

Escorted by Renee Roman. When fantasy meets reality, will escort Ryan Lewis be able to walk away from a chance at forever with her new client Dani? (978-1-63679-039-8)

Her Heart's Desire by Anne Shade. Two women. One choice. Will Eve and Lynette be able to overcome their doubts and fears to embrace their deepest desire? (978-1-63679-102-9)

My Secret Valentine by Julie Cannon, Erin Dutton, & Anne Shade. Winning the heart of your secret Valentine? These award-winning authors agree, there is no better way to fall in love. (978-1-63679-071-8)

Perilous Obsession by Carsen Taite. When reporter Macy Moran becomes consumed with solving a cold case, will her quest for the truth bring her closer to Detective Beck Ramsey or will her obsession with finding a murderer rob her of a chance at true love? (978-1-63679-009-1)

Reading Her by Amanda Radley. Lauren and Allegra learn love and happiness are right where they least expect it. There's just one problem: Lauren has a secret she cannot tell anyone, and Allegra knows she's hiding something. (978-1-63679-075-6)

The Willing by Lyn Hemphill. Kitty Wilson doesn't know how, but she can bring people back from the dead as long as someone is willing to take their place and keep the universe in balance. (978-1-63679-083-1)

Three Left Turns to Nowhere by Nathan Burgoine, J. Marshall Freeman, & Jeffrey Ricker. Three strangers heading to a convention in Toronto are stranded in rural Ontario, where a small town with a subtle kind of magic leads each to discover what he's been searching for. (978-1-63679-050-3)

Watching Over Her by Ronica Black. As they face the snowstorm of the century, and the looming threat of a stalker, Riley and Zoey just might find love in the most unexpected of places. (978-1-63679-100-5)

#shedeservedit by Greg Herren. When his gay best friend, and high school football star, is murdered, Alex Wheeler is a suspect and must find the truth to clear himself. (978-1-63555-996-5)

Always by Kris Bryant. When a pushy American private investigator shows up demanding to meet the woman in Camila's artwork, instead of introducing her to her great-grandmother, Camila decides to lead her on a wild goose chase all over Italy. (978-1-63679-027-5)

Exes and O's by Joy Argento. Ali and Madison really only have one thing in common. The girl who broke their heart may be the only one who can put it back together. (978-1-63679-017-6)

One Verse Multi by Sander Santiago. Life was good: promotion, friends, falling in love, discovering that the multi-verse is on a fast track to collision—wait, what? Good thing Martin King works for a company that can fix the problem, right...um...right? (978-1-63679-069-5)

Paris Rules by Jaime Maddox. Carly Becker has been searching for the perfect woman all her life, but no one ever seems to be just right until Paige Waterford checks all her boxes, except the most important one—she's married. (978-1-63679-077-0)

Shadow Dancers by Suzie Clarke. In this third and final book in the Moon Shadow series, Rachel must find a way to become the hunter and not the hunted, and this time she will meet Ehsee Yumiko head-on. (978-1-63555-829-6)

The Kiss by C.A. Popovich. When her wife refuses their divorce and begins to stalk her, threatening her life, Kate realizes to protect her new love, Leslie, she has to let her go, even if it breaks her heart. (978-1-63679-079-4)

The Wedding Setup by Charlotte Greene. When Ryann, a big-time New York executive, goes to Colorado to help out with her best friend's wedding, she never expects to fall for the maid of honor. (978-1-63679-033-6)

Velocity by Gun Brooke. Holly and Claire work toward an uncertain future preparing for an alien space mission, and only one thing is for certain, they will have to risk their lives, and their hearts, to discover the truth. (978-1-63555-983-5)

Wildflower Words by Sam Ledel. Lida Jones treks West with her father in search of a better life on the rapidly developing American frontier, but finds home when she meets Hazel Thompson. (978-1-63679-055-8)

A Fairer Tomorrow by Kathleen Knowles. For Maddie Weeks and Gerry Stern, the Second World War brought them together, but the end of the war might rip them apart. (978-1-63555-874-6)

Holiday Hearts by Diana Day-Admire and Lyn Cole. Opposites attract during Christmastime chaos in Kansas City. (978-1-63679-128-9)

Changing Majors by Ana Hartnett Reichardt. Beyond a love, beyond a coming-out, Bailey Sullivan discovers what lies beyond the shame and self-doubt imposed on her by traditional Southern ideals. (978-1-63679-081-7)

Fresh Grave in Grand Canyon by Lee Patton. The age-old Grand Canyon becomes more and more ominous as a group of volunteers fight to survive alone in nature and uncover a murderer among them. (978-1-63679-047-3)

Highland Whirl by Anna Larner. Opposites attract in the Scottish Highlands, when feisty Alice Campbell falls for city-girl-about-town Roxanne Barns. (978-1-63555-892-0)

Humbug by Amanda Radley. With the corporate Christmas party in jeopardy, CEO Rosalind Caldwell hires Christmas Girl Ellie Pearce as her personal assistant. The only problem is, Ellie isn't a PA, has never planned a party, and develops a ridiculous crush on her totally intimidating new boss. (978-1-63555-965-1)

On the Rocks by Georgia Beers. Schoolteacher Vanessa Martini makes no apologies for her dating checklist, and newly single mom Grace Chapman ticks all Vanessa's Do Not Date boxes. Of course, they're never going to fall in love. (978-1-63555-989-7)

Song of Serenity by Brey Willows. Arguing with the Muse of music and justice is complicated, falling in love with her even more so. (978-1-63679-015-2)

The Christmas Proposal by Lisa Moreau. Stranded together in a Christmas village on a snowy mountain, Grace and Bridget face their past and question their dreams for the future. (978-1-63555-648-3)

The Infinite Summer by Morgan Lee Miller. While spending the summer with her dad in a small beach town, Remi Brenner falls for Harper Hebert and accidentally finds herself tangled up in an intense restaurant rivalry between her famous stepmom and her first love. (978-1-63555-969-9)

Wisdom by Jesse J. Thoma. When Sophia and Reggie are chosen for the governor's new community design team and tasked with tackling substance abuse and mental health issues, battle lines are drawn even as sparks fly. (978-1-63555-886-9)

Lightning Source UK Ltd.
Milton Keynes UK
UKHW041541060322
399573UK00008B/28